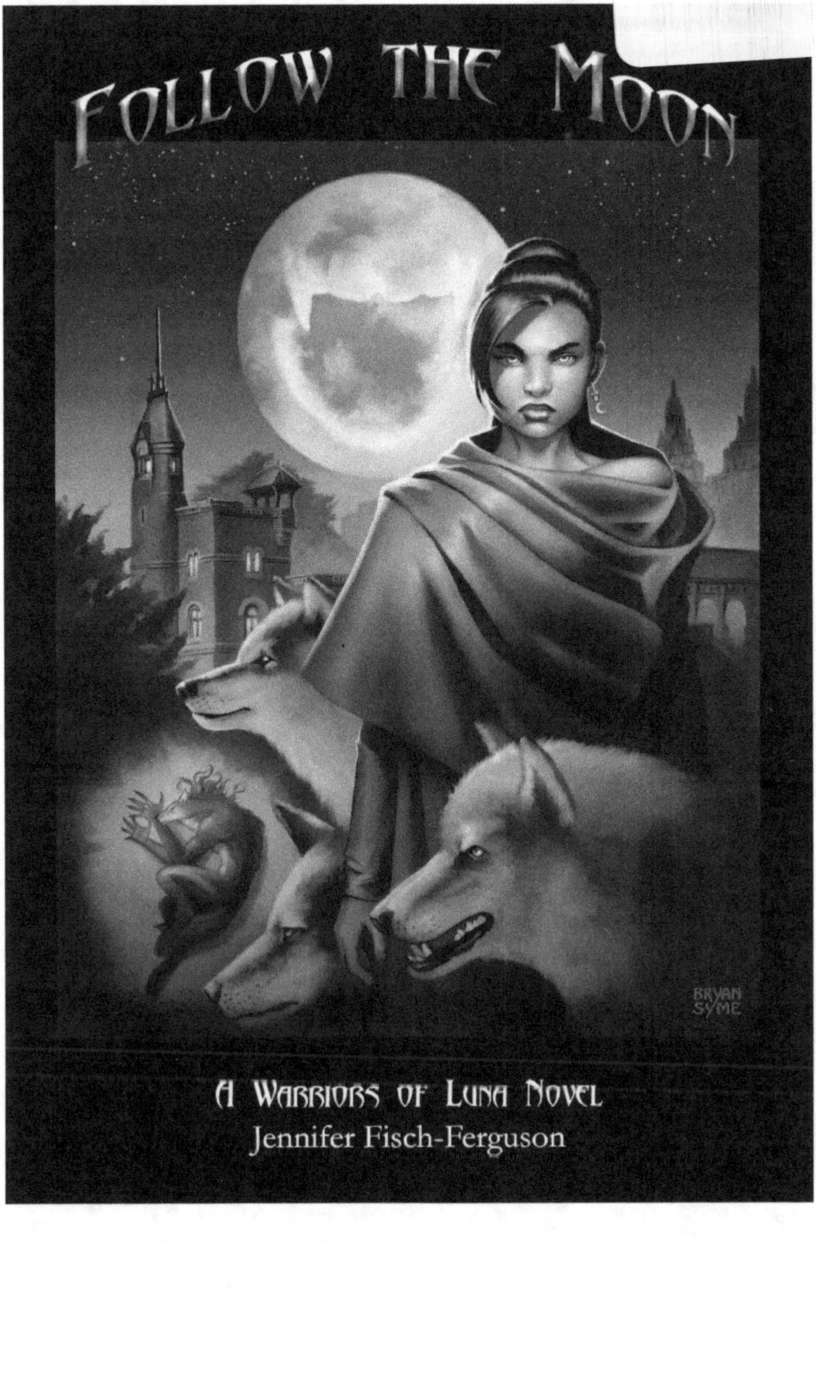

FOLLOW THE MOON

A WARRIORS OF LUNA NOVEL
Jennifer Fisch-Ferguson

FOLLOW THE MOON

A Warriors of Luna Novel

Book 3

Jennifer Fisch-Ferguson

DEDICATION

To Don, Xander and Grayson thank you for always brainstorming and breathing life into this world with me. To Artie- raptor claws, semi colons and all the stops and commas I try to refuse... You have always been amazing and generous and I couldn't imagine a better partner. To the rest of my family- this doesn't mean you don't have to hear about these people anymore- there are still more works. To my "fallen" friends- thanks for letting me take parts of your life and fictionalize them- I am glad you are still here with me. To Jessica – You are amazing! I asked for help and you answered and have just blown me away with your insight and excellent ideas! Here's to many more. To my Beta readers- thanks for keeping me true to my rules and SB- your reactions are the best; the readers are missing a whole other laugh by not seeing your notes. To my readers- thank you for investing your time and emotions with these characters with me.

Contents

CHAPTER One

Kama hefted a box onto her hip and grunted as the corner dug into her flesh. Once upon a time, she used to be excited to see packages, but that thrill had waned.

"One would think being Loup would make moving much easier," she groused into the air. "Although, after training for three hours and walking up and down the stairs twenty times with all my worldly possessions, it is bound to be difficult. I don't understand these people who move every other month and find it fun. They must have movers or something."

She set her current load on the kitchen counter and looked around. The apartment filled slowly with the sum total of what she had, but it didn't feel like home. Yet. Even though she had had it painted from stark white to warm jewel tones, it didn't seem quite real. Her own things, her own rules, and her own space.

I really never imagined I would live in my own place. I guess I kinda figured I would stay home until I made it big on the stage, and then I would live in hotels during my whirlwind, global tour. I never wanted to live on my own. I just knew I would take the world by storm and be the new operatic sensation. Instead, I found out I was a werewolf. Talk about things that derail your plans.

She opened the box, sighed after reviewing the contents, closed the flaps, and took it to the bathroom. Kama placed the various hair ties and barrettes in a drawer and shook her head at the amount of things she had. She laughed at herself for her hoarded collection of scented soaps, scrubs, and lotions. She put towels away and smiled with satisfaction. The simple act of putting her personal style into arranging her place soothed her. When she looked at the closet, she tilted her head and pulled everything back out. Out of habit she had arranged the linen closet just like her mother would have. She scrunched her nose in thought and then put all the towels up high and the soap and beauty supplies on the bottom shelves.

Much better. I want to have my own vibe for this place. Crazy to think only five months ago the biggest worry I had was finding the perfect performance gowns for my senior recital at Julliard. My shopping vacation meant I needed to focus on finding some new and intense fashion choices. For my senior year, I intended to be bold and edgy. Even that wasn't as easy as I expected. I missed an appointment, went through twenty-five stores on Rodeo Drive, and still didn't find a gown. Instead, I found a date.

The last thing she had on her mind had been meeting a man, but he had found her sitting in the hotel bar as she read a romance novel. Deciding she wanted to experience romance — bodice-ripping aside — she took advantage of her vacation and immersed herself in something she knew nothing about: dating. Kama had dedicated her life to becoming the best Opera Diva the world had ever known. She had attended the renowned Julliard School of Music since gaining admission at the young age of seven. She trained diligently to attain her goal and had not let anything detract her. Men and romance had not been anywhere on her radar.

Meeting Jack put me on the biggest and most exhilarating roller coaster ride. It wasn't the easy, vacation flirtation I thought it would be. I will say, I had no idea what to expect. He made the best impression possible by taking me to see my all-time favorite jazz duo. Such small-world syndrome to know that his favorite musicians were also mine; not quite kismet, but a connection nonetheless. Someday I will gain enough courage to actually call them, like Charlie asked me to, and then I can tell the world that I sang with them.

Kama could only imagine the surprise and pride her father would feel knowing she had sung with them—something she might not have done if she hadn't been persuaded to do so. She had gotten her deep love of jazz from him, listening to Charlie and Rainbow Bird for hours together. She hoped she might be able to tell him about the encounter someday. She would keep the secret of the special engagement with their favorite musicians until she was ready to explain how she had met Jack. Nothing good would come from her parents discovering she had been sneaking out to go on dates.

My dear father would probably fall over if he realized the first man I had dated was a bit older than me. Of course, I could offset the whole age thing by telling him Jack is a werewolf. Then I might have to explain how I even know about the Loup and why werewolves are real. Heck, since Mom never bothered to tell him, I guess I can leave Dad in ignorance. Although, she really could have done me a solid and let me know. I still giggle when I think about the look on Jack's face when I accused him of infecting me. I wouldn't change that for anything. A lot less laughing happened when I learned it was all genetics. Amazing that, out of five kids, I got the wolfy goodness short straw. So, yes I'm a, werewolf. And my newly found boyfriend? The pack Alpha.

Kama walked back into the living room and stared balefully at the monstrously huge pile.

"Seriously, I should not have ever let my mother shop for me. I have enough stuff for five people. I only moved one floor down from her; it's not like I moved around the world. I wonder if she would be upset if I returned it all. Just like a DeKosse to buy rations for an imagined catastrophe. That woman has a serious lack of self-control."

The snort inside her head made her laugh. As a true DeKosse, she had entered her Pack in spectacular fashion. Kama learned about her werewolf heritage after being brutally attacked. She had gone for an evening run and stumbled upon a drug deal in Central Park. Had she not shifted to warrior form and fought back, she would have been dead. When she woke, she learned the truth Needless to say, she didn't take the news about her Loup nature with any sort of grace or aplomb. She got into a heated fight with Jack and refused his offer of sanctuary with his Pack. She was determined to ignore the whole being a werewolf thing and tried to live her life as she had before. A run-in with a vampire changed her attitude, and she went back to the group. Before that dust had settled, she found herself in an altercation with another werewolf.

To be fair, I didn't plan for her mouth to wipe the chess table. It was more like I helped her facepalm into it. It wouldn't have happened if she hadn't been such a bully. Who grabs for another person's food, anyhow? I mean, low class, shitty stuff. Beth is one of the nicest people I have ever met, and having her as my bestie is so worth it. Granted, I did think I would be in trouble for beating up a packmate. Come to find out, it was a mark in my favor and, all of a sudden, I got christened as the Diva.

Kama had settled into her new routine of navigating both worlds. She worked hard to hide her paranormal activities from her parents, meanwhile acting like all was normal. She had almost gotten used to being with her Pack, learning the rules, and dealing with being Loup, when life threw her another curve ball. Just as she had accepted Jack being Alpha and having to fight against the things that went bump in the night, the maternal grandfather she had never been allowed to meet showed up. The one who happened to be a werewolf. Of course, an argument with her mother erupted. Kama was stunned to learn that her mother had known all along about the Loup, but had denied her the knowledge. She felt betrayed to have been left unaware for so long. It only got worse, as her grandfather wanted to whisk her away to Michigan to teach her to be a "real" Loup. Desperation pushed her into a rash decision.

I can't believe I thought taking my Rite of Passage six weeks after learning about being Loup was a good idea. Then again, I guess everything I have done concerning Jack has been rather spontaneous. I swear, being in an illicit relationship is damn hard work.

Kama pulled herself out of her headspace and sat down at the small kitchen table with a snack. Moving was much harder than she had expected it to be. The heavy boxes were no issue, but the constant walking up and down the stairs to relocate everything made her muscles scream.

Then there was the emotional aspect. Kama figured moving into her own place would just jumpstart the whole "being an adult" thing. Instead, she found being alone meant she felt lonely sometimes. Something she had never experienced before. She held onto the notion of having her own sanctuary, and it drove her to make it amazing and sacred.

After taking my Rite of Passage and literally killing my dream of ever becoming an Opera Diva, I thought life would get easier. I agree with that snort. What the heck were we thinking? The reality of being successful meant taking on the full, adult responsibility of protecting the Pack and Park. I bet people would laugh if I tried to explain that our Pack is run like the military. Who could have imagined me being in the armed forces? At least I don't have to get up and run at four in the morning.

Tears welled up and spilled over as she thought about Jack. She wiped her face and quickly forced herself to think about other, less stressful things. Such as her brother finding out she was a werewolf when she sat on his chest in her full, naked glory. It happened because he had been with a friend at a drug deal. The very same drug deal the Pack had been sent to bust. When she realized her brother was in the fray, Kama stood her ground and refused to let the others kill him. Amazingly enough, Ajani grew up after the experience.

I expected he would never speak to me again. I. Instead, we made amends, and he started dating my best friend. I would have never imagined he would turn around and stop smoking pot and hanging out with his dilettante friends. I suppose having to confront the fact that werewolves exist was hard enough, but realizing he had the genetics as well—I guess it gave him the motivation and reason to do something with his life. He moved out, got a job doing patisserie work in mom's catering hall, and became serious about the culinary arts again. Funny how I forgot he used to do sugar work.

Kama finished her snack and looked around. She had initially resisted when her mother set up her kitchen without asking, but after the hard work of moving, she was glad for one less room to do. Ajani's decision to move out a few months prior made the discussion with her parents about moving into her own place easier. Her father had bought the entire floor of apartments underneath their home. She remembered him explaining that he always wanted his children to have a roof over their heads, but he didn't want them to live with him forever.

Thankfully, it ensures me the freedom to come and go unchecked. I mean, my curfew was really more of a guideline than anything else. Now I can work the crazy overnight shift at the Park and not have to explain it to Dad,, on the off chance Aturus decides to make me go on any more runs or have special training. I know I need to get up and actually finish that last load of stuff, but here I am not moving. It's probably just a box of clothes, and it's not like I have been banned from ever going back up to my parents' home. Hell, I plan to be there at least once a week for dinner. Maybe twice.

Kama smiled, feeling slightly more grown up. She pushed herself to her feet and climbed back up the stairs. One of the few downsides to being Loup—aside from run-ins with vampires—was the whole claustrophobia thing. While walking up fifteen flights of steps every day for the past five months had the benefit of a nice, firm tush, the option of an elevator would have been great. She went to her old room and grabbed the last box. Tears came again as she looked around.

When did I get so damn sentimental? I wonder if Mom felt like this when she moved out. I mean, she moved to a whole other state and everything.

Her nose wrinkled as she thought about the ambassadorship forced upon her by The Judge. Essentially, he sent her to the ass-end of northern Michigan to meet the Loup family she didn't know. She had imagined all the worst things possible, but had no idea how alienated she would feel. She found an ally in her cousin, Nula, while the rest of her family treated her much like an unwelcome guest. Kama had tried to connect with her grandfather and get to know him. Overall, she learned to really like the man, except when he had insulted her Pack.

Whew, that whole situation got nasty. And then to find out why Mom never went back…mind blown. The absolutely crappy things we do to the people we love. I was glad to have met some of them, even Uncle James, despite his being a total Asshat at first. But he did come home with me and fight in our war against the mutants. Who the hell would even think it was a good thing to make mutant creatures, let alone set them free in Central Park?

Kama bit her lower lip and quickly left her room. There was no way to avoid thinking about the war and the destruction at her hands. She had taken the life of a mutant, bear creature. Even though she had been protecting her uncle and her packmates, she didn't know how to process the fact that she had killed someone. She had been sent into a war and expected there to be casualties. But to see evidence of humanity in a being labeled a creature had shaken her. She knew she had seen intelligence and understanding in it. It still kept her awake at night.

I'm sure screaming into pillows isn't the end answer, but it works for now. Plus, the nightmares, night sweats, and overall feeling like a terrible person have to be rectified for me to move on. Whoever said "kill or be killed" was either a psycho or someone behind the scenes and not on the battlefield. Though, Uncle James liked me much better after I saved his life. I'm not sure if I will ever forget the ride back to Michigan with him and my mother. That woman can never ever say anything about me and Ajani fighting again. The vitriol they spit… I hope I never make her truly mad at me.

She made it back down to her place, set the last box in her bedroom, and lay on her bed. Kama took a deep breath in through her nose and out through her mouth, like Beth had been teaching her as a relaxation technique. Her friend had been a great support system since she had gotten back from the Facility. Things were just different now; so different that she couldn't even begin to make sense of it all in her head.

I wonder if I can actually spend a night by myself. Then again, one more nightmare and Mom will probably toss me into a mental health facility until I get it under control. How do people deal with this?

Kama firmly pushed her thoughts to the back of her mind, but they wouldn't stay put. The reflections rebelled against her efforts and went to the forbidden place. To Jack. Despite all the focus on inhaling and exhaling, emotions flooded over her, and she gave in and cried. She still couldn't understand any part of his leaving. The wolf snorted, and she growled mentally in response.

I know you don't think we should be upset, but I don't understand what could have been so important. He was gone for six weeks, with no word. Then we had the raid. If he cared, he would have at least waited for me to heal before he just up and left me. How could it end like that?

After her sobs had silenced and the tears dried, she made herself a mug of tea and sat at her table.

So yes, Jack left me, and then Cade came into the picture. Not quite a white knight or anything. More like a smartass with a nice car. And in a city of twenty-two million people, I met up with another supernatural. I lived here my whole life with no idea. Then I tazzed and both my boyfriends end up being paranormal. Granted, he does magic tricks with coins and is not Loup, but still—what are the odds?

She drank her tea as she mulled over the highly amusing dates with Cade. He had been a lot of fun and even took her to her first and only school dance—dressed as a pirate, no less.

I didn't think I would ever attend a school dance. They seemed so juvenile that I never wanted to go, but I had fun with Cade. It actually took my mind off what happened.

Kama looked around and got back to work. She had been forcing herself to stay busy ever since she had returned from the raid. There was no way not to think about the atrocities she had seen.

And done. At least, that is all the unpacking I am willing to do today.

She worked hard to keep her body in motion: painting, moving, training, running. Anything to keep her mind from going back to the scene where her friends were killed. Back to the moment when she chose to embrace being a warrior.

It was us or them. Always remember that. This is what Aturus trained us so hard for. I wish we had been prepared to deal with the emotional backlash that refuses to leave. Instead, here I am, fighting to convince us that what we did was okay. Meanwhile, I have to suck it up and put on a pretty smile so my family doesn't worry. I can't control the nightmares or the jumpiness right now. Our Pack is divided into those who went to war and those who did not. They can't understand how we need to be around them but not with them.

Kama went to her kitchen and looked around. Finding nothing to take the edge off of her thoughts, she changed into her running shoes and headed out. She paused after she closed her front door, hearing Beth and Ajani having a soft conversation in the apartment next to hers. She put on her shoes, but en route to the Park, she changed her mind, turned around, and made her way to her mother's catering hall. As she walked into the huge industrial kitchen, she smiled at her mom and put on an apron. She looked at the huge pile of potatoes by the sink and sighed in relief. She started to peel and allowed the rhythm to let her mind go blissfully numb.

CHAPTER Two

Kama tensed as the bear rushed toward her. It rose up, tall and strong, roaring its challenge. She could see the crimson stain patterns on the thick pads of its paws, and the hot odor of copper permeated the air. She knew it was Rosanne's blood and trembled in horror, realizing the scent meant the death of her friend. She went from being scared to furious. She lashed out and dug into the mutant's belly. The intestines pooled over her claws like warm pudding. The bear dropped, looked up at her, and gave a piteous mewl.

"You were supposed to save me…"

She woke up as she fell to the floor with a painful thump. It took her a moment to recognize her new bedroom. The smell of fresh paint tickled her nose, and she rose into a seated position, leaning against her bed for support. Slowly, she stood up and sat back on the edge of her bed. She looked around her place and shrugged to no one. The numbers on the clock showed five thirty in the morning. At least she had slept through the night.

Somehow, we didn't think living alone would be like this. Okay, fine. I know you are here with me. We moved out for the sake of independence. It is rather odd. If we were home, we could go and make a cup of tea, knowing full well that Mom would wake up and talk to us. This is just… just what I asked for, I guess.

She stretched and tried to relieve the tension in her neck and shoulders. Waking from nightmares before a recital had become an unwanted, but predictable ritual over the past ten years. However, they had always been about being on stage. She worried her dreams of late focused on the guilt she felt over Rosanne's death. She recognized grieving the loss of her team leader as a healthy emotion. After all, it had only been two weeks. Things were different at the park while everyone tried to deal with the deaths of their packmates. There were lots of questions and even more tears.

After turning her phone back on, she waited for the updates. Her mother had sent a reminder text about her event late the night before. Kama smiled and dialed, figuring it would be faster to talk.

"Hi, Mama. Thank you for the reminder," Kama said.

Brenna rattled back in her ear for almost five minutes straight before Kama got in another word.

"Yes, I'm sure the after-party will be lovely. I hope you kept it to family and those who are like family. I can't handle a huge group. Especially after all I have been through."

Kama knew it was a cheap shot, but the only one that would keep her mother from randomly inviting the entire music department back to the restaurant to celebrate her senior concert. Since the return from Michigan, Brenna had been in constant communication. At least every two hours, her mother called to ask a question or to remind her of something or to ask her to bring something up to her. Her mother's fears had been compounded by her Uncle James's rendition of the story. The over attention to her well-being suffocated her.

Fortunately, she doesn't call all hours of the night. I bet she thinks we're going to crack and fall apart. Though some days, I think she might be right to watch out for us. Still, we have been working towards this moment for a decade. There is no way we are going to choke. Especially since this will be the final recital I give. I know there will be some hard feelings after I make my announcement. Professor Ralston will lose his mind with anger, and my father...my dad will never begin to understand why I am giving it up. I just don't see how I can pretend I will ever have a career in opera when I have Pack duties. I will make damn sure to go out on top, though.

She went to her closet and fingered the soft material of the silver and royal purple gown she had bought in Los Angeles six months before. The material shimmered as she caressed it, and she stepped away before she rubbed bare spots into it. Kama grinned, remembering the big panic during her trip to find the perfect performance gown, one that would be amazing and different than any other student's style. When she thought about all of the changes she had gone through in such a short amount of time, she wondered how she had managed to get through it all.

Her phone rang again and pulled her out of her memories. She wondered if her mother would miss being nervous for her. The constant phone calls were Brenna's way of soothing her own nerves. Kama had never had the heart to tell her how frazzling it was.

"Hi, Mama. Yes, I remembered my hair appointment. No, I don't need you to go with me," she said.

Another five minutes were spent listening to what her mother thought she should wear and do for the evening.

"Okay. Yes. You can ride with me to the concert. Have the driver come by at five. I will need my two hours. No, I already made my own coffee. I will see you later tonight. I love you."

Kama hung up and wiped tears out of her eyes. Her mother had always been affectionate but now more than ever.

The day progressed slowly: duties at the park, stopping by the catering hall to eat lunch with her mom, home for a quick shower, and then off for a few hours at the hair salon. She went back home to grab her performance gown and rode in blessed quiet with her mother to Julliard. She hummed, partially to warm up and partially to leave no openings for a conversation.

Kama went through her performance rituals by rote. For a moment, she thought about all she would be ending and gave a sad smile. Everyone had choices to make in life, and she was making hers.

The audience erupted into loud applause when she walked out onto the stage. Kama held her head high and smiled widely. She then gave the performance of her life. She used all her emotions to the fullest extent possible as she went through her repertoire of songs. She began with "Belle nuit, ô nuit d'amour,"," hit her stride midway through her program with "Ebben? Ne andrò lontana,"," and ended with "Casta Diva." It almost seemed that divine intervention arranged the selections for the evening. The songs started out dark and lonely; heartache, loss, and despair were easy emotions to carry through her music. The minor chords and chromatic notations sounded of horrors seen and lives taken. It healed her in ways she didn't quite understand but still brought her peace. The happier songs towards the end gave her hope that eventually her life would come full circle and she would find a place of peace to reside in. It would be different—oh, yes. It would be hers again.

I feel our connection more deeply than ever before. Sure, you can sing with me.

Kama tilted her head back and held the final note for as long as she could. When the note died out, she wiped tears of every emotion from her eyes, smiled at the audience, and gave an elegant, deep curtsey.

This might be the end of my singing career, but I'll be damned if anyone ever beats my performance.

Despite the amazing evening before, Kama paced around her room. Her nervous energy had returned. She had been stunned by the reception from the audience. She had not had the heart to break the news of her final concert after the applause and calls for an encore.

I feel guilty for not inviting Cade. However, I do know he would have been bored to tears. If he really wants to hear me sing, I will give him a private performance. Oh wait, that will never work. I just need to stop thinking about him. It has to be over, he can't be in my life any more.

The after-party packed her mother's restaurant and lasted until midnight, when she bowed out and went home. She expected to be exhausted after giving everything to her songs, but instead, she had been worked up and tossed and turned all night.

At six the next morning, she leapt out of bed and went for an early morning run at the park. It had released some tension but not enough. Kama returned home and showered under the hottest temperature she could stand. Still, she felt caged and trapped. The apartment shrunk in on her, and she had to get out before she reached her breaking point. Ever since she had gotten back, she had tried to stay busy and to forget, but it hadn't worked. She had tried to talk to the others who had gone to the Facility, tried to engage in conversation that might let them reconcile their actions. But no one wanted to talk, so there had been no chance to heal.

Cade had tried to understand the crisis. He had empathized with her as she tried to make sense of the carnage she had participated in. She also knew, with all the changes she had been through, she couldn't keep pretending to be a normal girl.

I guess this means concentrating on being Loup. I can't indulge the dream of singing on the stages of the world anymore, nor can I just date whomever I want. Cade may have magic or whatever it is, but he's not Loup. I might as well scrub it all clean and start over with a fresh perspective on what my life is going to be.

Waiting until nine o'clock in the morning had been nearly torturous, but when the time did arrive, panic accompanied it. Kama called a cab and gave them general directions. After a few twists and turns, she finally found the small shop and thanked the gods she had, since she had only been there twice. It was dark and quiet. She took a deep breath and knocked. She could hear him moving around inside and waited patiently for him.

"Yeah?" he called through the door.

"Hey, there," she said.

"Kama."

She heard him breathe her name almost reverently and grimaced.

"Hold on. It's going to take me a second to get there."

She heard a lot of shifting and rattling of metal. A few bumps, scattered curses, and a scraping thunk later, he opened the door. She drank in the sight of his face. His dark eyes caressed her, and a lock of dark brown hair fell over his forehead. She brushed it back before the reason for her visit crashed down on her. She pulled her hand back.

"Well, thanks," he said in a quiet voice and pressed his lips to her palm. "I have missed you."

Kama didn't protest when he pulled her into a deep kiss. She meant every emotion she gave him through the connection.

"I missed you, too. I'm sorry I haven't called. Things just got…well, complicated. I couldn't even begin to describe it," she said, gesturing as words failed her. "It's been messy and awful."

He moved aside to let her into the shop. She walked past him and hopped up to sit on a worktable to avoid more touching. She tried desperately to keep in control of herself. She took a deep breath and focused. Hot tears burned her eyes. Cade shut the door and turned to approach her. He stood in front of her and gave her the easy smile she had come to know and adore. He leaned in close and looked at her, and Kama felt he could really see her.

Crap, there is no way to avoid this next kiss. If I move away, it is going to force the conversation I am trying really hard not to have right now. I just want to enjoy a few moments of being with him.

She got her few moments as she leaned into his caressing hand. It skimmed over her cheek, turning her face to meet him halfway. Kama kissed him back with desperation and couldn't stop the tears from falling. She snuggled close to him, even after Cade broke the kiss, not wanting to see the concern in his eyes. Taking a deep, shaky breath, she allowed him to hold her and in his quiet, steady embrace, she realized she trembled.

"What's wrong?" he asked.

Kama bent her forehead onto his chest, trying to get composed. She found it harder than she expected as he gently rubbed her back. The simple gesture not only comforted her, but made her feel like a girl, just a normal girl…which was all she wanted. For a second, she again flirted with the idea of keeping him in her life. The lie rang hollow to her, and a stream of tears started again.

"Shhh. Easy, hon. Just tell me what's wrong." he said. "You were gone for almost a month. I know something had to have happened. Are you okay?"

"I had to go to Michigan to meet my family. I am certain my grandfather loves me, even though the rest of them looked at me like I'm trying to come in and take over. They must hate me because I chose my Pack over them. They don't understand how my Pack saved me. Then I get back here to find out we have to go and declare war on this laboratory," Kama whispered. "It was full of the kind of creatures who attacked our Park a few months back. Like the creatures that gave me my scar. I watched a woman I know get flattened in two seconds, and my uncle, whom I'm not even sure I like, got hurt defending my group as we escaped."

She pushed against Cade, who continued to hold her. As much as she wanted to feel his arms around her, she needed to have space. He kept looking at her with pity, and she didn't want to meet his eyes

"This is a lot to take in," he said in a low, serious tone.

Kama wanted to tell him all of it. She wanted to talk about the roars of pain still echoing in her ears. She needed to describe in detail the spatter covering the walls and floors, blood of her friends and enemies. She tried to reconcile the ache in her heart, because there would be many more battles in her life. But the suffering stopped before it left her lips. This is why she had to end things. Not because he couldn't possibly understand, but because he wasn't part of her world and didn't deserve to be dragged through it with her.

"Thanks for sharing with me. I went batshit crazy not knowing what happened to you. I thought you had to go and visit family for a few days, but then you didn't come back. Even Ajani didn't have much information. He thought you were going to be gone just for the weekend, too. He had to ask Beth. She said you were gone doing Pack stuff but didn't explain anything else. I'm pretty sure your brother is tired of hearing from me."

Kama laughed at his statement in surprise. In no world ever had she expected her brother and her boyfriend to communicate. The laughter ended quickly, and quiet surrounded them.

"We train for this, you know? Aturus works us into the ground every chance he can get to make sure we are ready to fight in an instant. But damn, how could I ever be ready to watch people die? I certainly had no idea taking a life scars your soul so deeply. I killed a mutant bear to save my uncle, but in the end, I still took a life. As we left, the poor bear crawled over to where its fallen companion lie, so they wouldn't die alone. Does that make it less than us?" Kama whispered, finally looking up at him.

"I don't think there are any easy answers," he said.

She didn't want to find comfort and understanding in his eyes. Kama wanted him to be repulsed and judgmental, shouting damning words at her, so she would finally hear it from somewhere else besides her inner voice. She got no reprieve.

"We can't date anymore," she said bluntly. "I can't be with you anymore. I'm sorry, Cade. I never thought it would go this far. I never thought I would fall so hard for you, and now I can't be with you, not with the crazy my life has become."

"Why?" he asked, obviously confused at the turn the conversation had taken.

"Because I can't do this anymore. I know you think it will all be okay, but I am not so sure. All I know is that I have become someone else. I can't meet up with you at school and have lunch like it is all okay and then go and kill some vampire because my Pack demands it."

"Kama, we have something special here. I can't believe you can just suggest we give it up," he said, holding her chin and forcing her to look into his eyes, to feel his truth. "I don't understand what you are going through, but I know I have been and will be here for you day in and day out. No one ever promised this life would be easy. No one ever said you had to do it all on your own, either."

"It's not like I ever planned this, Cade," Kama said, sobs sneaking past her carefully hardened defenses. "Do you think this is easy for me?"

"No, Kama. I think this is one of the worst things you have ever experienced. This means you are pushing away from everything you know, because you don't know what to expect anymore. Your carefully planned life has been turned upside down and gotten so rough you can't find your balance," he said. "I don't understand why you won't let me help."

She forced herself to be calm as his eyes pierced into her. Guilt surged up and choked her. She didn't want him to fight for her; she wanted him to storm away, furious with her selfishness. Anything would be easier than him showing care and understanding her chaotic mindset.

"I do not for one second regret what we had together, but I also know it cannot continue. I am sorry this is hurting you," she said with a tone of finality.

"Why are you making this so hard? You act like you can't have anything because you might go into another war. Do you not understand it should be the opposite, Kama?" he asked. "If you are afraid you are going to die, then don't do it alone. Go be serious with them, but come back to me and feel like life is okay. Embrace the moments when we are silly together to balance out the horror you have to see. Don't let your life be consumed with training and killing. It will eat your soul one bit at a time."

Kama slowly slid off the worktable. She stood toe to toe with Cade, staring into his unwavering gaze. She wanted to fold into his arms and take his words at face value. She wanted to say okay, toss all caution to the wind, and see where it all went. She also knew it would never be easy. She and Jack might not be dating, but he was still her Alpha. She would have to disclose her relationship, and she had no doubt there would be trouble. Cade's eyes searched her face. Kama took a breath, forcing her resolve not to waver.

"I am just trying to do what I think is right. I know with every fiber of my being that we cannot date anymore. We might both be on the freak scale, but flipping coins is way different than ripping the spine out of someone who is trying to kill you. What happens when I have a nightmare and shift on you in the middle of the night?"

"It won't happen. I have been with you while you are stressed—and you know what? You relax when you are with me because you know I am safe. I am the person who knows about your hidden life, and I offer you something different," he said, hands gripping the edge of his empty work desk. "You can't tell me you accidentally invited me to meet your family. You wanted them to know you had someone in your life. You want a sense of what is normal? So go with what is good for you. Maybe even have a little fun along the way. Just don't give up because one part got messy."

Kama watched him pace. She knew Cade really thought she had a choice. While it had never been expressed that she couldn't date outside her Pack, she had a strong suspicion if they found out Cade worked magic all hell would break loose. Considering she had only ever heard about vampires, she wasn't sure Jack or the Betas actually knew about Cade's kind.

"This is the only choice I have."

"Well, I don't think it's the right one. You keep telling me you don't want to hurt me, but how did you think I would feel?" he grated out.

"Like I betrayed you," Kama said, tears streaming down her face.

"So, that's it? Sorry, Cade. Have a nice life," he said, his sarcasm lashing out to inflict some reciprocal pain.

"I don't know how to explain it any better than I already have. I don't even know what choices I have anymore. I am trying to be fair, and it's not working," she said "I don't know what to say."

"Say you want me," he whispered.

Kama let him pull her close and hold her, until she realized she had started to relax and then pulled back. She watched emotions flicker across his face and finally settle on patient. She wanted to scream at him until he screamed back. Anger she knew she could handle. But caring and patience? It made her feel worse than she already did.

Don't we get a break from this? Don't you have some plan? We need him to understand why this is best for all of us. No, we can't just walk out on him...Well, actually, we can.

"Please do not ever think I took our relationship lightly. It was just the wrong time and wrong circumstance. Otherwise, I think it could have been forever," she said.

Kama had almost made it out of his shop before she felt his hand on her shoulder. Her hand shook as she opened the door, but she didn't resist when Cade turned her to face him. She saw concern and panic in his eyes. Gently, she shrugged off his touch. She pressed her lips together in a tight line to stop herself from giving in to him. She pushed him back off of her. She backed away and turned to go home.

"Stop. Kama, please, just stop."

"Don't do this," she implored. "You are making this harder than it needs to be."

"Don't you dare shut me out," he said.

"What do you want from me? I can't be your girlfriend," she said.

She allowed Cade to grasp her hands and hold them tight. She knew nothing more she could say would matter. She knew he wasn't willing to let her walk out of his life forever. His hands were warm and soft as they rubbed hers. Kama steeled herself and pulled away from his comfort.

"Okay. You are making a hard choice, and I am being selfish," he said. "You need time and space to figure this all out. I will give it to you. But I am not going to give up on you. You feel the need to do this to help you recover? Okay, I won't push you into a relationship. If I can't have your heart, I will take your friendship."

The words burned her, and she sighed like her world just ended. He tugged her hand and nodded at the bench near his worktable.

"Let's just sit together. We can spend some quiet time with each other," he said softly. "You have been through so much. Please, don't just drop this on me and leave. I accept your decision, but at least give me some time to deal with it."

"So, we are going to sit and stare at each other?" she asked after a heavy pause.

"I do have snacks," Cade said, leading her towards the bench.

She gave in, knowing full well that despite his offer of friendship she wouldn't ever see him again. Kama nodded with a small smile, ran up to the bathroom in his tiny apartment space, and spent the next ten minutes throwing up repeatedly. Cade quietly stood by her side, holding her hair back and talking softly to calm her down. Kama sat back against the wall and wiped her mouth with some toilet paper. She started to say something and leaned back over the bowl.

I cannot believe our nerves are this bad. Right, we have never broken up with a guy before. I don't know how people do this. Dating is all well and good, but being broken up with and breaking up with people is just hard. How are you supposed to look into the face of someone you like and just be done with them? I'm not sure whose heart is breaking more right now. If it feels like this, maybe I am doing the wrong thing. Oh, hell, he is rubbing my shoulders to make me feel better.

"So much for Loup healing abilities," she said, giving him a watery smile.

"Guess the almighty regeneration powers don't include frayed nerves. Seems like a big loophole to me," Cade said, offering her a wet washcloth.

Kama grinned at the pun as she sat back and took a cleansing breath. She watched him look her over. She knew the stress showed in the way she carried herself and the tense energy pouring off of her. She had no idea how Cade thought he could fix any of it. She didn't even want to deal with her experiences, but recognized she felt the safest and most comfortable around her Pack.

"I guess not," she said, refusing to give in to the guilt as he cared for her.

For once, I just wish he would be a jerk. He really should have been turned off by our throwing up and crying. It would be so much easier if he would take the out we gave him instead of trying to help us.

"Do you want anything to eat? Crackers, cheese, or something?" he offered. "It might not sound great, but it will help to settle your stomach."

"Probably a good plan, I guess. You know, up until this whole experience, I rarely got sick. Now, it seems like every time I have to think about what happened…what I did… I'm forever puking. Maybe some water will help. I'm sure I am dehydrated," she said, feeling unsteady. "I just hate the whole situation."

"I can't even begin to imagine," he said. "Kama, you have to give yourself a break. You just went through war. Sure, you were trained, but nothing ever gets you mentally ready for carrying out actions that were just exercises before."

She looked around and smiled when she noticed the pirate hat sitting on the table. Just being in his space, with his calming energy, allowed her to relax. Kama sat on the edge of his bed and closed her eyes while memories flickered by. Despite not having spent a lot of time there, what had transpired had been poignant. He walked the few steps between the impromptu kitchen area and the bed and handed her a bottle of water and a package of crackers. Kama grinned as she noted the crackers were her favorite kind. She didn't ever remember telling him what she liked. Then again, Cade was like that.

"I almost wish you wouldn't be so nice," she said as she nibbled. "Hopefully, this will pass over soon. I doubt it, but maybe."

"What? The sickness?" he asked. "Don't you have a doctor or someone who can check you out?"

"I have been sick almost every day since I got back," Kama said bitterly. "This is the aftermath: nightmares, vomiting, and pretending like nothing is wrong."

She watched him sit and knew he wanted to offer her haven again.

"You know I busted my ass to get promoted to the harder class? Somehow, I thought it meant I had made a lot of progress," she said. "The moves got easier, so I allowed myself to think I was a great fighter. Some big warrior."

Cade reached out to put a hand on her shoulder, and Kama knew he wanted to take her pain. He would give her room to vent and spit until she calmed down. She also knew the time had come to break it off. Each moment gave him false hope that she might change her mind.

"Well, thanks for the snack. I've got to run so I'm not late. Good-bye, Cade."

Kama walked out of his garage in a hurried pace.

Crap. We don't have a ride. Note to self, when breaking up with someone—have the car wait. It probably would have made for a shorter experience, too.

She forced herself to keep moving, so she wouldn't waiver and walk back to him. She didn't look back because she already wondered about her decision and had a hard time justifying her actions to herself. Her resolve wobbled a little, and she almost got run over when she stepped into the street to flag down a taxi. Quietly, she stared out the window. The bright lights of Manhattan drew closer as the taxi raced towards home and emptiness.

Her phone rang, and she didn't have to glance at the screen to know it was Cade. She silenced the call. The phone buzzed a few times indicating she had a new message.

Crap. And now we need to change our phone number. I can't deal with seeing missed calls and messages from him.

She shut off her phone and spent the rest of the ride in silence. Kama walked up the fourteen flights to her home and sighed in relief. She had actually expected to see Cade waiting at her door. She nodded at herself when she realized he did not know she had moved. If he had planned to wait, he would be at her parents' place.

She turned her phone back on and ignored the eruption of buzzing when it updated her missed calls and messages. She had two phone calls to make before she could shut it off again. The call to her carrier took only a few minutes. Kama doubted her parents would really understand her reasons, but in twenty-four hours she would have a new phone number.

Take a mental note, Wolf-Girl: we need to let Beth know our new phone number. I also need to tell Ajani that I broke up with Cade so he doesn't try to get my brother to help out with a "Win Kama Back" campaign.

The next call went better than she could have imagined. The news lightened her mood and made her smile. Things were going to change for the better. She just had to make it to January.

CHAPTER Three

Jack walked out of his office and, with a stretch of his shoulders, began to make his way to the Lounge. There were lots of popping noises as his joints tried to find their proper place again. His whole body still ached, and he spent a lot of time helping the Pack recover—both from his long absence and the fight against the mutants at the Facility. The unending activities expended all his energies. The mental fatigue consumed him just as much. He had conveyed the events of his Quest to Lorna, hoping she might have some insight for him, but when he tried to relay what he had experienced, it fell flat. His Pack Witch explained that each Spirit Quest had to be tailored for the individual person.

Of course, he still had a business to run, as well. Carla had also demanded his presence as the CEO of Twist Industries to accompany her to a dizzying array of holiday business parties. Thus, he spent each evening uncomfortably stuffed in a tux, groomed to perfection, and attentive at her side. He had to reestablish to the skeptical business world he was alive and well.

"Face it, Jack," Carla had said. "You don't have the luxury of not attending parties this year."

"I go to the blasted things every year," he said. "I am damn exhausted, Carla, and my Pack needs me."

"I understand, but you know we have the expansion deal coming up in January. There is no more time for you to be absent," she said calmly. "People noticed you weren't around. No matter how much I covered for you, people were starting to pry into our affairs. Go out, be social, and have a good time, dammit."

He nodded as he gave in. Carla had not only kept the company running for the last six weeks, she had been integral from the beginning. Realistically, he never would have made Cypress Steel Mills into Twist Industries if not for her strong, business acumen. He smiled at her and took a deep breath.

"I know you're right," he said. "I just hate making small talk with small-minded people."

"And now you know why I prefer to be the Executive Assistant," Carla laughed.

Jack had been offering her the title of Vice President for decades, but she turned him down time and again. Finally, she had explained, as his Executive Assistant, people would ignore her. She had gained valuable information over the years in this manner. Rather than fight to gain even a grain of acceptance, Carla often took advantage of being discounted and underestimated. Until she had the upper hand. Those who made jokes about Carla being in charge of Twist Industries while Jack played frontman had no idea how close to the truth they were.

He decided the best course of action would be to do the items Carla assigned him and show up at the parties. Arguing with her would be pointless and only add to his stress.

At the Park, things weren't much easier. He called his Betas together to debrief and nearly growled in frustration at the frenetic energy in his office. Lorna and Aturus had never liked each other, and during his absence, it had gotten worse. As he listened to the happenings, he had to resist the urge to visit harm upon both of them. In the end, The Judge had stepped up as de facto Alpha and kept things smooth. He dismissed Gabe and The Judge when he had heard enough. He stood and looked at his two remaining Betas, letting his fury fill the room. When they were properly cowed, he spoke.

"What the hell is wrong with you?" he asked.

Lorna and Aturus stared straight ahead without flinching. The last duty Jack had expected to have to do upon his return was to discipline two of his top warriors. They had presented a united front to the Pack for so long, and this digression pissed him off.

"I thought you two squashed this rivalry years ago."

He glared at them, not even sure what to say. He agreed with his wolf—who wanted to smack them both down—but he had no intention of fighting with his pregnant Beta. He paced a moment before turning to face them again.

"Here is where I'm at. I am too damn tired to deal with petty bullshit from leaders of this Pack. So…leave now, end your squabble.

Or Challenge me. You don't have to like each other. But if you ever disrespect me like this again, I will take your throats. Get out."

They walked out without a word, leaving him to the task of getting his life back on track. He managed to get through each day by counting down to Christmas, when the parties would end and the insanity would ease.

Working with his Pack to get people resettled and being seen had been hard enough. After his daily ministrations, things were beginning to get back to normal. The sense of panic had calmed, and people were returning to their customary sense of security. He didn't get to enjoy their relaxation, because he had to endure four to five hours of fake pleasantries, torturous small talk, and socializing with people he didn't like. It seemed each holiday party had someone waiting and watching for the smallest clue to validate the circulating rumors:

"Jack Twist has been off the radar, because the mob is looking for him."

"Jack Twist went to China to plot the demise of a competitor."

"Jack Twist went to Hell to renew his contract with the Devil."

And his all-time favorite: "Jack Twist went to the Philippines to get work done on his face."

He pretended he couldn't hear the hushed comments as he walked by with a smile on his face and Carla on his arm. They chatted, danced, and made sure to be seen long enough at what she deemed the most important parties. He wanted to laugh, albeit bitterly, as he had become the darling of gossip again merely by picking and choosing which parties to attend. He shook his head when Carla told him how his selections had set a new bar for popularity in their crazy business world.

"We can use this to our advantage," she said. "We will continue to be exclusive and only allow those who have sent in their RSVP to attend."

"Why would we do that? We know most of the people anyhow, and they are just lax about responding."

"Well, it's time for Twist Industries to change the trend," Carla said.

He nodded as he snagged another canapé off a tray. He knew he would not have been effective in changing her mind about the policy. He recognized the benefit to both him and Twist Industries, because the party would be magnificent. Carla had insisted they go old school: wandering carolers, chestnuts roasting in a mocked up fireplace, and even a performance troupe dancing signature pieces from *The Nutcracker*. At midnight, there would be snowfall and musical selections from a children's choir. Each guest would be ushered outside for a horse-drawn carriage ride. In September, when she had mentioned the lavish ideas, he had scoffed but ultimately let her make all the choices. He knew she asked out of protocol, because she always arranged the entire event anyhow.

Mostly because my relationship with Christmas is slightly marred. The holidays were great when I had a home and a family, but being in the orphanage was terrible and depressing. Losing Melissa two months before our second Christmas together didn't help at all. It is hard to pretend to feel the holiday cheer, like the others, when all I want to do is forget what happened. Just a moment to breathe and readjust to all of this.

There were going to be about two hundred and fifty guests in attendance. As they strolled through the venue, Carla updated him on the new security plan, and he made a mental note to add another bonus to his security team's paychecks. She wanted three separate checkpoints to ensure only the guests on the list made it through. He quietly laughed to himself at the diligence she had shown to exclude people.

"Get real, Jack. People will be talking about this until next year."

He let her ramble for the next few hours, choosing to think about how he would surprise Kama with her Christmas gift. He had meticulously crafted part of it and loved the finished product.

Two nights later, he found himself wandering the tunnels aimlessly until he had to get ready for the Twist Industries Gala. He had spent a lot more time being around his people and listening to what they had to say. For the most part, the mid-level Pack members were nervous since he didn't interact with them often. It made him realize just how large of a group seventy people were. Some of the tension had left his Pack and, somewhere along the line, he had been put up on a pedestal. It surprised him, because he had always thought himself to be approachable.

He enjoyed getting to re-meet his Pack members, some of whom he realized he barely knew anything about. Since he had gotten back from his Quest and the war, he had clocked more miles around the tunnels than he could remember. He had taken to spending time in the Lounge when possible, because most of them hung out there. It worked to his benefit as well; the more he interacted with his Pack, the closer her felt to them. Above all, he wanted to see Kama.

I understand we are all busy. The last time I saw her was in the trailer, as she slept. Then she went off with her mother to take her uncle back to Michigan. I wonder if she's had her winter recital at Julliard, yet. I haven't even had a chance to talk to her since I got back, to explain everything. Six weeks and no word—she's going to be upset with me. Of course, all of my time is now spent soothing the business world and the Pack back into a sense of normalcy. I don't have any free time; hell, I don't remember the last time I actually had a full meal.

Because he had been forced to attend half a dozen fancy parties in the last week, Jack hadn't had enough rest or food. He expected to have more time during the week, but something always came up.

I just want a break…

In a completely humbling moment for him two weeks later, he reached his breaking point. The night of the Twist Industries holiday party had been as exceptional as Carla could make it. He almost didn't recognize his own building. She had hired a company to decorate the entire thing, from the entryway and lobby all the way up to the second floor, which had been transformed into a winter paradise. The holiday events, per fashion dictates, had multiple waiters winding in and out of the guests, offering tiny sandwiches, canapés, and a variety of sweets. Having missed lunch and dinner that day, he resisted the urge to take a tray from a waiter and eat all of the contents.

After the very last guest had left, Carla excused him, and Jack stumbled back to his house at two in the morning. He made it to his room and changed carefully out of his tuxedo, only because rumpling it would mean Carla-the-She-Demon would force him to go shopping for another one. He pulled on some pajama pants and called it a night. Halfway to bed, his stomach clenched in a hard knot, reminding him it really needed some food.

I swear, if they are going to force us to spend evenings dressed up and interacting with the people who tried to destroy our business all year long, they should feed us real food. No more of these puffed pastries with a dab of cheese and some, fancy, red thing. Dammit, I am hungry.

For a few moments, Jack contemplated pulling clothes back on and heading back out to find a restaurant. The one benefit of living in New York? The city really didn't sleep, and there had to be some place open to feed his hunger. His bone-weary tiredness reminded him leaving the house would mean less sleep, so he found himself shuffling down to his kitchen. He was too tired to do more than give a disappointed sigh when he found nothing in the fridge.

Right, Twist, your kitchen is not going to be stocked after you've been gone for six weeks. Seriously, did you think it would magically replenish itself? Holy crap, can I just get a burger or something? A big, juicy burger with cheese and bacon... shut up, Jack.

He rifled through his cupboards one more time and, after reviewing the pitiful offerings with disdain, pulled out a can of baked beans. After two minutes of fighting with the electric can opener, he realized it had a pop top. Jack laughed and opened the can. He stared at the watery, dog food-like contents and weighed the costs of moving across the kitchen to pour the beans into a bowl and heat them in the microwave versus eating them cold. As a ripple of weariness blanketed his body, Jack gave in. He leaned against the counter and, using his fingers, scooped his makeshift meal into his mouth.

Yes, kids. This is how an overly exhausted, billionaire, ex-marine, Loup Alpha lives the big life. Eating beans from a can.

He let his thoughts spiral around, without forcing them into anything coherent, and the world slowly went gray around him. Weak beams of sunlight penetrated his eyelids, and, as Jack blinked them open, he realized he must have fallen asleep mid-meal. He sat slouched against his cupboards, can of beans on its side on the floor next to him. He shook his head and pushed himself to his feet.

Yes, I have definitely hit a new low.

Jack felt immediately better when he realized his party-going hell was almost over. His company event had fallen on the night before Christmas Eve, and the only party left to attend would be New Year's Eve. He had made it through the holiday season, bean incident aside, mostly unscathed. He climbed the stairs and went to shower.

After two days of no parties, food in abundance, and long hours of uninterrupted sleep, Jack had returned to the Park. He took a deep breath and walked out onto the large platform. The Lounge was crowded, but more subdued than Jack wanted to see. Losing eight members of their Pack had taken a toll on the survivors. Hushed conversations lowered even further as he looked around. His own desire to see Kama would have to wait just a bit longer; his people were hurting. Over the past few weeks, he had spent more and more time at the popular meeting place, driven by what he assumed to be his instinct to help them. Jack went to the group in the center and sat next to a sobbing, young girl. He gently placed his hand on her shoulder, to connect with and comfort her. Their wolf nature needed the physical reassurance, and the human side would need his words. He felt a pressure on his own shoulder and peace settled over him.

Just as the Goddess showed me how to come to terms with my experiences, I just need for each and every person in my Pack to know their Den is a place of safety. I get it. I know they have lost a sense of well-being and trusting us, their leaders. Damn, I am going to have to ask Lorna what else can be done. Of course, there might be nothing else but to let time heal them. I just took a bunch of children into war. What did I really expect to happen? Okay, let's see what my Pack has to say.

He sat talking with the girl until the group stood to go on rounds. She thanked him for his attention and excused herself. He tried not to stare openly at Kama and Beth walking into the Lounge. Another group called him over to chat, and he moved towards them. Jack saw Kama pull out her phone and talk animatedly into it and wondered why she had changed her phone number. He had been frustrated with the three weeks of zero contact with her. Instead of being able to go directly to her, he made small talk and gave reassuring touches to various shoulders, reasserting himself as protector, friend, and most importantly, as their Alpha. By the time he had made it around the platform, Kama had already left. He shook his head. They kept missing each other, but when they did get together…

Sometime later, Jack prepared to leave. He saw Lorna approaching and put a smile on his face. Despite the harsh words a few weeks before, leading to her avoiding him as much as possible, she seemed to be in a good mood, and he intended to enjoy the upswing. He greeted her warmly and told her of his plans to have a memorial service for the entire Pack. After she left, he got some hot coffee and made his way back to his office. Jack was lost in his thoughts as he wound through the tunnels. He hoped to never have to take his Pack to war again. For all of the training and keeping them ready as troops, he had never actually planned for more than a few raids on vampire nests. He had been proud of them for fighting without question or qualm. He also felt a profound sadness that they had to have gone through such horrors.

No, "sad" isn't quite the right word. There just isn't another to describe it in detail; there is nothing to describe making people who trust you go through something that will haunt them for the rest of their lives. My pack members who participated are still suffering in silence due to fear of repercussions of telling what they experienced. They are afraid to seem weak from unresolved emotions and pain. There is no way my Betas or I could have impressed upon them the magnitude of responsibilities they would have to adopt when they became part of the Pack. I know this will take time.

He forced himself to calm his mind. It wouldn't do anyone good for him to appear to be frazzled. Instead, he would work with the Betas to create a new training program, to better deal with the many aspects of death they would have to live with. A flicker of movement caught his attention in the tunnel ahead of him. He looked up and met Kama's gaze. A smile covered his face, and he began to walk slightly faster toward her; he exhaled a breath, releasing tension he didn't even know he held. He had a lot of things to say to her. They could walk back to his office together, where he would explain his idea and how she could help him out. Then he would kiss her breathless. Jack rehearsed the words in his head carefully, there would only be one time to deliver them. He waited for a return smile, but instead received a hostile glare before she turned and fled down the tunnel. Away. From him.

What the hell? I can't believe she just ran away from me.

His mind churned all the way down the halls back to his office. He didn't understand what had just happened. He all of a sudden needed nothing more but to get in his office and get his head around what had happened. He had a moment of hope when he saw a lean figure leaning against the door.

"Alpha."

The soft greeting dashed his hopes. He looked up and met the soft gray of Olivia's eyes. Jack sighed inwardly. He didn't actually want to deal with her right then; he wanted to talk to Kama. Ever since saving the girl from the mutant facility during the raid, she had become his ward, as he had promised Janus. He didn't mind the job. She was quiet and followed orders without question. The problem came from her needing orders to do everything. In the facility, she had had no freedom to do anything, and that mentality followed her to his Park.

"Olivia," he said and forced some warmth into his tone to hide the disappointment. "Come in."

He opened his door for her and followed her in. He walked around his desk while she stood at attention in front of it. Jack wished she would relax, but he doubted she knew how.

"How can I help you?"

"I hate to have to ask for this, Alpha, but I have no food in my room, and I am not sure where to get any more."

Jack nodded and sighed. He had allowed Lorna and then Tina to take over supervising the girl after they had returned from Pennsylvania. He had made sure to have someone get her acquainted with her new surrounding while he got his Park and his business back in order, but he had never once considered that she had no idea of how to take care of herself. It would become a wearisome chore to make sure Olivia had enough supplies. He also suspected she would need to learn how to do the basics, such as shop and cook. Then all the puzzle pieces fell into place and a soft smile creased his lips. He knew the perfect person to help show Olivia around. He bade her sit while he called Karl and sent him off on a search and recovery mission.

Why did he sound so eager? He can't possibly be petitioning another stake-and-take. Oh, hell. His vocabulary is rubbing off on me. I suppose it doesn't hurt for me to speak a little less formally with my Pack. Perhaps he is hiding from The Judge. Either way, he can run this errand for me. I suppose the best thing is that Olivia will stand here quietly until Karl gets back.

Jack didn't bother to make small talk with Olivia. From the few interactions they had had in the past, she didn't seem to need the filler most people did. He did want to take time—maybe after a few months, when she had acclimated to their Den—to get information from her. He couldn't shake the feeling of needing to remember important information. He had been having déjà vu since coming back from his Quest. Pieces of information flittered through his mind, but it didn't make sense just yet.

He waited as patiently as possible for Karl to return from his mission. Olivia sat still on the sofa, so he picked up a sheaf of papers and tried to read about some of the raids that had been done. He had missed the routine of taking care of affairs at the park. Unlike business paperwork, it was simple and plain. There were bribes to be paid to keep their secret and other money donated to societies and organizations to help smooth the way. He collected himself as a knock on the door sounded.

"Come in."

He watched Kama walk in and smiled at her. Jack then had to offer the same smile to the Omega, Beth, who trailed behind her. He hadn't counted on her bringing her friend, but it actually worked out better.

"Hello, ladies," he said with a smile.

"Alpha," Kama and Beth said in unison.

"This is Olivia. She is new to our Pack from the facility," he said. "She is Loup and needs some help acclimating to our city and how we do things around here. She has worked with Tina for training, but I would like you both to show her around. Omega, take Olivia out to get some food for her room. Make sure she has anything else she needs."

With a smile, he handed a credit card to the young woman. She still seemed nervous around him, and he hoped it would fade soon. He waited for the two to leave the room and shut the door after them.

"Her name is Beth."

He paused before turning around. The tone of Kama's voice went beyond frosty and into downright hostility. Jack faced her and placed a calm smile on his face. He knew she was upset with him, so he settled himself to wait out what he rather expected would be a tirade.

"I'm sorry. I shouldn't have been so degrading toward your friend," he said.

"You mean your Pack member, don't you, Alpha?"

Her sneer put him on alert. Jack swallowed back a sharp retort. He would let her vent so they could talk. But he had no intention of waiting for too long. He approached her gently.

"Yes, I do. She is a valued member as well," he conceded. "You're right. I should call her by her name."

He walked closer and stood in front of her. She met his eyes, and he saw the fury. He knew he had earned some anger from being gone so long, but not the amount she blazed at him. Jack knew it would only be a matter of time before she let him know what was on her mind.

"Is that all, Alpha?"

"No."

She raised an eyebrow but waited.

"I really would like you and Beth to make Olivia feel welcome. She has been through a mess, and I want her to feel like a member."

"I cannot believe you expect me to take your new girlfriend around the Park."

Jack flinched, not so much from the words being said, but from the absolute hiss they were issued with.

"It is bad enough you would leave me—injured—but to come back after we almost died and have me take her around is just damn insulting."

"Wait a minute. Girlfriend? What are you talking about?" Jack asked. He could not figure out how asking her to help someone would warrant this kind of reaction. The anger had more behind it than his absence. Maybe being sent on the raid and the injury to her uncle drove it.

"Which part didn't you understand? I'll speak slowly this time."

His wolf growled low in his head, and all his hackles were up.

"Why don't you explain everything," he said.

"Alrighty, then."

Jack watched as she paced and then stopped in front of him, her spine stiffened more, if possible. He watched her give him the once-over with her eyes and then take a deliberate step back.

"As you might remember, I had a run-in with a mutant. I got hurt, defending this Park and this Pack. Doc had to cut away parts of my arm to make sure it would heal properly. But you wouldn't know about those grisly details, would you? No. Because you decided that, rather than let your precious Pack know we were dating, it would be better just to leave. To be done with me. All because I wouldn't stay and follow your orders. You made it clear if I chose my family over your Pack, you would be done. You said good-bye and left."

Jack stood there, stunned. He didn't actually have an answer right away, because never once could he have imagined she thought he had left her. Still, he waited for her to get it all out.

"What I don't understand is why you want me to take her around? Why do you want me to get to know her? What kind of sick games are you playing, Jack?"

The rapid-fire questions were flung at him like knives, and he decided to straighten some things out.

"Kama," he began gently, then got more firm as she cut her eyes at him. "What do you remember about your injury?"

"I got attacked in the tunnels by the mutant, and he sliced my arm up. You took me to Doc and then left."

"How much time passed?" he pressed.

"What?"

"How much do you remember from the attack? Do you even know how long you were in the med bay?

"Well, Doc said about four days," she said, shrugging.

"Okay. Do you realize you were unconscious for almost a full day before I even got to see you? Doc had to work on you nearly four hours just to get you stable."

Jack watched confusion cloud her face. He hoped walking her back through the timeline would help her realize the truth.

"You waited a whole day to come and see me? Do I mean so little to you, Jack? I got hurt defending *your* Park. The least you could have done is made sure I was okay. You could have checked in or something."

He wanted to shake some sense into her. She held on to her anger with a vengeance he didn't understand. He tried to give her more facts to help her realize the truth.

"I carried you through the tunnels, with your blood running down my arms. I stayed until Doc took you into surgery and threatened me with great bodily harm and worse if I didn't leave," he grated out. "I left while you were in surgery to make sure the rest of the Park was secure."

A small frisson of doubt creased her face but went away too quickly for his liking.

"Yet you come back, throw me a pretty excuse, and then expect me to be her private guide. There are plenty of people willing to kiss your ass and teach her the Park rules. What is wrong with you, Jack Twist? Let me tell you something. No, never mind. I will take your little girlfriend around, because you are my Alpha and I have to do what you say," she said. "However, understand this: you aren't the only one who found someone new. While you were away, I dated someone, too. I guess it is pretty easy to find a replacement."

No other words she said had impacted him more. Fury rose up quickly, and his wolf pushed forward. He stepped in close to her and glowered as she stepped in as well.

"You what?"

"You may have left me, but I moved on," she said. "And do not expect me to leave this Pack just because you can't handle being my Alpha while I date someone else."

Jack growled low in his throat. He wanted to believe she spoke with fake bravado, trying to make him feel as out of sorts as she. However, the taunt of her dating another man crossed the line, and he stalked even closer, forcing her to take steps back to look up at him.

"I never left you," he said in a quiet tone, forcing himself to stay calm. "I was sent on a Spirit Quest to protect this Pack and had no choice about it."

He cut her off when she started to protest.

"As for Olivia, she was held captive in the Facility. I promised to rescue her in order to get the plans so we could take down that evil place."

Jack paced, his fury rose, and he shook as anger coursed through him.

"What gets me the most is not the fact that you felt free enough to date," he seethed. "What kills me, Kamaria, is you think so little of me. You actually thought I would just walk away while you were hurt. Apparently, my morals and ethics are so lacking and deplorable, you thought I would walk away from our relationship, from you—my Mate—when you needed me most."

He watched her mouth open and close as reality crashed down on her.

"Let me clarify it for you. I didn't leave you, I didn't break up with you, and I still love you," he said. "However, I am going to take a cue from you and walk out of this room before I say things I cannot take back."

Jack turned, walked to the door, and pushed it open.

"For someone who swears she is grown, you might try acting like it."

He walked out and headed… somewhere. Despite hoping he could calm down enough to go back and get some work done, he knew it wasn't going to happen. Instead, he walked around the city for about an hour, until his stomach gurgled.

"I am going to get enough food to feed eight people," he muttered to himself. "I cannot believe this."

Jack set his phone to priority calls only, made his way to his favorite restaurant, and hoped December would end soon.

CHAPTER Four

Kama walked along, lost in whirling thoughts. She had tried to focus on the loud city around her, but it only made her mind shout louder. She had been wandering for at least an hour, trying to make some sense of the emotional maelstrom from her meeting with Jack.

Somehow, I didn't expect our first meeting to end up with me shouting at him. He didn't leave me. Or course he didn't! How could I ever have imagined he would just walk out? He is not that kind of man. The man I know him to be is honorable and caring. Being hopped up on drugs with a major injury doesn't make for the best sense of what is real. Oh, damn. This is just a big, fat mess. Why the hell did I throw Cade at him? He was pissed. I don't think I have ever seen him—oh, wait. When I didn't want to believe being Loup, he got all dominant. Definitely the Alpha there.

She grinned. Jack had never been anything but playful or kind with her, so seeing his strong, governing side actually comforted her on an instinctual level. She didn't enjoy being yelled at or cornered, but her wolf radiated an extremely smug and satisfied attitude at his behavior. Kama knew she would sort through it all later. For now, she needed to apologize and make reparations. She walked with slow, dragging steps and hesitated before his house. Feeling nervous about seeing him again unnerved her. She'd never had a negative emotion about Jack.

This is the other side of being walked away from. This bites. Okay, no answer for the door buzzer. I guess we sit here and wait. At least it's not snowing today. We are done with the holidays; it can all melt, and spring can come back.

She sighed, reached into the basket she had brought, and found a roll to nibble on. It could be hours before he returned, but she would stay to have a discussion and get things sorted out. About forty minutes later, she looked up at the sound of footsteps and met Jack's eyes. The air seemed to thicken around them as emotions rolled off each of them. He walked up to her without hesitation and stood before her. She rose to meet him, not sure if she should say anything or even smile. Minutes rolled by as they stood there, looking at each other. She sniffed appreciatively at the scent of Thai food swirling in the air.

"I would like to finish our discussion," Kama said. "And I am hoping you brought enough for both of us."

Jack gave her a quizzical look and a small smile. He pointed to the picnic basket sitting on the porch.

"Didn't you bring a lunch?" he asked.

"I wasn't sure how long you would be…and I got hungry," Kama said with a shrug. "I've been waiting a long time."

Relief swept over her as she watched him shake his head. He opened the door and gestured for her to enter. Kama walked to the kitchen, put the basket on the counter, and then turned to look at Jack with scrutiny and concern. His face looked drawn and tired, but she could tell something else haunted him. She could only imagine how slowly he had to be recovering after his Quest and going to war. She felt exhausted all the time from a lack of uninterrupted sleep and knew he must be suffering the same. She wanted to blurt out all of her apologies and get it done, but tried to approach it differently than she had last time.

Yes, we do need to listen to him completely. Let him finish explaining. No, I will not accuse him again. Sheesh, for a non-verbal component in my head, you sure are chatty. Yes, let's go in and have a nice talk.

She followed him to the living room and stood awkwardly in a place so familiar but at that time, so unforgiving.

"I am glad you came," he said.

"Me, too," she said and blinked against her misting eyes.

Kama took a silent, deep breath and tried to get down to business. It all felt very weird, and she didn't know where to start. She didn't want it to sound like a bunch of lame excuses because she got called out. She wrung her hands and blew air through clenched lips. Nothing made sense, and after a few false starts, she hung her head. Kama refused to give up but couldn't find the words. Looking into his olive green eyes, she found hope.

"Well, if it's any comfort I don't hate you. Nor am I pushing you away," Jack said quietly.

"Why?" Kama said, looking at him in surprise.

"Why?" he tilted his head in confusion. "You honestly don't understand?"

"I betrayed you. You should hate me," she said and paused until the silence suffocated her. "I am sorry."

"Apology accepted," he said simply.

"It is? Just like that?" Kama asked. "It's this easy?"

"As I said before, you are my Mate," Jack said. "And no, this won't be easy, but it will be worth it."

She let out the anticipatory breath tightening around her chest like a vice.

"So, I don't have to figure out how to get over being in love with you anymore?" she asked.

"It doesn't mean we go right back to where we were. There is a lot that needs to be said and worked through. I love you. That is the simple part. The rest will come along as we re-learn each other."

She watched him set the food on the coffee table, not sure what she felt. Nothing prepared her for the wash of emotions flooding over her. Kama sat when he did and kept sneaking glances of him out of the side of her eye. She had been impressed with his firm stance; it felt secure. She realized his quiet strength calmed her, even though the past few hours had been disastrous. Kama tried to figure out how his being mad at her made her feel like everything would be okay. She decided nothing about being in love made sense.

I'm crazy. Something is broken in me. At least Jack is being calm about it all. Who likes confrontation? Maybe wolf nature has something to do with this. Maybe I should learn more about this side of us.

"Should we have red or white with dinner?" Jack asked.

"You finish setting out the food. I'll grab a bottle of red."

She tried not to run into the kitchen, sighing in relief. She took a bottle out of the fridge and popped the cork. Kama smiled, despite the emotional blender running in her body. She remembered the last time they had eaten at his house—before this mess. She wanted to stay in and cook dinner, so she made sloppy joes. He had teased her mercilessly about being a gourmet cook. Leaning against the prep island, Jack took great pleasure in mocking her.

"Sloppy joes." he sneered.

"What?" she had asked, confused.

"Nothing. Miss Gourmet Cooking Camp Champion."

"I like sloppy joes," she said dismissively. "Tell you what, if these aren't the best you have ever tasted, I will make whatever you want."

She watched Jack take his sloppy joe and make the point of an exaggerated bite. Satisfaction filled her as his eyes widened in surprise. She knew a complex array of spices and textures had exploded in his mouth. Kama grinned smugly at him and ate her own sandwich.

"This is superb," he said, with real surprise lacing his voice. "I mean, it's really good."

"This is what happens when you spend your summers at a cooking camp," she said. "My mother's idea of giving back was to sponsor city kids to go to some dude ranch and learn to cook. She also sent me and Ajani. She swore we needed the experience, but, not surprisingly, it coincided with our increasing sibling spats. I only went for three years, and then Julliard took over. My brother attended until he turned fourteen, and until the cool factor of being a chef vanished."

"Your mother sounds like an amazing woman," he had said.

"Yes, she is."

Kama shook her head clear of the memory and went back to the living room where Jack had laid out the Thai food. As he sat down next to her, she noticed he moved stiffly, as if tendrils of discomfort affected his whole body. Kama hadn't heard of any injuries to him on the raid, so she wondered what the whole Spirit Quest had done to him.

"Can we talk about your journey during dinner?" she asked. "Afterwards, I have a whole bunch of explaining and groveling to do."

"Sure, I can answer a few questions."

Kama caught his eyes and the pain he didn't bother to mask and took a sip of wine.

"What happened to you?" she asked quietly, focusing deep within the glass but having to say something as his stare became more and more intense. "You were just gone."

"I am sorry I couldn't contact you sooner," he said. "Lorna set up the Quest, but at the last minute we learned I was the one who needed to go. I had no idea it would take six weeks of time here. As you can imagine, everything is different in the Spirit realm."

"I didn't even know the place existed."

Despite trying not to just shoot glances at him, she found she couldn't. She filled a plate and then got up, moved around the coffee table, and sat on the floor. She didn't want to try to have a conversation without eye contact.

"What did you find there? I mean, what did you do? Did you physically leave, or were you in some kind of trance?"

She watched him take a few bites of food. Emotions warred across his face, and she wondered if she could handle what would be said next.

"Kamaria, I really think we need to address the hard stuff first. I will happily tell you all about the Quest, but let's get the big talk done first. We will both feel better."

"Damn, I hate when you use my full name like that," she muttered. "You are going to have to use it periodically when you aren't upset with me."

She saw the grin before he squashed it and realized they could have a talk without it turning into a shouting match, if they both tried to be civil. Kama took a breath.

"Okay, then let me address a few things you said. You are correct. I didn't think. I know you are an honorable person and you never would have left me injured if you had a choice. However, I would also ask you to look at it from my side," she said. "I think this misunderstanding has been building since we met. It only got worse when I found out I was Loup and you became my Alpha."

She pushed her plate away from her and locked eyes with him.

"Since we were waiting until I turned eighteen, no one knew we were dating, which meant I couldn't ask about you when you disappeared. The last words I remembered you saying were good-bye. When I finally had to talk to someone about our break up, I vented to Beth. She warned me not to say anything about dating you, because I could be Challenged and killed for it. All this hiding and sneaking around is horrible. Having to pretend this—us—isn't happening is just crap."

Kama watched a frown tighten his mouth and sat up a bit straighter.

"Kama, you would not have been killed for dating me. I suppose there could have been a Challenge, forcing us to be public with our relationship in the Pack. However, I doubt it. None of the other women in the Pack have shown the least bit of interest in dating me. As for one of them killing you…" Jack said. "Why would Beth think it's possible?"

"As Omega, she sees things you don't as the Alpha. I mean, she gets picked on when someone needs to feel better about themselves on any given day. No one sees her as a worthy person or even Pack member. But I do. She is my best friend and always offers unique insight to situations. So, I believe her about this. A Challenge over the coffee pot is one thing, but a Challenge over dating you is different. Essentially, it means I claim to be strong enough to be with you. No female who wants top spot would let me live, because it means she would have to watch her back for when I wanted to Challenge her again," Kama said, and then added after a pause, "And, Jack? There are a lot of women in our Pack who want to date you."

She ate as she watched him consider the information. She couldn't believe his blindness to the flirtatious looks and glances tossed his way.

Hell, even as new to dating as we are, we can see it. I mean, we aren't good at dating by any means. We just caused… yes, we, not just me. You do not get to be exempted from this mess. We are one. Remember what Nula said? Anyhow, we were saying, at least we can tell when someone is attracted to us. They aren't throwing themselves at his feet—but seriously? They lift a metaphorical tail every time he comes around.

Kama found him giving her a dubious look. A small flicker of satisfaction ran through her. Dating was hard for everyone.

"Anyhow, it only got worse. A lot of rumors started going around our Pack. The Betas announced you were gone on business and for the first few weeks, things were normal. But the longer you were away, the more agitated people got," Kama said with a small shudder. "There were talks about the Park splitting into smaller packs, until The Judge took over. Most people were pretty certain he killed you. Of course, things calmed with him calling the shots, because everyone is afraid of him. The whole feel of the place got all tense, and people started to act weird. Is that normal for Loup?"

Jack shrugged, even though the look on his face betrayed a whole other set of emotions. Kama relaxed a small bit more as she realized she could still read him.

"It's one of the oddities of our nature. Despite having the high-end intellect of humans, we also have the instinct of wolves. We take poorly to the leader being gone. Wolf packs in nature get very skittish when the Alpha is gone too long. It's the reason the Betas didn't tell you all much," he explained. "Although, in hindsight, it might have been better for everyone to know I was on a Spirit Quest. Then you would have known I planned to come back."

"So, I found myself upset to have been attacked, confused about why you left, and, not for nothing, still figuring out how to be Loup," she said.

"I can understand your confusion and pain, but—you dated another man?"

The hurt she saw in his eyes made Kama want to fix everything as soon as possible. She had been careless with his feelings and it felt devastating.

"Yeah, well, I cried for about a week. When Cade asked me out, I was at a low point. My wolf wasn't at all happy, but we had been friends at school, and I saw no harm," she said. "And then you brought Olivia back. I saw the care you gave to her and jumped to conclusions. I had just learned I could have been killed for dating you and yet you walked her around in public. I couldn't handle it. It pushed all sorts of wrong buttons. I felt very much like a hidden mistress, instead of your girlfriend. I thought I was over you and done being mad at you."

"Olivia is a child and part of the mission," Jack interrupted.

"I know that now," Kama said. "How did she end up there? She's Loup. It doesn't make sense."

"It's a tale for another time. Let's just finish this. Obviously, I am not at all happy you dated someone else, but I can understand. I am sorry you feel like you are a hidden shame. I'm sure we both could have handled it better."

Kama nodded and finished her dinner. They sat in silence for a moment.

"I am damn tired of feeling guilty about every damn thing," she said, her shoulders slumping. "Just so you know, I broke it off with Cade after we got back from the raid. Of course, my anger spoke in loud volumes, and I only threw it at you because I didn't understand how you could ask me to be friends with my replacement. I was even angrier at myself for not being over you. I didn't want to be in love with you if you didn't love me back."

She flinched when Jack grabbed her hands. She hadn't expected him to move so suddenly.

"Okay. It's done. I cannot pretend it won't take more time, but I can say I am not going to be without you again. If you want to announce it to the Pack tomorrow, we will do so."

"I have waited five months. I can wait one more," Kama said. After a small hesitation, she released his hands to reach across the table to refill her plate. She felt ravenous after working things out.

"Can I ask you a question?" Jack said.

"Yeah?"

"Why did you change your phone number?"

"Oh, yeah. I broke up with Cade and I didn't want to see any missed calls or texts from him."

"But you go to the same school," Jack said.

"Not anymore. I'm graduating in two weeks," Kama said. "I have enough credits, so I decided to take the January ceremony instead of June."

"I had no idea you could graduate early," he said. "What else has changed since I've been gone?"

"Well, let me think…"

Kama started to fill him in on all the adventures she had. She told him about the sketch mission with the vampire, and then telling her brother about being Loup. She moved to sit next to him on the couch and spoke animatedly while she explained how Ajani had been brought into the know. She moved through some of the daily minutia and frowned slightly as she recalled some of the minor scuffles she had been in.

"You know, you have some rotters in this Pack. Some of these people never got over some internal emotional crap and pick on other people," she said. "Anyhow, Juan decided I would be his favorite whipping girl. I mean, not literally, but he certainly enjoys forcing me to tap out any time he can."

"All of this in six weeks. I have lost so much time with you," he said. "So many things you have experienced without me here."

She placed a hand on his arm, hating to hear the sadness lace his voice.

"Jack, we will have a lifetime to make new memories."

"I missed your final concert."

"Well, then, rent Carnegie Hall, and I will give you a private one," she said. "I mean, my mother will probably be there, because that woman has never missed a single concert I have given."

Warmth filled her as Jack broke into laughter. The sound healed and soothed her all at once, and she joined him. Though she did want to warn him, she didn't say it in jest; Brenna didn't miss her daughter's concerts. She easily went to his embrace and snuggled against his chest as she finished talking about her time in the Park without him. Recounting it all, Kama noted she had done a lot of training. Every time she turned around, one of Aturus's crew was roping her into some kind of exercise. She wondered if they would ever forgive her for defending her brother.

"Okay. As much as I have enjoyed our talk, it's time for you to get going," Jack said, interrupting her internal ramble.

"What? Where am I going?"

"Home?" he ventured. "You have a curfew."

"No, I don't. I moved out," Kama said. "After I got back from taking Uncle James to Michigan, I realized I needed more freedom to come and go."

"Wait—you what? Where did you move to?" Jack asked.

"Downstairs a floor from my parents," she said and explained the situation to him.

Kama snuggled in closer and kept talking until yawns punctuated her sentences on a regular basis.

"Okay. Now, I'm going," she said.

"You're welcome to stay," Jack said. "I have a guest room if you want to sleep alone."

"No," Kama said after a moment. "I'm going to go home. We need time to process."

She stood and found the shoes she had kicked off. Hand in hand, Jack and Kama walked to the door.

"Let me at least offer you a ride home," Jack said and called for his driver.

They waited in the foyer, Kama leaning back against him in comfortable silence. When the driver showed, she turned to give Jack a hug but eagerly accepted the kiss he offered instead. The passionate embrace reconnected their energy, which surged between them. She broke it off, breathless, and looked at him.

"I need to go."

"Goodnight, Kamaria. I'll see you tomorrow."

"Ahh, the use of my whole name in a good way."

She walked to the car and waved to him. Slumping back in the seat for the ride, she exhaled slowly.

I expected it to be much more complicated. Maybe I need to just accept this at face value. Perhaps I make things a bit more dramatic than they need to be.

Her wolf snorted in agreement.

Gee, thanks.

Kama woke early the next morning and lay in bed. For the first time in weeks, she felt calm and settled. She smiled as she thought of her good-night kiss, but it faded when she thought about the task she faced. Jack had asked her to help Olivia acclimate. She doubted he would have asked her to do it just because they were Mates, however, she had no idea how to deal with the girl.

First things first, we are going to have to get to know her. I wonder if she likes shopping. It would be a fun way to get to know each other. Not to mention, I am sure she needs new outfits. Actually, I wonder if she has anything.

She pushed herself out of bed, took an amazingly short shower, and got dressed. She walked out her front door and knocked politely on Ajani's door. Kama could hear the clatter of dishes going into his sink. Her brother opened the door, and she held out her coffee mug and tried to look piteous.

"Please?"

"Really, Kama?" he snorted. "You know how to make coffee as well as I do. Fine. Come in."

She smiled and walked in with a slight bounce.

"You made waffles. Can I?"

She laughed as he sighed deeply, handed her a plate, and then opened the fridge. She loaded the plate with two, huge waffles and drowned them in butter and syrup. She forked a huge piece into her mouth and made appreciative noises. Kama nodded to Beth as she came into the kitchen and sat at the table with her. Ajani placed two mugs before them.

"You two eat like teenage boys," he muttered. "I was one. I should know."

"Gender biased much?" Kama laughed. "We eat like Loup girls; we can put teenage boys to shame."

Beth agreed from deep within her coffee cup.

"Today's mission is to learn all about Olivia," Kama announced to her. "I figured we could take her shopping and help her get stuff for her place. I've seen Karl's room, which is kind of nice, considering he lives in a subway tunnel, but I have no idea what her space looks like."

She went back to eating with gusto and didn't think of much else until the silence forced her to look up.

"What?"

"You're in a good mood," Ajani said. "It's nice to see."

"Thanks."

Kama finished her waffles and the eggs her brother had generously made. She sat back and sipped her coffee.

"Do you two live together?"

"No, I still have my own place," Beth said, finishing her own plate of food. "Why?"

"Just wondered. You are here a lot. I think it's cute," Kama said. "Okay, let's get ready to figure out Olivia."

Despite her eager and ready-to-go attitude, she had to wait for Beth and Ajani to say their good-byes. She rolled her eyes and finally walked out of her brother's apartment to wait. Beth joined her soon after, and they made their way down the stairs.

"No sounds of derision this morning?"

"Would it stop your kiss-fests?" Kama asked.

"Not really," Beth said with a grin.

"I can't be mad. He's clearly smitten with you, and he did cook me breakfast. I mean, he cooked it for you but made more for me."

They laughed together as they complimented the food. The idle chatter carried them all the way to the Park.

"Do you know where Olivia stays?" Kama asked Beth.

"Yes, she's up in the northern section."

"How do you know these things already?"

"Why did you ask if you didn't think I knew?" Beth said with a laugh. "I did spend the better part of yesterday with her while you met with the Alpha. How did your conversation go?"

Kama hesitated. She had never lied to her friend. She also didn't see any point in having an argument with her just then. They hadn't even talked about her breaking up with Cade, yet. So much had gone on in such a short period of time that Kama's head still spun thinking about it all. Instead of answering, she deflected.

"Rough and uncomfortable. Needless to say, the Alpha wasn't very happy with my attitude," she said. "But he did task me—us, really—to help Olivia get settled, and I plan to do so."

She was thankful her friend didn't push the issue. The crisp, December air invigorated them, and they moved quickly north. Kama loved the way the snow clung to the trees and laughed as Beth took a face full of snow when a branch dumped onto her. She didn't even mind when her friend took the initiative to throw a few snowballs at her. When their hands were nearly frozen, they resumed their walk.

"Where do you think we should take her first?"

"I don't know about taking her anywhere, Kama," Beth said. "Maybe we should bring some food to her and sit and chat for a while. It might be easier to take her places if we know more about her."

Of course. It makes perfect sense. The poor girl probably has had a miserable experience being there. I think she needs to have a family; we can just adopt her into ours. Look, the Blockhouse. I swear the Park gets smaller each time we walk through it. It really is home now.

"You go and grab some food, and I'll chat with Olivia," Kama said, handing Beth some money. "I'm thinking groceries are a better call than restaurant food. I have no idea what she eats, but I can work with components."

She handed Beth more money.

"Get a hotplate or something, too. I doubt she has anything to cook with."

She walked down the narrow stairs and then pulled open the hidden door. The Central Park Historical Society hosted tours to the basement room of the Blockhouse, so it wouldn't be strange to see someone going in. She made her way to the ledge, found the metal ladder embedded in the rock, and scaled down a few levels. While Kama didn't really spend time in the living areas in the northern section, she at least could find them. As her eyes adjusted to the darker space, she began walking down a tunnel that probably hadn't been used by anyone other than Loup for at least three decades. She hated the dank smell; being close to water left the area perpetually damp. She passed one platform already converted into rooms and got directions to the one where Olivia stayed.

"Hello?" she called, after finding her way.

She heard a light growl and then a grunt. Bones popped in the distance, and Kama's brow furrowed.

"Hi," Olivia said a few moments later.

Kama noticed she wore only a robe and looked drawn and skittish.

"Can we talk?" Kama asked.

"Sure. What do you need ?"

"How about we sit and have a chat? The Alpha asked me to help get you settled here. I sent my friend to get us some food, and I thought we could figure out what you need."

Kama followed Olivia to the back of the platform and hoped Beth would be able to find them. Two lanterns cut the darkness around them, and she tried not to groan aloud when she saw three mattresses that made up Olivia's living area.

"Oh, wow. You don't even have blankets," Kama said.

"I don't need any. My body is warm enough."

It took Kama a minute to process her words.

"Oh. You sleep shifted?"

"Yes, I always have," Olivia said. "You do not?"

Oh my. We are going to have a lot to talk about, methinks. Instead of jumping right in with what she needs, I'm going to start with who she is.

"No, I have my favorite pair of flannel jammies," Kama said and sat on the floor. "I have to imagine this is really different for you."

"Yes," Olivia said. "Especially speaking so much. You all seem to talk quite a bit. Is this normal?"

Kama laughed, until she realized she laughed alone.

"Please don't be offended. My family tells me I never stop talking. But, yeah, I suppose we do talk a lot. It's how we communicate, so there is usually a lot to be said. How did you communicate before?"

"We didn't. It wasn't allowed."

Oh my damn. Add "sheltered to a fault" on to her description.

"Well, feel free to talk here. It will make it easier for you to acclimate," Kama said and then clarified for the confused look.

"People around here aren't really good at guessing what you need or want. You will have to talk to them to let them know. If it feels like too much, just start with me and Beth. We are here to help you."

"I don't want to be a burden. This is just all so chaotic compared to what I knew."

Kama looked at the younger girl with compassion. Olivia sat quietly, without much movement, and her eyes reflected profound grief.

"It will take time to see this as your home, but trust me, you are not alone here. And look, here is Beth with some food. Let's have a snack and talk some more."

Kama smiled as Beth brought bags onto the platform.

"You need some more light," Beth said, setting the bags down.

"Oh? Do you stay in lighted areas most of the time? I'm used to it being dimmer."

"Well, a lot of us like to be topside most of the time and really only come down here for sleep," Kama explained.

"Don't worry," Beth said quickly. "You are welcome to stay here until you feel comfortable. It is quite loud up there."

Kama rummaged through the bags.

"Would you like a sandwich?" she asked. "Beth, I think maybe we need to see if we can get her a microwave."

"I don't think there is electricity in this area. Maybe a camping stove?"

Mental note to self: Talk to Jack about this living arrangement. This is terrible. She is living like a homeless person. We have to do something about these tunnels. If we are going to call them home, they need to look like it. I can't believe I ever thought she was his new girlfriend. She's a kid. I feel bad for not liking her.

She let her thoughts ramble while she made food for the three of them. Kama handed the sandwiches out and began to ask Olivia questions about her life. She put on her best performer's face and listened carefully. She tried not to react with outrage and horror as her new friend calmly explained her experiences. The more she heard, the more Kama hated scientists with a level she had never known.

She sits and talks about these horrors like it is something to be expected, like it is normal. Don't snort. I know it was her normal, but dammit—How could someone do those terrible things to them? How did they get to decide her life meant nothing? I guess so they could dissect her and not feel guilty. Yeah, I doubt guilt ever entered the equation. It is a good thing that damn facility is gone, else I would go back and burn it down all over again. Worthless because she is Loup, not human enough for their standards, but envied because of the abilities she has.

Kama took a breath and settled in to spend time with her new friend. As she watched Olivia carefully, she realized there would be no quick fixes. Shopping for an outfit took a backseat to making Olivia feel like she had a family.

CHAPTER Five

Kama woke and smiled. She and Jack had started to work things out. She knew it would take time, but they were on the healing track.

Not that I want to fight with him again. He is kind of scary when he's being all Alpha Jack. Granted, I suppose I should have figured there was no way he could keep a Pack seventy deep by being the nice guy. But the look on his face...yes, You. I am going to giggle. Did he really think we could be a match and I would not have an Alpha side, too? Though stepping into his space might have been bad, I think I might have peed a little when he moved in and towered over us.

She rolled over and looked at the clock. Having free time felt odd to her because, for as long as she could remember, her life had been according to a schedule: school, practice, homework, performances, and more practice. Kama knew she would have to find new things, else she would go stir-crazy.

Well, we can now move forward. Jack will never cease to surprise me. I acted like a jerk, and yet he still heard me out. Though, I doubt he expected me to leave after he learned I have my own place now. What am I going to do with Olivia? I know Jack said to tread carefully, but I really am curious about it all. Maybe just a few more answers will help me figure out how to help her here. Okay, taking it easy or not, I am not going to lie around all day in bed.

Kama finally pushed herself to get up and take a shower. As she started the water, out of habit, she reached for the waterproof speaker she had mounted on the wall. She had not touched her music since her final concert at Julliard, because it felt too hollow. Ten days after her finale, she finally started to grieve her loss. She squared her shoulders, turned it on, and, as she got into the shower, began to sing.

No one said I couldn't stay at Julliard, but it seemed like an empty promise. I can't be a part of our Pack and have a huge, ole spotlight shining down on me because of my career. I'm sure I will find something else to do; for now, I am going to work through giving up my life's dream. However, it doesn't mean I have to give up singing. Guess they better get used to hearing my dulcet tones in those tunnels.

Kama stayed in the cascading heat to accommodate all the good songs rotating through her playlist. She enjoyed not being in a hurry. She dressed for the ever increasingly bitter weather and got ready to go hang out with her friends for a while before her shift started. She walked out of her apartment, smiling because it was hers alone, and, as she pulled her door shut, rolled her eyes. She could hear her brother and Beth kissing on the other side of his door. In typical youngest child behavior, she walked the few steps to his door and pounded on it much louder than necessary. The spike in heart rates made her grin, and she waited for the door to open. When it did, she grinned widely.

"Damn, Kama," Ajani muttered.

"Sorry, brother. Beth, we need to go," Kama said.

"What are you talking about? I don't have rounds until this afternoon. Neither do you. So, what's up?" Beth asked, still snuggling against Ajani.

"Yeah, but he has to go to work, and I wanted to go spend some more time with Olivia."

She watched Ajani sigh and smiled at him. He ushered Beth out the door, followed her, and shut it. He shook his head at her.

"And here I thought living in our own spaces would mean less intrusion by you," he said.

Ajani made it a point to kiss Beth in porn-show worthy fashion. Kama smirked at him as she pulled Beth's arm until they stood a few feet away from him. Kama leaned in and gave him a brief hug and a kiss on the cheek.

"She will be back to give you sugar later, but for now, she's all mine."

"That would have sounded sexy, if you weren't my sister."

"Ew," Kama and Beth said together.

"I love your sister, but the idea of kissing her..." Beth said. "No thanks."

She heard more under-the-breath cursing as he jabbed the button for the elevator. She linked her arm through Beth's, and they made their way to the stairwell. She filled her friend in on all the items she thought Olivia would need as they made their way fourteen floors down. With a sigh, Kama had to relinquish Beth as they exited for a few more lip-smacking moments. She wanted to be impressed because Ajani waited at the bottom for them, but watching them make out creeped her out. After her brother left, she grabbed Beth again and they walked toward Central Park.

"I wonder if she might want some audio books as well as music for her alone time. Oh, we definitely need to make sure she has enough towels and linens, too."

"Kama," Beth said. "Do you think she will be overwhelmed if we just barge in and change everything?"

"Yes, I did think about scaring her, but I think if we take our time, she might be okay. Besides, she needs to have more in her living space than some old mattresses and food," Kama said. "She is used to being on a rigid schedule, so all this free time has to have her going crazy with boredom. I figure we can start working her up to getting topside, and it will help her make some sense of this new existence."

They began to walk and Kama shivered. Despite having a faster metabolism, December in New York had proven to be colder than ever. She rolled her eyes at the snowscape the wolf showed her from Michigan. It had been the first time she had ever been in snow that literally came up to her knees. There had been a lot of firsts in Michigan: first time she had shoveled snow, first time she had hunted, and the first time she had bit a deer in the ass. She chuckled and then flinched when a hard poke to her ribs grabbed her attention.

"Beth," she squealed.

"I know you are up in your head a lot, but you can't keep the joke to yourself," Beth said, poking her again. "Spill, sister."

"Remember when I told you about the snowfall?" Kama asked. "Well, I left out a few tiny details."

She proceeded to tell Beth all about the hunt during the remainder of their walk to Central Park. By the time they reached the border, they were nearly bent over from laughing so hard. Kama wiped tears from her eyes and took a deep breath. She was glad she could laugh over the events; at the time, they had quite a different feel. They walked through the park, chatting and laughing as they made their way to an entry point. Kama stopped up short as her location caught up with her. She stared at the bronze Balto statue. She took a deep breath and walked down the slope until she stood in front of it. With determined steps, she walked under the bridge and stood before the door panel. A frisson of panic surged through her, as her mind's eye saw the fight with mutated wolf creatures and flashed forward to the fight at the Facility. She shook her head to clear the vision and pushed the panel open.

"What is it?" Beth asked gently.

"I haven't been here—well, to this exact location—since I fought with the mutants here and got hurt," Kama said.

Flashes of the mutant attacking her and falling backwards into the tunnel crossed her memory. She felt her fingers tremble against the cool rock of the panel. She took a breath, blew out a stream of cool air, and stepped into the darkness. A moment of panic gripped her, and Kama forced herself to breathe. The large platform area surprised her. It had felt smaller. She had no danger of falling accidentally, and no one waited to attack her. She turned and began to climb down the metal ladder. She had not thought about the event since it had happened; truthfully, she had not had a chance to replay it in her head too often. Once she had been cleared to leave from Doc, she had been too upset about Jack that she hadn't thought about the physical fight.

Yeah, stupid misunderstanding making me think we were broken up. Stupid mutants caused much more trouble than they will ever know. I should have realized Jack never would have left me sick and injured if he didn't have to.

Kama stopped those thoughts before they turned the corner and started to focus on Cade. She didn't know if she could handle the feelings of guilt along with the panic, sadness, and fear flooding her mind and overwhelming her. She scrubbed tears out of her eyes and allowed herself to fall the few inches left to the floor. Her feet splashed in a shallow puddle of water, and she kicked at it. What started off as irritation became a frenzy of motion until the puddle stood empty and the tears had stopped. She felt a cloth pressed into her hand and whirled to face Beth.

"Crap, I forgot you were even here," she said.

"Seems like you were just working stuff out," Beth said. "It's only natural that you would have some strong reactions to the place where you were attacked."

Kama nodded and suddenly felt a rush of anger take over. She wanted to throw or hit something. She stomped around the area a few times, growling as she processed what had happened to her. She had killed two of the creatures and almost died doing so.

"Those stupid things attacked me here. They almost killed me," Kama snarled. "They forced me to kill them. It's not fair. I didn't ask those freaks to come here. They never should have been here. I'm glad we took them out."

Kama paced more, feeling her anger rise even more.

"They had no right to be here. They should have stayed in their freak cages and died there."

"Olivia, too?"

Beth's soft-spoken question drove right through her brain and stopped Kama's tirade. She whirled on her friend.

"What?"

"I asked, if Olivia should have stayed in her cage and died with the rest of them. I mean, she lived there, too. She had to have known the two who came here. She grew up with them."

Kama stopped and stared at her friend. The words had deflated her rampage, and she shook her head. She wanted so badly to hate the whole group, but based on her heartbreaking conversation with Olivia, she knew they had had a life of imprisonment and pain.

"Dammit."

"Just reminding you, this girl you want to help so much is still fragile from her loss. The event that makes you so angry is the one where we destroyed everything and everyone she knew. And now we are asking her to be one of us," Beth said.

Kama stifled the urge to scream and kick the walls for only a moment and then gave in to temptation. She still wanted to be mad and be able to fling hate and rage unfettered. She also wanted to help Olivia acclimate to her surroundings. She didn't want to think of Olivia as one of the mutants; she wanted to like her. She railed against the walls longer and, when her voice sounded hoarse even to her, she stopped.

"I think I am good," she said to Beth.

They walked down the tunnels, twisting and turning through the underside of the park, and Kama told Beth all about her experience. Her friend offered soft sounds of compassion, but mostly let her talk.

"We should probably have a support group or something for those of us who came back," Kama mused. "Then again, I really don't want to have to remember it any more than I do. Let's go finish this. I want a nap before tonight."

Kama gave one more look in the mirror. She found herself excited about the New Year's Eve party. The original thought of being alone had become increasingly depressing, and, after learning Jack would be at some corporate affair, she had taken up Karl's suggestion to join her packmates in celebration. She decided to dress up, despite knowing most people would be casual.

We are not going to have many opportunities to dress up from here on out, so we might as well do it up while we can. What a stupid thought. I can dress up any damn time I want to. My life is what I make of it.

Her wolf agreed wholeheartedly. Kama wasn't sure when the big change had happened, but it seemed like her wolf agreed with her more often than not. The thought got some major eye-rolling, and she smiled. As a method of coping, she had begun meditating and trying to blend herself as one whole being in her mind. It did seem to have the added benefit of giving her easier access to her gut feelings and instinctual musings.

Are you sure about wearing the green? I really did like the orange dress we wore for Jack in LA. Okay, right, I know it's sleeveless, but surely it is going to be crowded and hot in the Lounge? Right, you don't have ESP, either. Even though I know we are one in the same, I do like talking to you as a separate because it feels just a bit less crazy.

She turned once more and smiled. She chose yet another old performance gown, a simple green and gold sheath dress that came to her ankles but wasn't form fitting.

Good thing I have shoulders like a football player thanks to these workouts.

Kama opted to wear her hair down, instead of her established, patrol ponytail. Light makeup and a simple, solitaire pendant finished off her look, which was almost ruined by her nice, warm, fuzzy, black boots. She still warred with herself about whether she really wanted to bring heels. Ten minutes later, she settled on kitten heels and walked out the door. She directed her driver to Columbus Circle and, after wishing him a happy New Year, exited the car.

Seriously? It's busier? I know people flock to the falling ball, but wow. I can't believe I have never been out in this chaos. It seems private parties are the way to go to avoid the huge press of bodies coming here to celebrate. Tourists...

She walked through the Park's gates and encountered many people walking around the park as well. There were double the amount of carriages driving through, and Kama smiled. Everything seemed to pulse with the city's energy of excitement. She found her way to the castle and waded through another huge crowd of people. She finally made it to an entry point and made her way into the tunnels.

Kama walked into the Lounge and was suitably impressed with the transformation. Her packmates had been hard at work. The long tables were still present, but the hordes of coffee machines had been replaced with punch bowls and trays of food. Despite having seen plenty of sentries as she walked through the park, it felt like the rest of the Pack had shown up for the party. She took a deep breath and looked around to see if there were any friendly faces to hang out with. She saw Mary and Dan sitting nearby and went to chat with them.

I know, I know. This is just weird. Usually, we have Beth around us, but we have to make more than just one friend. Besides, I know these two already, and it won't be too painful to start a conversation with them. Why did we think it would be a good idea to come to a party by ourselves? We don't even like parties. Then again, most of the ones we have gone to have been corporate affairs for my family. I am beginning to realize how much I just don't know. I'm sheltered, I guess. Oh well, New Year's is a time to start new things.

"Hey, Kama," Mary said warmly. "Come sit with us. This is Lani, Damien, and of course, you know Dan. Guys, this is Kama, the lifesaving Diva. To think I assumed the electric grid room assignment would be the easier gig to take. Almost ended up applesauce."

Kama wasn't sure how to take the giggling fit Mary fell into, until Dan leaned in and offered her a flask in a loud voice. The fumes coming off him were almost enough to make her drunk.

"It might help if you catch up with us," he said but didn't push it when she refused. "Anyhow, this is Lani and Damien. They are some of the good people around here."

Kama looked at the tall man sitting next to Dan. He looked like he could have been related to all of her cousins, with his pale skin and red hair. He had an easy grin and warm hands as they shook. Lani had huge, brown eyes and a skin color a few shades lighter than Kama's. She stood and gave her a hug, leaving Kama surprised at how tall the girl stood. At five foot eight, she was used to being taller than most women, but Lani dwarfed her by at least four inches. She sat down at the table with the group and looked around. Damien touched her hand, and she looked over at him.

"They have been going strong since about six. However, they aren't drinking quite enough to get completely smashed. Granted, it is much harder at three-quarters waxing, but considering the bender they are on, it might be possible before the New Year comes in," Damien said in a surprisingly deep, gravelly bass voice. "Thank you for saving her for me, and I suppose him, too."

Mary pouted until Damien leaned over and gave her a long kiss. Dan shrugged and gave Mary a kiss as well. All three raised their shot glasses and continued drinking. Kama must have blinked more than she thought because Lani laughed loudly at her, a genuine, rich, earthy laugh. She pointed at the two drinking and raised her eyebrow.

"Yes, those three are a unit, although I have no idea how they deal with Mary," Lani said and leaned in conspiratorially. "I do hold the belief that it is impossible for only one man to date her; they need to split time with her, because she is so high maintenance. Oops. She might have heard me. Do you dance? I've been waiting for hours for Mary to get buzzed enough to join me, but no luck so far."

"Sure, let's go dance," Kama agreed. "They don't mind people knowing their business? I mean, not for nothing, but saving them or not, I barely know them. I certainly didn't know they were a trio."

"I forget just how new you are," Lani said. "This Pack is worse than any other gossips they could be compared to. You think high school is bad? Once a single person knows, most likely the whole Pack will know. Especially Sophie. I mean, I knew all about you and your drama before I had ever laid eyes on you. Then again, I haven't heard much from her about you since you busted her face.

Of course, it's old news now and nothing compared to the rest of what had been said about you."

Kama's eyebrows rose.

Okay, so people will be people, even if they are Loup. And I didn't bust her face. The table did all the work. Not to mention, it wouldn't have even happened if she would have left my food alone. Who takes another person's food? Apparently, no one ever taught her manners. I can't believe she said anything about me. Even though I don't want to be the topic of gossip, it's kinda nice to know we are normal. Oh, she is waiting for me to talk to her.

"I am almost afraid to ask what else you are referring to."

"You have been on the radar ever since you tazzed after those drug dealers attacked you. There were all sorts of stories after you cussed out the Alpha and stormed off. Just when we thought you were all done, you came running back after a vampire attack. And in wolf form, no less," the young woman said. "Then the whole taking your Rite early, telling off Tina, and the like. The best rumor? You cussed out The Judge, and he had you taken off to be killed. But you are still here, so no truth to it. There are a lot of people who are waiting to see what happens next."

"I'm not sure my eyebrows are going to leave my hairline anytime soon," Kama muttered.

"Come on. Let's dance."

Lani laughed and grabbed her hand. They wove their way through bodies and tables to the makeshift dance floor. Kama gave in to the thudding beat and loud, pulsing rhythm. She didn't recognize the song, but music was predictable for her, and she lost herself in her movements. It gave her the catharsis she had needed for a long time, and as the music moved from one song to another, she danced harder and moved freely around, not caring what anyone thought. They stopped after some dozen or so songs to get a drink and food.

"I am so glad you showed up," Lani said. "I wasn't looking forward to being stuck sitting like a non-trio wheel all night."

Kama filled her plate with deli sandwiches and chips as she moved down the line. She grabbed a cup of punch and precariously held it in one hand. With so many people in the area, she hoped she wouldn't spill. As they walked back to the table where Dan, Mary, and Damien sat, Kama paid more attention to keeping her food from falling off her plate than to her surroundings.

"Watch it, you stupid cow."

The sneering of the voice made Kama's head snap up. Lani had tripped over a chair leg and dumped most of the chips off her plate and onto a girl sitting in the obstructing chair. To Kama's surprise, before Lani could say anything, the girl reached out and slapped her hard across the face.

"Too stupid to be anything but useless. Now, there is grease and salt all over my new outfit," the girl seethed.

She reached up to swing again, and Kama stepped in front of her friend.

"Hey, it's crowded in here. It's not like she dumped her plate on you on purpose."

The girl looked up at Kama, and her eyes narrowed into angry slits.

"Mind your business and let go of my arm."

"I will when you calm down," Kama said.

The girl slowly stood.

"It's okay, Kama. Let's go and sit down. We're not trying to cause any trouble, Raye," Lani said in a soft voice.

As Kama watched, Raye turned back toward Lani and knocked the plate out of her hand and onto the floor. Then, to add insult, she took her glass and splashed the liquid on her. Before she could react, Raye turned and flipped the plate out of Kama's hand.

"Sorry. Not so sorry. You probably should hang with better company."

It took a moment for Kama to process that her snack was now splayed all over the floor. She looked down and then back up, just in time to see Raye step on her chips and feign dismay at her.

"She's drunk. She doesn't mean it," said another girl sitting at the table.

"Yes, I do," Raye insisted. "Because of *her*, we had to run extra laps for not paying attention. And what did she get? Promoted up to Juan's class. Do you know how hard I have been working for a promotion? Miss Thang just walks in here and expects everyone to love her."

Kama tried to move past the woman and get back to her table with no further incidents. She had come to have some fun and party with her pack, not have a fight. Instant regret for declining Beth and Ajani's invitation to go with them for the night filled her. At least with them, she would be sitting in some loud bar against the wall by herself. She maneuvered Lani through the mess of bodies, until she felt an icy liquid cover her shoulders and cascade over her front and back.

It just keeps coming. How big is the cup she is holding? Okay, now we have to do something, because I am not about to get crapped on for being too good again. Question is, how much is too much? Can I shove her and be good, or will I need to, like, bust her in the eye?

The continued icy torrent of liquid raining over made the decision easy. Kama turned to face the woman and looked into furious, honey-colored eyes.

"Aww. Poor Kama. Your too expensive gown is all ruined. All messed up," Raye scoffed. She made a point of putting the plastic cup down gently on the table. "At least now you look like what you really are."

Did she just call us...

Kama reached out and grabbed the woman's arm, stopping her from reaching toward one of the two still full cups before her. Raye struggled to free her arm, but Kama held on tight. She easily blocked the blow as the woman swung her left hand. She was still pissed about her food and dress. She twisted Raye's right arm, pushing hard into a sharp angle, and pulled it up until Raye knelt.

"I suggest you cool down. I don't want any trouble. It's New Year's Eve. Let's just party."

She released the woman's arm with a warning shove and made her way back to the table where the group smiled at her.

"Whoo hoo. You told her, Kama," Mary cheered too loudly. "She's been mean with Lani here, because she won't admit she's got the hots for her. Too stupid to realize everyone else already knows the truth and too damn scared to admit it to herself."

"Shhh. Mary stop it. She's already a mean drunk," Lani whispered. "Oh, no..."

It was all the warning Kama got, but all she needed. Her instincts were already on high alert after having been doused in drink. She felt the air ripple and turned in time to dodge the punch that would have hit her square in the back.

"Oh, look. The Rock Star has moves, too," Raye slurred.

Kama couldn't believe someone so drunk could move so solidly. The others had cleared out of her way, and Raye used the extra room to throw punches. After the third swing, Kama caught her fist.

Did she just Challenge us? Fine. Challenge accepted.

She looked the woman in the eyes and increased her grip until she felt bones pop and crunch. Raye fell to her knees. Whimpers of pain came through clenched teeth, and Kama stood tall.

"It's Diva," Kama said. "And the next time you come near me or mine, I will break more than your hand. And heads up, you aren't getting promoted, because you have no damn idea how to fight. I suggest you walk away."

Somehow, I didn't expect my first Pack party to be like this. Now we are wet and need to go find some clothes and change. This sucks. I didn't want to ring in the New Year all by myself. I really hope the salle has a good cache of sweats handy. I am so done with this.

She dropped the woman's hand and walked away without looking back. And yet, she was not surprised when an enraged bellow sounded behind her. She whirled to face the furious woman, whose eyes were clearly shifting amber. As Raye lunged for her, Kama pulled her arm back and then connected solidly with a punch to the woman's throat. She turned around and kept walking, despite the woman gagging and trying to catch her breath on the floor behind her.

She made it to the training room and, to her relief, there were sweats for her to pull on after a quick shower. Even better, no one asked her to explain what happened. She went on her way quickly but resisted going and sitting alone. Kama wandered around the tunnels for a bit with no plan in mind, until she realized her meanderings had taken her path north.

I'll go and check on what Olivia is doing.

She made her way down the lesser used tunnels and found the platform. Again, the lack of lights was disconcerting, but she figured it might take a moment to get the area fixed up enough for electrical work.

"Hello?"

"Oh. Hi, Kama," Olivia said, appearing before her quickly enough to startle her.

"I thought we could hang out a while," Kama said. "Or we could go for a walk."

The young woman looked at her, and Kama tried to give a reassuring smile.

"There are a lot of people moving around tonight," Olivia observed.

"Yeah, New Year's Eve brings out the crowds," Kama said. "On second thought, maybe we should stay here."

"Okay. Can you explain what New Year's Eve is?"

Kama followed Olivia into her living area and passed the evening talking with her new friend. They even had the countdown at midnight, though Olivia didn't quite buy in to the tradition. Soon thereafter, Kama went home, took a shower proper, and went to bed. She thought about texting Jack but fell asleep before managing to act on it.

CHAPTER Six

Kama stood in her old room, looking in the mirror, trying out smiles. She had spent all but the last few months of her life in that room, and it felt right she would be getting ready to transition in the space she had grown up in. She looked around, feeling simultaneously out of place but at home. It felt empty without her belongings, and her parents hadn't done anything with it, yet. She looked at the ivory walls, devoid of her awards and achievements, and wondered for a moment how her parents were coping since all of their children had left. Before letting an emotional riptide consume her, Kama went back to practicing smiles. She finally settled on the most natural, relaxed one and got ready to go. Over and over, she reminded herself her choice was the best course of action, even though it felt rushed.

This is for Daddy, not me. Suck it up, smile, and pretend it's the best day of your life. Honestly, it is not a bad thing; we are graduating and moving forward. Really, who wanted another semester of high school? We are done. Think of all the free time we will have not having to do any more homework. I can't even say I will miss my friends. Face it, after twelve years of being in the same school, we aren't close with anyone. We haven't talked to Gianna in months. This just isn't my life anymore.

A knock at the door made her jump, and Kama shook her head. She still hated that she reacted to sounds so skittishly, especially when they should be expected. She squared her shoulders and walked to the door, grabbing her coat along the way. She opened it and found her siblings stood on the other side of the door. She had started the tradition when Dante had graduated from Pembleton eight years prior. Being a bright-eyed ten year old, she had been more excited at his milestone and roped all her sibling into standing outside his door while he got dressed. They had all showered him with love, pride, and a clap-out when he exited his room. Each sibling had been treated to the same accolades on their graduation day.

The perfect smile she had been trying to force came naturally as she received their applause. Dante stood first in line to greet her, being the oldest of her siblings. He was the idolized brother, and she went to his embrace eagerly.

"Congrats!" Dante said, reaching out to hug her. "I can't believe our baby is graduating. And early. Well done, *Arachidi.*"

Kama felt warmth and love being enveloped in his hug. No matter how old she got, she suspected he would always call her *Peanut.*

"Good work, Kamaria. We are so proud of you."

She turned to Twin and smiled at them. Her twin sisters were only two years younger than Dante. While Kama knew their names were Bella and Bridget, at two, she'd had a hard time discerning between them. No matter how many times they prompted her with their names, she called them Twin, and the name stuck. She could tell them apart now but secretly thought they were a single soul split into two bodies. They gave her an appraising look.

"New hairdo?" Bella asked.

"No," Kama said. "Why?"

"You look different but lovely. Changed somehow," Bridget said as they hugged her.

"Thanks," Kama said, unsure if she had actually gotten a compliment.

"You will do amazing things," they said in unison.

"My turn," Ajani said and hugged her close. "I get to be spokesperson, because no one else wanted to."

Light laughter sounded amongst the siblings; none of them had ever minded giving a speech.

"Mom and Dad always said you were the surprise baby, coming in hot, eleven months after me. And you have lived up to it. Constantly, you have surprised us. You were determined to go to The Julliard of School of Music at seven, when most kids wanted to play with toys. You wanted to be an Opera Diva. Let's face it, sweetheart, you have never wavered from your goal. You buckled down and showed dedication and discipline that made the rest of us—well, okay, maybe just me—look like slackers," he said with an easy grin. "The fact you are graduating early shouldn't have caught any of us off guard, but here we are, getting ready to watch you cross the stage. We send you off with a tradition you started—lifting up the ones you love. Also keep in mind, despite being an amazing and crazy talented woman, you are not alone as you follow new paths. You, little sister, make us proud. As you move forward, know you do so with admiration and love from your family."

Kama felt her eyes start to fill with tears. She looked at each of her siblings, precious faces that had been with her through her entire life. Twin handed her a package, and she smiled. In contrast to her otherwise orderly life, she had never been a careful un-wrapper. Instead, she ripped open the paper with gusto and gasped. Nestled on a small satin pillow, lay a necklace charm. Her sisters had fashioned a treble clef and five staff lines out of platinum. The jewelry was intricate and beautifully detailed. Kama knew it had taken them months of careful work at their shop to create such an elegant piece. A garnet represented high C, an opal for C#, a bloodstone in the high D, and the E over high C was an amethyst. Each stone representing the birth month of each sibling.

"You know I hate aquamarine," he said.

Despite pretending he wanted nothing to do with the family business of jewels, he knew the birthstones as well as any of them. He had staunchly refused the modern aquamarine, scoffing at it as a punk stone, and claimed the ancient Bloodstone, instead. The symbol and the gift overwhelmed her more than she could have thought possible, and Kama let the tears flow. After a final group hug, they took one more moment together.

"Let's go get you graduated," Dante said softly.

They walked into the living room where her parents, her sister-in-law Jill, and Beth sat waiting for them. Kama looked at them all and smiled again. They stood and clapped for her, as well. To her surprise, Jill stepped forward first.

"Congratulations, Kamaria," she said.

Her sister-in-law remained a mystery to her. Idly, she thought about having lunch with her, since she would need something to do with all of her new free time. Family meant everything to her, and she felt it might be past time to really get to know the woman who had stolen her eldest brother's heart.

"Thanks," she said. "Please call me Kama."

She saw the shock register in the other woman's face. Fourteen-year-old Kama hadn't been particularly thrilled when her beloved brother had fallen in love with someone. She had insisted Jill call her by her full name, even with the chastising from her family. Kama gave her a quick wink so she wouldn't start to cry.

"Very well, Kama," Jill said. "We are proud of you."

Kama moved on to Beth, who hopped up and down a bit and clapped.

"This is so exciting. I am so happy for you."

Kama laughed, and Beth joined her. The cleansing laugh felt good and light after so many tears.

"Who graduates early?" Beth asked. "Do you know how to do anything low-key?"

"No," her siblings answered, and Kama laughed harder.

"Job well done, my friend," Beth said, pulling her close. "I guess I am just learning this is your nature. Go all the way in glorious fashion."

"This is why we let you keep Ajani," Kama whispered in her ear. "Thanks, Beth."

She moved on to the sobbing mess pretending to be her mother. The proud, Irish woman mopped at her eyes.

"I do believe this is where I get my flair for the dramatic," Kama said with an exaggerated sigh and then squeezed her mother tight.

"I do believe you are correct," her mother agreed. "I am so proud of you. So much has happened, yet you rise above the challenges and continue to amaze us all."

Their eyes met, and Kama gave a small nod. A few, bumpy months would never sever the strong ties with her mom. They had been through too much together.

"I have a small story to tell," Brenna said and waved away the groan from Kama.

"We do have to be there in an hour, Mama."

"Hush, darling. As I got dressed today, I began to remember this feisty young one. We had just left Julliard, getting her all signed up for her first singing classes. I can picture her perfectly in my mind: hair in braided pigtails, a bright yellow sundress, and wearing her birthday crown, because she just knew Opera Divas wore them all the time. So people could recognize them off stage, of course."

The family chuckled around her, and Kama rolled her eyes.

"Well, as we stood waiting for the car to come round and get us, Kama danced around and sang. This tall...lady...came up to talk to me, remarking on what a lovely voice she had. To set the scene, my brogue was out in full. It had been an emotional day, and you know how it works. We had a short but rather nice conversation for a few moments, and then Kama came to ask how long it would be until the car came. I reprimanded her for interrupting, and the lady looked at me in shock. 'I can't believe you would speak so sharply to your charge. I would fire my nanny if she were as rude as you to my children.' Needless to say, I stood there, stunned at the slight, but my darling girl acted. Wee Kama reached up, adjusted her crown, and then put her hands on her hips. 'That would be my mother you are insulting. I'm sorry in your privileged world you have only been exposed to monotone families, but mine embraces a variety of cultures and avoids inbreeding.' And the woman walked away embarrassed. Kama then turned to me, exasperated of all things, and said 'Mama, apparently you just can't buy class.' And with her irritated proclamation, I knew my daughter would do anything she set her mind to."

Kama watched her mother take advantage of the laughter to again wipe her eyes. They locked gazes, and she felt a lump in her throat.

"Obviously, the child had overheard a rant or two of mine. But I am proud our family always has been important to her. Still is. We stand here, getting ready to watch you graduate and move into a new phase of your life, I need to tell you I am very proud of you. Sometimes, we are too alike to appreciate it, but I have had the pleasure of watching you grow from a precocious child to an amazing woman. As you continue to mature and go through this next phase of your life, I am excited to see what you will do."

Kama went into her outstretched arms, and they both cried. She had known it would be emotional but not like this.

It almost feels like we are saying good-bye to everything. I know this is my family just giving me the graduation send-off they feel like I want. Funny, I think this is exactly what I needed to have. And…here comes Daddy.

"*Cara mia*, I have to say, I expected to have at least another five months to prepare for all this," her father said, giving her smile that didn't quite reach his eyes. "However, as I stand here today, I know I would not have been prepared then, either. What I have come to realize is my daughter will always be seven in my mind. I have watched her grow into a young woman who is capable, talented, and mature; a father's blindness means I see her as the bright-eyed child who loved to pretend to read business reports on my lap."

Kama laughed lightly as her father cleared his throat. She noticed when his speech shifted to ultra-formal, it meant his emotions were overwhelming him.

"Then, all of a sudden, she requested to move into her own place. For a minute, I regretted getting those apartments, but when reality came back, I realized how very lucky I was to have my children close by. I am privileged to watch you grow and make choices to advance your future. The only regret I have is my own mother never got to meet you. My daughter, you are special and gracious. Sadly, we get to spend less time together, I am always amazed when we do, because our conversations are so rich. As you prepare to graduate, know I am proud of all you have done, and I can't wait to see what you will do."

The rest of the family applauded, and she hugged her father tightly. Kama relaxed against him, having been given his support even though she hadn't known how much she needed it. He pulled back and stared at her. She felt he looked for something. He nodded and allowed her the floor.

"Somehow, I expected a lot more snarky jokes," Kama said and cleared her throat. "Despite my penchant for talking a lot, I almost don't know what to say. Almost. Today, I realize what a luxury I have been afforded by having you all as my family. And I do mean *luxury*, something you just expect to have and don't recognize. Yes, I may have decided to be the best Opera Diva in the world from a young age, but only because I was allowed to believe I could be anything I set my mind to. I have had the shoulders of kings and queens to stand on. Not that there weren't squabbles and learning lessons along the way."

The family chuckling gave her a moment to breathe before she continued.

"I go to my graduation today, realizing I wouldn't be here without all of you. And then you shower me with kind words and praise. I am overwhelmed in the best way possible. While this feels like a huge ending in my life, and it's a bit scary, it also feels like things are just starting to begin. I am excited and nervous to find out what comes next," Kama said and took a deep breath. "As I get ready to do this, as the kids say, I find it easier knowing you all stand with me. When I offer my thanks, know these words are a poor substitute for everything I mean to convey. This is the best day of my life, and I am honored you all have chosen to share it with me."

Somehow, in the haze of sniffling and hugging, they did make it out to the cars and off to graduation on time. Kama sat silently between her parents, the ride punctuated now and again with a quiet sniffle from her mother. They pulled up to her high school, and Kama stared at the building's front. Twelve years of her life had been spent there, but there wasn't any attachment pulling at her. A soft hand on her arm made her look back at her mother.

"Are you okay?"

"Yes, Mama," she said. "Are you?"

She almost laughed at the wry grin her mother gave her.

"My youngest is graduating from high school. Of course I am a mess," Brenna said.

"Guess you can't pretend to be thirty, anymore," Kama joked.

"Sure, I can. I am certain I can pass you off as adopted."

"Mama!"

"What? There seems no reason not to use the ignorance of others to my youthful advantage," Brenna said.

Kama started to giggle.

"You are horrid," she said.

"Pot...kettle," Brenna said as she gestured between them.

"A black joke? Really, Mom?"

"Naw, darling. Just needed a real smile from you. I made your favorites for your reception after."

She hugged her mom close.

"Love you."

"I love me, too. Now, let's get in there so you can strut across the stage. Be sure not to trip and fall."

"Mooother!"

Kama exited the car and walked into Pembleton with her head held high.

Two hours later, and she was ready to be done with all the boringness that constituted graduating from a high-end preparatory school. She had sat through some notable business person giving a speech about what an asset to the future they would be. Kama looked around the ballroom, refashioned to hold their ceremony. A small stage, complete with podium and displaying the school crest and colors, had been positioned at the northern end of the room. In the southern portion of the hall, small, round tables were dressed for the party after the ceremony. She sat quietly by herself, wishing she had brought her music to listen to.

I know it would have been rude, but for the love of cheese, is this the last test before graduating? Sit through some boring prattle and pretend to be interested? Yeah, this really does sound like a business meeting. Okay, so we have heard from the Salutatorian, and this dude—thanks, Karl—and now on to the Valedictorian. Almost done, and then we can eat. I wonder if Mom was being literal when she said she made all of my favorites, because if so, she and Meghan must have made enough to feed about five hundred people. I am really hoping she kept the party invites limited. I understand there are some people who should be there, but I would appreciate nice and quiet after all this. Oh, wait. Why are we standing?

Her rambling thoughts had carried her through the last speech and up to the point where she could see an end to the very long ceremony. Despite this being the early graduation, almost half of her graduating class was in attendance.

Of course, we are twenty-eight out of sixty students, but I didn't realize there would be so many. Stop snorting; I know we really had no idea what this would be about. I thought graduating early would mean all of two people in attendance.

She smiled at the thought and then paid attention as her row stood and walked toward the stage. The one benefit she saw to having a small graduation was each senior got to take the stage alone and have a few seconds in the spotlight by themselves.

"Kamaria Celeste DeKosse."

She walked up the stairs and over to the Headmaster to shake his hand. She moved her tassel from right to left with a grin. Her family made the appropriate amount of noise on her behalf, especially Beth. She gave them a grateful look and, as she walked off the stage, almost tripped down the stairs when she noticed Jack sitting in the section reserved for some kind of important people to the school. She smiled at him and then at the whole section. Kama schooled her face not to grin too widely as he gave her a wink.

It's really too bad he couldn't have sat with my family and made a whole bunch of noise with them. Although, we are pretty damn impressed how he managed to be here at all. When did he choose to affiliate himself into the school? I'm sure it's all donation based and such, but I do wonder when he made the decision. Not like I didn't tell him only six days ago this is what I would be doing.

As she sat through the rest of her classmates walking across the stage, it became increasingly harder for her not to turn and stare at Jack and make faces. Just as she had worked up the nerve to maybe try to look over in his direction, her attention was grabbed.

"Carnegie Xavier."

She looked over into the audience of parents and loved ones, where a petite, dark haired woman stood and clapped loudly. Kama joined the others in polite applause, but her mind reeled.

What the hell is Cade doing here? I forgot his full name was Carnegie. I bet that is his mom over there. I never did get to meet her. Oh, crap. I wonder if Jack is going to put those two together. Did I ever mention his last name? There is no way Jack and Cade can ever meet; Jack would kill him. Why is Cade here? Did he always plan to graduate early? Oh snap, he just made eye contact with us. Smile, Kama. You don't hate the man. Remember, you broke up with him. Well, don't smile too much. You might encourage him to come over and talk. Just look ahead and pretend you find the rest of this stupid ceremony interesting.

She sat still, facing forward. All urges to turn around and look at Jack were gone. She would talk to him later. Kama stood with the rest of her class and cheered as their graduation ceremony finally completed. She walked toward her family quickly. She needed to make sure she wouldn't run into Cade. She hoped he would go over to his mom and leave her alone, but she didn't take any chances.

"*Complimenti, figlia,*" her father said, sweeping her into a hug. "Make sure to call your grandfather, so he can have his moment to congratulate you, as well."

"Thanks, Daddy."

Safe in the bosom of her family, Kama dared to look around. Jack had already left; in fact, the whole section had emptied quickly. However, as she watched Ajani move determinedly through the crowd, she grew nervous. She watched him intercept Cade before he could weave his way back to where her family stood. She watched her brother reach out to shake Cade's hand and strained to hear their conversation over the din around her. For once, she thanked the gods for her enhanced Loup hearing.

"Hey, Ajani. I was coming over to say congrats and all."

"Hi, Cade. Congrats yourself. Let me save you the trip over. Kama doesn't want to see you."

"I just wanted to say hi and congratulate her."

"Look, I like you. I think you are a decent guy. I even think you were really good for her, but she has made herself clear. She told me she had broken things off and does not want to see you. I know it sucks, and I know you are worried about her. She is my sister, and I've got her back...in all things. Seeing you is only going to upset her, and, given everything she has been through, I want her to have just one day where her smile is real and she can relax."

Kama watched Cade's head droop a bit and felt a stab of pain at the look on his face.

"I get it, Ajani. Just let her know...never mind. Take care of her; don't let her push you away, too. She needs support and is bad at accepting help. Just keep her safe, man."

Kama wanted to burst into tears from Cade's dictate to her brother. Why he couldn't be a vengeful bastard was beyond her. It certainly would have made her life much easier. She watched Ajani weave back through the rows to return to their family. She made eye contact with him and mouthed *thank you* before turning to accept another well-wishing about her graduation. She and her family made it over to their table to indulge in strawberries and cream, per Pembleton tradition. Light conversations filled the room as the delicacies were consumed.

"Thank you all for coming. I mean, you're family, and it's expected, but I appreciate you all suffering through graduation with me. While the berries and cream are all good, can we go to my real party and get some food?"

Her family laughed along with her, and they moved their celebration to DeKosse's, which, to Kama's great delight, held only forty people.

Later, as Kama left the restaurant, her phone chirped at her. She felt slightly bad about lying to her family. She had convinced them she had to go to a senior party. She just needed space. Being the center of attention overwhelmed her more than she thought it would.

~Unless you are too exhausted to come over, my driver is waiting for you at the corner. ~

Kama smiled at the message from Jack; he had reluctantly given in to texting her instead of calling and leaving voicemail. She began walking to the corner, seeing the familiar, black car.

~I'm fine and walking to the corner. How long did you make the poor man wait? ~

~He's been there only ten minutes. I took an estimate of how long you would be. I'm just that good. Oh yeah, I also had Kincaid ping your phone, so I knew when you turned it back on and figured you were getting ready to leave. ~

~Really?!? ~

~Just come on. My thumbs are cramping. ~

Kama laughed, shook her head, and got into the car. Fifteen minutes later, she made it to his house. As she walked up to the door, he opened it, and, before she made it past the threshold, pulled her into a deep kiss.

"Congrats on graduating, Kamaria."

She smiled up at Jack.

"Thanks," she said and kissed him again.

When they came up for air, Kama found they had moved into the foyer and her coat lay on the floor.

"How did you manage to be there?"

"Pembleton likes my money," he said with a dismissive shrug. "They liked the ten scholarships I donated enough to invite me to all formal functions."

"Ten? Why so many? Do you have people lined up for them?" Kama asked.

"Well, I think we have a few Pack members who would love to finish their high school years there."

"Wait, there are others in the Pack who are still in high school, as well?"

"Yes, despite you being the newest member, you aren't the youngest."

"Huh."

Somehow, it had never occurred to her. Beth was close in age, being only a year older, but Kama had just assumed she was the youngest by default. She didn't spend much more time thinking about it. Jack grabbed her hand and led her into the dining room. She had only been in the room a few times, because, more often than not, they ate in the living room when she had been over. Her mouth dropped open.

"Jack…"

"Happy graduation, My Love," he said softly.

"But, I thought we were taking things slow," she stammered.

"Some things don't allow for slow. Graduation is one of them," he said. "I missed your final concert, but that is the last thing I plan to miss where you are concerned."

She stared around at the room, which had been impeccably decorated. Candles on the table highlighted two, silver domes. Soft music played in the background and enhanced the romantic feel.

"And to think some people prefer going out and getting drunk on graduation night," she murmured.

"I have some Scotch. It's the good stuff, too," Jack laughed. "Though the last time you got drunk, you fell asleep."

Kama tried not to roll her eyes at him, since he had made such a lovely gesture in having dinner made. She failed.

"Jack, I said *some*," she said. "I can't think of anywhere else I would rather be."

He seated her at the table and lifted the dome to reveal a dinner plate filled with steak, potatoes, and some vegetables. She watched him hold up a bottle of wine, and after she nodded, he filled a glass with a rich looking, red liquid and then sat with a smile.

"I offer congratulations and want to say how proud I am of your accomplishment."

Kama returned the smile, touched by his gesture. After all they had been through in the last few weeks; she noticed she felt truly comfortable with him again. As they ate dinner, she regaled him with stories about her time at Pembleton. She laughed at his many questions about her alma mater.

"You gave scholarships to a school but know nothing about it?"

"I knew you were there. I knew it had to be top notch," he said.

Kama sat back and sighed in contentment.

"Delicious," she said. "I am stuffed."

She wanted to say she had been eating all afternoon but didn't want to remind him that he couldn't yet be seen with her. She accepted his hand and moved into the living room. Kama took her normal space on the couch and looked at him. Jack held up a deck of cards, and she nodded. She had enjoyed their new, nightly ritual of playing cards and her filling him in on what she had done while he had been gone.

"The Judge made me ambassador to my family up north in Michigan," she started as he dealt.

I never would have thought I would enjoy pinochle. I always thought of it as an old person's game. Yeah, soon enough I'm going to have to tease him about it. Then again, I enjoy playing. Whatever, Wolf-girl, it's you, too.

"Just like him to create a new position while I am gone. I should stick him with being Alpha," Jack muttered.

As they played cards and took tricks, Kama filled him in about her visit.

"Funny, I always think of us in separate forms, too," Jack said. "Interesting way to reconcile all forms into one being. Maybe we should try to promote thinking of ourselves as wholes and bring some unity to people in the Pack. It might help them accept who they really are."

"It has helped me to think differently."

"Well, I will talk to Lorna and see how to best implement the idea."

Kama nodded as she scowled at her cards, which quickly turned to a smile when Jack discarded the queen of diamonds. She snatched it up and laid down her meld of queens all around and held her breath. He cursed lightly as he played jacks all around. With the final sixty points, she had reached twelve hundred and raised her hands in victory. She didn't quite crow, but she smiled widely.

"Ready for dessert?"

She nodded eagerly and watched as he reached back behind him and produced a small, covered dish. He set it in front of her. Kama lifted the cover and gave Jack a quizzical look.

"Taste it," he urged.

The tart, dark chocolate cake made for a rich bite and when the chipotle raspberry mousse hit her tongue, she met his eyes.

"I knew you enjoyed it the last time you had it," he said. "I figured it would be a great way to end dinner."

Kama eagerly took another bite of the cake. The sweet, sour, and spicy medley melted in her mouth as a rush of memories flooded her about their time together in Los Angeles.

"Thanks," she said after finishing the dessert. "This is an amazing graduation gift."

Kama stood, grabbed for his hand, and began walking. It felt only natural to her to have a repeat of the nightly activities that followed her first acquaintance with the delectable dessert. Jack paused, and she looked into his eyes, searching for any sense of doubt. She didn't want to rush things, but in meeting his gaze, she knew they were ready.

She leaned in to him and kissed him deeply.

"I'm ready for bed."

She grinned as Jack took the hint and the lead. For the first time in a long while, her wolf rumbled in contentment and sat back quietly to enjoy their Mate.

CHAPTER Seven

Jack felt an unusual sensation of nervousness prickle up his spine. It wasn't that he expected trouble, but as a person whose defense mechanism was burying grief until later, this gathering would be difficult. He had invited the entire Pack to an important meeting. Aturus and Gabe were none too happy with the lack of security topside, but even they understood the importance. People milled around the deep tunnel but in general were quiet. He stepped out onto the makeshift podium on the platform slab. It had been constructed for this purpose and looked out over what appeared to be almost all of his members.

"As a Pack, I know it is hard for us to gather today, because it makes the losses we have suffered real and now we have to face the reality that our loved ones are gone. Even though not all of us had to physically go into the raid, each and every one of us has felt the impact of our mission. This day asks us to take our mourning out of the silence and speak words which might not come out correctly. The good thing about today is how it brings us all together. We are sharing the silence, sharing our heartbreak and even sharing tears; but best of all, it allows us to share our memories of our fallen mates."

He took a moment while soft sobs filled the still air. The feeling of heaviness pressed against them. His Pack had many members, but they were young, and fear covered many faces. Jack despaired for them, for not having the lives they had anticipated and for having to go through hell. He pushed his anger back and tried to regain his calm. He was their Alpha. They needed his strength.

"We will all have our own, personal and special memories of those we lost. Each one of them has left a mark on our lives and in our hearts. I know sometimes you may think as Alpha I don't recognize you or notice all of the amazing skills and talents you bring to our Pack, but I do. It is very hard for me to be up here today, hearing my own thoughts spoken out loud, trying my best to focus on the happier times we all enjoyed, rather than face the fact that members of our Pack are no longer here with us. There has been a lot of speculation about what is happening in this Pack lately. Let me clear things up for you all. We are in this together, and you should know the truth. A mutant attack took place against the Park on Halloween. It left people hurt, and I needed to find answers. I undertook a Spirit Quest, and you will have to trust my journey is a story for a later time. But it did allow me to learn more about our pack and how very special we are."

Jack took a deep breath and looked around again, trying to make eye contact with every pack member who looked up at him. To his surprise, he met more eyes than not. Each set held a different emotion, but so far they were with him. He found Kama in the crowd and drew strength from her gaze; she looked calm, serene almost, and it gave him purchase on the slippery emotional slope he tread upon. He inhaled silently and continued.

"I am certain of two things. Each person who gave their life would have wanted us all to be here today, with our happiest thoughts of our times spent together. Second, they are still here very strongly in spirit. I know, for some of us, finding out about being Loup shook our sense of spirituality. What I can tell you, without a doubt, is that there is a Goddess who does care. Even though She may feel absent in the hurts we suffer, She allows us to make our own choices. She is there to help and offer guidance if we ask."

He looked around and exhaled quietly. He certainly didn't expect this to turn into a religious revival, not when he found himself still trying to figure out where his own beliefs stood. But he couldn't talk about his experience without talking about Her.

"I don't say this to convert you but only to tell those who need a sense of peace that we do have someone looking over us."

He cleared his throat and then, with sudden inspiration, sat down on the ledge of the platform. Even seated above them, he could see them all, but being closer felt like it made him accessible. Jack gestured for others to sit with him. He wanted to get comfortable for the next part.

"Let's talk about our friends and remember the people who touched our lives," Jack said and then took a pause.

Tension rolled in the air as the surreal feeling of loss began to settle in. He took a breath.

"Sara. Such a strong person housed inside a petite form. Her personable nature shone out through her caring presence. We are all here because somewhere, somehow, we have all been touched by her," Jack said, and then an honest grin covered his face. "Most of us with a tap to the arm as she talked to you. As you all know, we could always hear her coming, due to her habit of tapping her drumsticks against the tunnel walls. There was never a time where her location was a mystery because we could hear Sara tapping out the music she played in her head. It also made her one scary and lethal fighter. She had fast reflexes and commanded her sticks like they were weapons."

"True enough," Aturus agreed. "To that end, Sara was one of the most fiercely devoted warriors we had. She volunteered for many runs, not because she had thrill issues, but because she wanted our park to be safe. She wanted to know vampires would never move back into the area and torment any others. The first time I called her an itty-bit, she smiled up at me and explained to me how, if she shoved her drumstick under my third rib on the left side, it would puncture my lung. She calmly told me how it would fill with blood and no one would hear me scream. I knew she would be a powerful warrior, because few people are brave enough to threaten me."

Hushed laughter coursed through the group. Jack watched as people turned to each other and pointed out various places on their arms where they had been hit by a drumstick. People nodded in agreement at her prowess. He waited for quiet before moving on.

"Next, we reminisce about Donnie."

Jack had a fond spot for the young man; he had been there at his First Change. Donnie had engaged one of the older men up at the chess tables. He lost a game in which the old man clearly cheated. As they argued, the man called him crazy, and Jack had noticed his eyes changing. He managed to get him into the tunnels before fur sprouted, but barely. After a brief scuffle to keep the newly flipped Loup from hurting himself, Jack took him to see Doc.

"When I welcomed him and talked with him, I found an intelligent young man who had a true passion for science, especially physics. Mind you, my experience with physics came from watching Discovery Channel specials, and if I recall, they were mostly about gravity. He loved to talk about rotational motion to anyone who would listen. He made sure, over the course of the five years he spent in our Pack, that I learned about centripetal force and tangential velocity," Jack said with a laugh.

More laughter came from the group as they recalled that asking for his help meant a dedicated helper who would spend the whole time talking about science. Jack even heard a few members talk about harsher topics. Donnie's parents had him locked away in a juvenile ward when, at fourteen, he defended himself against his inebriated mother. He spent four years fighting with against the violent youths he had been housed with. He managed to survive until they released him when he turned eighteen. The conversations died down again, and Jack met Doc's eyes and noticed she had come up front. He gestured to her to share with the group.

"He took the time to paint different starscapes on the ceiling in the med bay, so the people who were in recovery would have something to look at instead of a flat surface. He also spent time explaining the systems and stars to those who were there healing," Doc said. "He had planned to paint all of the empty surfaces in tunnels. He wanted to recreate as much of our solar system as possible. I will always remember him, because I have never seen a person care so much about others despite having a lack of care given to him."

Many heads nodded amongst the group, along with quiet suggestions to pick up where he had left off. Jack wondered how they would get through all eight of their fallen friends. Tears that people had stoically held back during his opening speech were starting to fall. He could spend all day telling his Pack how lucky they were to have had their friends in their lives and how much they would be missed, but he knew he had to give a proper fare-thee-well to each person who had died.

"Today, we also honor the memory of Pam, and, once again, we know how keenly the passing of friends and loved ones affects us. To truly do her justice, I would have to explain her life's days as being described like the grass of the field in their brevity, but they also represent the flowering of some, great, cosmic urge that brings forth intelligence," Jack said as he adopted a terrible, British accent. "Of course, most of you will recognize those words as a quote from the short story she wrote out of a sense of love, duty, and responsibility to make sure our Pack had a sense of creativity to go along with all the *charlatan*-style fighting."

For such a quiet person, she had a firm, very firm, command of language. When I could get her to speak to me, I always felt two, distinct things: First, I wouldn't understand half of what she had said, and second, I would be quietly judged on how I responded.

People laughed at and with him. Pam's First Change happened after being forced into an exorcism to free her from her dark afflictions. She fled her very conservative home that night, traveling from Connecticut to Manhattan. A group of sentries almost missed her hiding in the crumbling remains of the Blockhouse. Near starving and frozen in the harsh winter, she surprised everyone by Changing as they tried to help her to a shelter.

"She always offered to help me with my newest writings. She even made me feel like I wrote decently. The last gift given to me was working with me to finish my book," a voice piped up. "She edited the whole thing in exchange for lunch."

Jack recognized her as Lorna's second in command, Rhea, and he smiled at her.

"Your epic, long thing?" another voice asked.

"Yes. All one hundred and twenty-three thousand words," Rhea said proudly.

Laughter sounded, and comments were made about her being long-winded. Jack could see some of the tension had left the group as they talked about their friends from the place of special memories instead of a place of loss. He could tell that, even though they had lost loved ones and were reminded their lives were precarious and definitely not guaranteed, they could promise to each other their memories would last forever.

"I know you all would agree with me on how we wish Rebekah would have had more than just two years with our Pack."

The group immediately began chiming in. Jack chuckled as he heard small clusters within the whole group begin to talk about receiving a tea cozy from her, and how she preferred the proper, English spelling of cozy with an *s*. He began to breathe easier as people interacted more. They would recover.

"She is the reason for the addition of tea kettles in the Lounge, because she very politely requested them. Though I had less interaction with her, I know I have her to thank for the variety of crocheted blankets made for our use. Beyond us, she also made them for each and every person she saw in need."

More stories were spoken, and he let it go on longer this time. There was no way to keep people from grieving a loss. He knew a few words wouldn't erase the months coming after, when the pain remained, but memories being shared was a positive. Jack watched them interact.

We are emotionally involved in the lives of these people who are like our family; we will grieve at our loss because it is difficult for us. Grief is an inevitable part of the life of any person. And that is all they want, to live a normal life. But life means grief, and the only way to avoid grief is to not live.

"In the devastating course of grief, we are going to experience feelings of pain, disbelief, and loneliness, which will lead to emptiness and insecurity. There are going to be negative and even hostile feelings which seem irrational and overwhelming. So we all understand there will be tears. Tears are not a sign of weakness. We should all know this, because Levi was all about the blood, sweat, and tears. Despite being the one Loup who managed to keep his exercise-induced asthma after his first change, he had a dedication to running every day. However, because of this workout, he developed a bad habit."

Jack waited for the spontaneous giggles and full-out laughter to die down a bit. He smiled as a small group of Levi's friends enjoyed this part. A very private memory surfaced of a young, soft-spoken cub, who escaped into the big city to find anonymity after his worst nightmare had come true. Like most lost cubs, Levi had no idea of his heritage, and his First Change had been horrifying. He had been the tall, awkward kid who played violin in the symphony and was a solid anchor on the bowling team. Being timid and quiet seemed to be a beacon to every other young man in his high school class who felt insecure about his own, perceived inadequacies. The constant bullying only made him withdraw further into himself to avoid being a larger target. A confrontation one night after school had turned into a bloodbath where Levi had been the only survivor. He had fled before law enforcement got there and took the first bus leaving the area. Guilt over the memories surfacing in his dreams made him fear for his sanity and made him desperate, but fortunately he came to the one place that could help him. Jack had found him sitting on a bench, ready to end things.

"Running the New York marathon had been Levi's biggest goal. As he began to train, he graced us with pictures of his running routes from his tracking program. Each one shaped like a dick. The more he ran, the more dick-pics we got for the Lounge," Jack continued the story when the chuckles died down.

A stifled gasp sounded deep from somewhere in the crowd, and he grinned. Apparently, the Alpha using the word "dick" ranked right up there with hearing it from a parent.

"Yeah, the boy could run," Tina said with a snicker. "He also was one of the best jo-stick fighters I have had the pleasure to teach. He used the fact that everyone thought him nice to push the advantage in a fight. He certainly thrived here."

Jack began to feel some of the sorrow ease. The tears from losing members wouldn't stop for a few weeks, but at least now they had talking points. They would be able to focus on the good and not just the tragedy. People were starting to come to grips with their new reality after the war. He hoped they wouldn't operate from a sense of fragility. Instead, as a group, they would have to rise above the hardships of being mortal. His Pack had gotten comfortable with the perks of being Loup—faster and stronger than others around them—and their sense of being vulnerable had started to fade.

"Bear with me, because we have three more friends to honor today. I know most of you knew Andrea. Her love of spicy food and cooking it for us all were common knowledge. Her amazing performance on the tennis court was just the tip of the secrets she hid," Jack said.

"Only because her parents thought it to be the only sport feminine enough for her to play," The Judge snorted. "It's too bad they never really understood that gal's potential. When I found her, she stood on the tennis courts, tossing a ball and letting it drop onto the middle of her racket. I figured I would wait until she missed and then approach her. After a half hour of absolute precision, I finally decided to interrupt her. Instead of being scared of me, like most of you, she grabbed the racket and held it like a weapon. I have never seen such fierce determination from anyone."

People in the crowd murmured and nodded. Quiet stories started to surface. One in particular, where Andrea stood in front of a group of tourists and gave them a speech about cultural appropriation and how Central Park had been built over Seneca Village. Everyone knew she always had a story—correction—a narrative to teach them about how where they came from and where they were now was part of a cycle. Slight laughter filled a western corner as a small group remembered how she had schooled them on letting red wine air in a decanter before drinking.

"At least a half hour," they chorused together and then laughed.

Other stories about her bartending skills began to surface, and as people compared their favorite drinks, a few fresh sobs began to punctuate the air.

"She came into her heritage after forcing a car accident. As she traversed a snowy road, she noticed a semi-trailer swerving and pitching all over because of the ice. The driver had fallen asleep, but rather than let the man careen to certain death, she turned her car to hit the wheel wells and force him to wake up and adjust into the snowbanks. The impact, along with the ice, sent her into an unrecoverable spin. Being Loup meant she survived. It also gave her the wake-up call to take control of her life, and she moved," Jack said. "She came to work for me as the Diversity Officer of Twist Enterprises. I figured out her heritage when she came to my office, eyes all yellow, about celebrating the federal recognition of a mass murderer. The rest is history."

Whew. Six down and two to go. This is the part of being Alpha that is hard. We train them to fight; we pretend they will never have to use the skills. This pain is from every member I have lost. It's not just talking about them in the past tense but realizing how much they trusted me and followed my orders without hesitation.

"Eugene Bartholomew," Jack said and grinned. "Many of you in the Pack may have heard of him but might not have seen him."

"He enjoyed sneaking up on people," Lorna said with a chortle. "I never even heard of parkour until him. Eugene took it one level further when he decided he wanted to do it in the tunnels."

"Ninja style," a small voice added.

Jack couldn't see who spoke, but Lorna chuckled. Other smatterings of conversations started breaking out, and rather than talk over them, he let the memories trickle out. He smiled at what he heard.

"I couldn't tell you how many times that young man nearly ran me over," Lorna continued. "As you all know, I'm at the southern end of the Park. He would use the corridor nearest my office to gather speed. Since he wanted to be a ninja, he dressed in dark colors. He perfected blending into his surroundings, thus the constant near misses. Though he did keep me on my toes, and I have better reflexes for it."

Laughter started slow, somewhere in the middle of the crowd, but worked out to the edges. Some laughed in remembrance, and others joined in as it caught on. It gave him hope for his group to rebuild and become okay. As they began to heal from such destruction, this conversation would be a starting point to give the group a unifying bond that had been growing weaker as the Pack grew in size. Jack waited for the cacophony to die down and then started again. This one would be rough for him, but he knew exactly what to say.

"Finally, we come to Roseanne. Her story is a bit more unusual than most. I know it sounds cliché, since we are werewolves, but it's true. Most of you know that years ago—yes, back in the Dark Ages to some of you—our Park was split into many, small packs. Some have compared it to roving street gangs, and it was kind of true. Some of us decided a unified Pack would make more sense. Others hated the idea, and we fought. When the dust settled, we regrouped and tried to figure out how to best make our situation work," Jack said and looked around.

He realized most of the Pack had probably never heard the story. Out of the seventy members, only approximately twenty percent had been there from the beginning. Four of whom were his Betas. Some had died on raids, and others had stuck it out a few years before deciding that the new, more rigid way of life didn't suit them. However, Jack admired the hard work of those who had stayed and made the transition. They had turned Central Park into a safe haven for the Loup. Since the 1980s, violence at Central Park had continually gone down.

"When we decided to go underground and set up our Den, we found her. Roseanne had escaped from a cruel Alpha just before our Civil War began. Thanks to her efforts, we have the amazing advantage of understanding our home base."

Jack paused for a moment and allowed the weight of sadness to press on him. Roseanne had been an amazing young woman. Not only had she mapped miles of the tunnels, but because of her efforts, they knew the tunnels were made up of multiple levels. At least four, differing depths existed, ranging from water level up to just under the surface. Her more important work had been finding lost cubs. Roseanne had started the taskforce. Through her many connections, she started rescuing cubs from the violence and themselves. She found them in ERs, juvenile detention centers, and sometimes sitting almost catatonic in the aftermath of their First Changes. With a small group, she had started patrolling on full moon nights to find those she could.

"More importantly, Roseanne was a real example of the best of us. She cared about this Pack and lived to help all of us," Jack said with a smile. "Her loss will be felt by each of us, because she made it a point to get to know everyone. As a tribute to her, I would suggest we all take that mantel on our shoulders. Get to know each other. It doesn't mean we won't squabble; we are a family, after all. We won't always agree, but we can do better for each other."

He watched as heads nodded and people looked around, trying to find a face they didn't know just yet. Jack stood up again. He had made eye contact with every member of his Pack. He had approached them as mentor and friend, but now he needed to unite them as their Alpha.

"We have suffered a loss as a Pack. We lost eight people. Eight family members. It is something you never get over, but we need to learn to live with this new reality of loss. It doesn't get better, however we can and will learn to live with it. I know some will feel it more deeply, so I urge you to be kind," he said. "At the end of the day, all we have is each other. So take this grief and recognize it. Don't be ashamed to feel and don't be scared to reach out. Look around. You are part of a special group. We will get through this, and we will survive, because it's what we know how to do best. Let's stand together. Thank you for coming."

Jack jumped down from the platform. He stood in front of his Pack for a few moments and then walked through them. He touched as many shoulders as possible while he walked through the group, which parted as he passed. He left the meeting area, but he could hear chatter and some sobbing. He continued with purpose until he reached his office. He walked in and stood still for a moment, staring at Kama. He started to ask how she had gotten there, but before he made a sound, she held her arms out to him. As he was held by his Mate, the weight of his own grief finally began to release.

Two days later, he sighed with happy relief. The memorial seemed to be what his Pack had needed to start healing. People were talking about those they had lost, sometimes with tears but often with fond memories. Even though the mood still felt heavy, everyone had started to get back to the basics and reconnect. Jack had met with more of his Pack in the last two days than he ever had before. His Spirit Quest proved to have longer lasting results than he had originally thought. Small moments of déjà vu kept cropping up and reminding him of the different aspects he had encountered. It almost unnerved him how accurately they related to each pack member he talked to. He was amazed at how much had been packed into his Quest and realized he had been given a gift. As he walked through the tunnels to unwind and just be visible, he realized that, for the first time, he really did feel alive. It wasn't going through the motions anymore. A smile creased the corner of his mouth, and he shook his head at himself.

He turned the corner and walked down to the meeting room. He went in and smiled at those seated around the table. As Jack noticed the bottle of Black Label on the table and tumblers in front of each of his Betas, he began to laugh.

"We're going right for the good stuff, eh, Old Man?"

The Judge took a long drink before placing it back on the table.

"You called us all here," the old man grated out. "What did you want?"

Jack sat down and caught the eyes of each person as he grabbed the bottle. He filled his own glass and took a long drink.

"I wanted to take the opportunity to thank you all," he said, and relaxed back into his chair.

He took a long sip.

"For thirteen years, you all have stood by my side, guarded my back, and helped me create and maintain a Pack. Each of you stepped up when you didn't have to. I really started thinking about this group when I had to plan for the memorial," Jack said.

The group sat silent for a few moments, thinking about their fallen members.

"Gabe. A man of few words by choice but amazing in action. You keep the security of this group and the Park running like clockwork, despite the fact that we have a large group and an even larger area to work with. You keep the tunnels safe. We know this because of how many times we have had to stop teenage pranks," he said with a grin to the man sitting on his right. "You have made our home secure, and I thank you."

Everyone raised a glass and had a sip.

"Lorna, I sure hope that isn't whiskey you are drinking."

"No, Alpha," she muttered while scowling at her glass. "I was given cider."

"You like cider," Jack said. "Besides, as Pack Witch, you know the importance of keeping the body and mind clear. You have the job of not only working with the Spirit Realm but also offering spiritual guidance. You take the scared, nervous, new cubs and help them understand their humanity is still intact. You help them understand they are not cursed nor evil but still the same person they were before. You take the thankless position of helping them take their first Rite, but you also act as Den mother. Being one of the two females in a higher position is hard, and I want you to know just how much I appreciate your dedication to this Pack."

The glasses rose again, and everyone took a drink.

"Aturus, you get the job of taking these kids and making them battle ready. It's hard enough to get them to understand that you push them, not to be mean or nasty, but to keep them alive. You take these kids, which maybe had played a video shooting game or two, and turn them into fighting machines. You have the job of preparing them to die, and there is no amount of thanks that will make up for the personal scar of losing each one."

He met the eyes of his Arms Master for a long moment and then raised his glass.

"It is probably a good thing our metabolism works off the alcohol before we can all get maudlin and have to talk about The Judge," Jack said and ducked to miss being hit with the old man's baseball bat.

"By all means, let's move on to the good stuff," The Judge said and pulled out a squat, clay bottle.

Jack watched him blow a cloud of dust about an inch thick away from the top. Using a knife, The Judge pried a cork out of the bottle neck. Lorna grabbed the cork and sniffed it. Jack laughed as her eyes began to water. Minus Lorna, they all pushed their glasses to the center. An amber liquid poured in a mesmerizing, undulating fountain from the bottle. It didn't smell like any whiskey Jack had tasted before. As they all raised their glasses, he met the older man's eyes, and they smiled.

"Okay. Now that we have the good stuff and apple juice, I want to say The Judge has been an amazing mentor and friend. I have learned much from him, even as he reminds me daily I still know very little. I am lucky to have you here, most days, to deal with the young needing more guidance than any of us can provide," Jack said with a grin. "Let's drink to our health, our unity as Pack leaders, and the hope that the next time we all sit down for drinks it will be in celebration."

His grin was quickly replaced with harsh coughing when the liquor hit his throat. Despite having a smooth and complex taste, the whiskey burned all the way down his esophagus and scorched his stomach. As he tried to inhale enough oxygen to breathe, he noticed Aturus having the same reaction, while Lorna, Gabe, and The Judge stared at them.

"It's good," Jack whispered from his seemingly charred lungs.

"Another?" The Judge asked as he let his head drop back and laughed loudly.

Jack knew without a doubt he would suffer a hangover in the morning, but in the moment, drinking with his friends was worth the price.

"Sure."

The Judge filled another round, and Lorna shook her head.

"I am suddenly glad I am pregnant," she said dryly.

"No worries, gal. It will just put chest hair on that boy," The Judge said.

"You're having a boy?" Jack asked, turning to her in surprise.

"I don't know. We can't find out for two more months," she said, rolling her eyes at The Judge. "Just drink, you old coot, and leave my offspring alone."

As the conversation entered the bounds of friendly jabs and insults, Jack sat back with contentment. He knew the steps towards healing had been taken by them all.

CHAPTER Eight

Kama squatted against the wall as she took a long drink of cold water. Sweat wound down her back in an itchy trail she chose to ignore. She stood to relieve her screaming quadriceps, pretty sure her hatred for kettle squats had to be universal. The music from the speakers thudded around her, and she argued with her wolf about which set of exercises to practice next. The idea to ask Aturus for a practice set crossed her mind. All of the reasons why she shouldn't follow through with her thought came to the surface as her thigh muscles seized in a small cramp. She walked it out, tossed a few objects out onto the floor for some footwork practice, and grinned.

Even though it's only been a few months, I'm pretty excited that even I can see the differences the training classes have made. Despite adding on a bit of bulk I'm not so sure I enjoy, I am faster and stronger than I ever imagined I could be. Juan insists on tossing me around like a stupid rag doll to try to prove I still need work, but I manage to surprise him. He's a jerk, anyhow. Okay, enough of a break. Let's start.

Her internal ramblings stopped as she began to move slowly and deliberately around the litter strewn on the floor. She worked hard to keep her form consistent and clean. As she sliced her knife across the guide marks on a practice bag, Jack walked into the room, shut the door with purpose, and stared at her.

"What are you doing here?" Kama asked, after a few moments of him standing there. She would have preferred for him to give her a hug but knew it wouldn't happen while they were at the park.

"Watching the star cub go through her forms," he goaded.

Her spine snapped straight as she kept his direct gaze. Her eyebrows rose, and she folded her arms over her chest with a scowl.

"I'm not a cub," she said.

"Oh, right. You're an *adult*," he said, dragging out the word. "Well, then. Let's see what you can do."

"What? Jack, what are you talking about?"

Kama caught the rattan stick he tossed to her and jumped back in time to miss a hit to her midsection. He swung again, and she leaned out of the way but didn't move; her feet and her stance remained steady. She watched carefully as Jack circled, hefting the stick in his hand. She schooled her face to be passive and tried to figure out what he would do next.

Why doesn't Aturus train us on these stupid sticks more? We take all these defense classes with knives and such but not these. I know Karl said some of the upper level people use these for fun sparring. Who the heck spars for fun? Oh, sure. Let's grab a big stick and smash each other's fingers. Then again, it's probably the people who enjoy fighting who want the challenge of a stick battle. I guess it's better than fighting him with a knife. I sure hope he doesn't expect me to give into him. Ha, silly man, I saw your wide, sloppy swing coming.

A smile quirked her lips as she tapped him between the shoulder blades with her stick and shifted her weight between her feet to stand firm. He swung again. Kama side stepped just out of his way, still watching.

"Alpha."

The title rang out with all the snarkiness she intended, but Kama didn't expect him to reply. As he shifted his balance onto his left foot, she waited for him to lunge in an attack. She was surprised when he crouched and swept her legs. She fell, rolled toward him, and lashed out with the stick. The sharp rapping sound meant she had hit the floor and not him. She got to her feet and carefully circled around him, leery of his casual posture. Again, he reached out toward her. Kama easily deflected his attacks and used her wrist to catch and guard against the volley of blows. Jack increased the speed and began to intrude into her space. She noticed the subtle shift of his facial expressions go from amused into what she knew to be his professional face. As he struck, she used her free hand to cross her body and pin his stick with his own free arm.

She didn't anticipate his pulling her in closer and striking at her neck. She raised her arm to deflect, and he used her momentum to push her down to the ground. She scuttled back and jumped to her feet.

"Not bad," he murmured.

She didn't answer, leaning back just far enough to avoid the punch he swung at her face. Kama not only recovered but also took a forceful shot at his throat, which he barely avoided. Before she could get too comfortable, Jack spun his stick even faster, and she carefully followed the flow of his shoulders and arms, to track what path his movements would take. He stepped in quickly and forced her to rapidly adjust. She veered to the left, hoping to confuse him, because the natural flow of the fight would have had her ducking to the right. She was caught off guard as he landed a blow to her midsection.

Stunned, she folded over and didn't resist as he pushed her head toward the floor. Kama dropped to her knees and pulled him off balance. She struck back with her elbow to the side of his knee and put distance between them. She didn't make it far enough away. Jack grabbed her arm and twisted it up until she rolled over and fell to the floor. She met his eyes as he put the stick against her throat. Kama titled her head just a bit, and he pushed the stick harder into her wind pipe and raised an eyebrow at her.

"Alpha," she said softly, trying her best to make it sound like she meant it. Kama met his eyes and realized he looked like he wanted to shake her.

I get it. Our lives are serious, and fighting has consequences. I do not take this lightly. I wasn't even certain if I would come back from that awful place in Pennsylvania, but it doesn't mean every practice is life or death. This man needs to find some kind of balance.

"Not bad," he said. "You shouldn't drop your guard. Even when we are sparring, you need to follow through."

"Agreed," she said. "Next time, I will do better."

"You pull your blows in a real fight, and there won't be a next time," he snapped.

"Yes, Alpha, I know," she said calmly. Kama wasn't sure what Jack thought in those moments because his mood had shifted from almost playful in the beginning to life-and-death serious as they sparred. "I also know you have twenty years of training on me. If I could easily take you in a fight, we would have a problem. I am still learning. What is going on?"

She waited for his answer, watching the brief frowns and scowls as he worked through his response.

"I don't understand why Aturus sent you out on those missions," he said.

"Because I am good," she retorted. "The only way I will ever get better is to continue to push. I may not be as trained as your veteran fighters, but I'm not bad."

Kama stared at him until he removed the stick from her throat. She extended her hand to him and waited for him to help her stand. She thought he looked overly pensive but still turned and went to get a bottle of water. When she looked back, Jack appeared a bit distressed, but she couldn't imagine their spar to be the cause. The air thickened around them as emotions rolled off each of them. Minutes seemed to slow as they stood there looking anywhere but at each other. Even though they had made up weeks ago, they still had odd moments like this. It all felt very weird. He cleared his throat, and she tensed up again, expecting round two to start with no warning.

"Relax, Kama. I'm not going to start another session with you," he said.

"Okay, then. Care to explain why *you* don't think I am ready to be sent out on missions? Because it makes no sense. I am a warrior in this Pack, Jack," she forced herself not to giggle at the rhyme. "Aturus sends me out because I work hard. Unlike some people, I practice daily to get better. I push myself, and he sees it. What was this sparring session really about?"

"Honestly? I wanted to see how good you are," he said, and she relaxed as he finally grinned at her. "You have been here since October, and then I was gone, so I know almost nothing about your training here. It's weird to think that you are part of my Pack and I've never seen you spar. I know you as a woman. I just want to know your warrior as well."

She nodded her head. Kama also found it odd to realize they were both Loup, but she had never thought of him as such.

"We don't interact here. Remember? We are actively trying to keep our life together private," she said. "Although, people have noticed you have been trying to socialize with them more. I hear them talking about it. They were impressed with the memorial and how much you knew about people."

Silence hung between them for a few more moments. She almost made a face at him just to ease the tension, but he gave her a questioning look.

"Do you want to go home and have dinner?" Jack asked.

Kama stared at him in surprise and then laughed.

"So much for not interacting. Your place or mine?"

"I think mine is still a safe bet. I mean, you have your own space, but what happens if your mom decides to make an impromptu visit?"

"I think it would be called a shotgun wedding," Kama said dryly.

She appreciated that Jack laughed with her. As she began to pick up the clutter on the floor, she looked back to see him lean against the wall.

"You could help," she said.

"I'm the Alpha," he mocked.

Kama rolled her eyes and finished the quick chore.

"I am going to take a shower, *Alpha*," she said in an overly sweet voice. "It will take me about a half hour of suds and nakedness to finish. Once I am done, I will walk to your place. Shall I cook?"

"Do you want to? We can always bring in some Guyanese food if you want. The place with the cassava bread you like is still open."

Kama was slightly disappointed he didn't rise to the bait of her teasing comments.

"I enjoy cooking. By the way, your kitchen needs a huge makeover. I think my closet is bigger. Not to mention, all your tools are primitive. I'm pretty sure my birthday present to you is going to be an overhaul. Either way, it will be my pleasure to make dinner. Do you have groceries?"

She loved the way his face relaxed into the smile he gave her. There was a look in his eye, one she guessed meant she only had some of the information.

"What?"

"Just remind me to tell you about the beans," he said with a laugh.

"What else?" she prompted.

"Nothing. See you soon."

He turned, pulled the door open, and then walked out before Kama could get any more answers. In retaliation, she took a nice, lengthy shower and chatted with various people as she exited the park. Still, she made it to his home in forty-five minutes—not quite the show of defiance she had wanted. She nodded to him when she walked through the door. She had almost made it to the kitchen before he pulled her into a hug and kiss.

"I really wanted to do that in the *salle*," he said.

"Ahh, but you were being the Alpha," she teased.

Kama ran one finger up his shirt and laughed at herself as it caught on a button.

"Don't you ever wear t-shirts?" she asked. "Someday, I am going to break a nail on your fancy shirt buttons."

"We can't have you injure your delicate, little hand," he mocked. "Should I take the offending shirt with the nail-breaking button off?"

"I thought we were going to have dinner?"

"After," Jack said.

Kama leaned into the kiss he gave her and offered no objections as he maneuvered her toward the living room.

Screaming woke her. Kama sat up in a panic, realizing the screams were hers. Her eyes flew open, and she stared into Jack's olive green ones. She looked around and fought against what constrained her.

"Kama. Kama. Wake up, babe," he said softly.

She realized his hands were on her shoulders, holding her tight. Kama found it odd she was still screaming, even after she woke. She stopped the noise and then took a deep breath. It had been weeks since her last nightmare; long enough for her to forget how twisted they made her feel.

"Kamaria, are you here with me?"

"Yes," she said and pulled back enough to sit up.

Looking around, she realized they were still on the floor in front of the fireplace in the living room. She pulled a blanket up over her body and tried to process.

"What did you dream about?" Jack asked.

"What time is it?" she deflected.

"It's almost ten."

"So, I didn't even make it through the whole night," she said.

Kama noticed he moved closer to her but slowly, as if he were afraid to spook her. She was torn between being mad she still had nightmares and being embarrassed because he saw her have one. She didn't know what to say, so she sat there, avoiding his scrutiny. Silence filled the space between and threatened to suffocate them both. In not talking, she found the sound of the clock in the room to be extra loud and nerve jarring. After more than a few moments, Jack cleared his throat, causing Kama to jump and look up at him.

"How about we talk about what just happened," Jack said in a soft and imploring voice.

"What do you want to hear?" she asked quietly, her eyes wide and lips pressed thin in stress.

"You have a lot on your mind. I want to hear what you are thinking and feeling," Jack said, keeping his eyes locked on hers. "I am used to being privy to what's going on."

"I think I should probably put on some clothing," she said.

She kept his gaze until his eyebrows rose in question.

"Look, these are not new. I've had a few nightmares since I came back from the raid," Kama said. "I thought they would go away. Then you had to go and see this, and it's embarrassing."

"Nightmares are a way of processing. Don't be embarrassed." Jack said. "I never wanted to take you into war. For that, I am sorry,"

Kama hated the soft expression on his face. The compassion and understanding from him didn't make it easier for her. It felt like pity. She had pretended she could just block the events from her mind. After returning from dropping James off in Michigan, everything changed. It was calmer around the park, which left her time to think. Too much time. Trying to deal with her loss and anger on her own proved pointless, and nothing seemed to make sense. When her stress levels peaked, she had nightmares until she physically worked herself into forgetting.

"Well, it is not like you could help it, but it doesn't make what happened disappear. I am just trying to deal with it all," she said, reaching out to grab her clothes off the couch where they had been tossed.

"I can understand that, but I *am* here now. If you need to get things off your chest to deal with them, please do. I don't want our night to be spent in awkward silence."

Kama got dressed and then braided her hair back. She stood and looked at him, still sitting on the floor.

"I don't know what else to say."

"How about you tell me about the nightmares?"

"Yes, because I am sure, after having mind-blowing sex in front of a romantic fireplace, the next awesome thing to do is talk about what is keeping me up at night," she said dismissively. "Are you hungry? I'm going to go make a snack."

Pull it together, Kama. You, too, Wolf-girl. I am not going to babble and cry all over Jack. I know he said we could. I don't want to. We just got done convincing him about our great warrior abilities. Lots of people go to war and do things. Okay, let's go and do this.

Kama stood and walked into the kitchen. She opened the refrigerator to peruse her options and nodded to herself as she decided that lemon cream chicken sounded good to her. She found anger the easiest emotion to push the blues and the urge to cry away and took out her frustration on the hapless vegetables in front of her. She could hear Jack dressing in the other room and realized her reprieve would be short. She didn't look at him as he walked into the kitchen and sat at the bar across from where she worked.

"Explain something?"

"Sure," he said.

"How are there groceries in the house? I mean, you don't cook. Last time I was here, we had to order in food because the cupboards were so empty. Now I have enough ingredients to make real food."

"Well, I called Carla and told her I needed some food in the house. She had a market service deliver."

Kama shook her head. The thought of having someone make the food choices for the kitchen amused her. A shopping trip to the Food District would be in their near future.

"Do you mind garlic?" she asked, happy the conversation had moved on to a safer topic.

"Love it," Jack said quickly. "I used to have nightmares, too. Especially when I first came back after being a prisoner."

She didn't respond and instead focused on chopping and pushing the minced onions into a bowl. Kama moved on to crushing the garlic, peeling potatoes, and slicing mushrooms. It gave her a convenient excuse to stare at the cutting board. The food went into a pan on the stove, and she set the timer. Done with preparations, she sat at the bar. She forced herself not to flinch when Jack put a hand on hers. She looked up and met his concern-filled eyes.

"You were not the only one scared. No one goes into war and feels secure. When I got back from my Quest, I knew what we had to do. But as plans were made, real fear gripped me," he said. "Aturus informed me that you were coming with us, and I couldn't breathe. For the first time in more years then I care to admit...I felt like I would lose something priceless."

She swallowed hard and saw something almost unreadable pass over his eyes. She didn't want to give in to the tears the look evoked. Too many nights she had cried alone.

"It takes time, but it does get better," he said.

"If I felt I had someone to talk with, it might be better," Kama said. "But no one at the Park ever talks about it. Until you did the memorial, people acted like it was just an everyday thing. We talk to each other now about those who died, but for those of us who lived, it still sucks."

"Survivor's guilt," he said. "Kama, this is a form of PTSD. Every warrior who goes to war will experience this emotional onslaught. It stays with you. You witnessed death and destruction, and you were forced to make a choice I hoped you never would."

She didn't like the nightmares and the upset. After talking to Jack, she felt like at least there was a start to some changes. Not only for her, but perhaps a start to the healing for everyone in the Pack who had been a part of the confrontation and had been affected as well.

Kama nodded to herself and got up when the timer chimed. She grinned at the slight confusion crossing Jack's face. She met his eyes and gave a short laugh.

"Yes, you do have a timer," she said, glad that the silly kitchen gadget had broken the tension.

The flurry of utensils and pans clattering intensified for a few minutes. When she finally finished, she walked around the bar to Jack and kissed him. She relaxed against him as his hand curled behind her back and pulled her closer. Kama wrapped her arms around his waist as his hand moved up to the back of her neck, caressing it as he deepened their embrace. All the words unsaid were conveyed through the touch of togetherness, rocking them to their cores, and neither wanted to break contact. However, the timer chimed again, and Kama straightened up reluctantly.

"We will work through this," Jack said. "And I think you are correct. The Pack needs to be able to talk about this more. Perhaps a therapist or someone of the like to help us recover."

"A werewolf shrink?" she scoffed. "Yeah, the idea of counseling is going to go over well. We're together, and yet I didn't want to talk to you about what has been happening. It makes me look weak, but I trust you. Being weepy and dependent doesn't fly in our group."

She watched Jack mull over the information while she put dinner on the plates in front of them.

"How many battles have you gone into?" she said after a few moments.

"As Loup? A few. As a man? Many more," he said.

"Despite the form, you still are just you, Jack," she said and then grinned at herself for borrowing Nula's wisdom. "I hope there won't be any more encounters for a really long time."

They ate in silence until she dropped her fork. The clatter jolted them, and Kama winked at Jack. She grabbed it from the floor and tossed it toward the sink. She raised her arms in victory as it rattled around the basin. She laughed at the roll of his eyes and directed the conversation to her last concert at Julliard. Kama made sure to describe everything in as much detail as possible, since he hadn't been there. She pointedly ignored him as he asked her for a mini concert. She got up to refill her plate, refusing to give in to the stare he had continued to give her.

"Okay. You have a very serious choice to make," Kama said. "Crème puffs with ice cream or whipped cream?"

She put on a serious face. His eyes roamed over her body in a slow and suggestive manner. She tried to up the ante by returning the lascivious gaze with a seductive smile. An ill-timed belch on her part made her laugh, and the mood broke.

"Puffs and ice cream," Jack said, then after a slight pause, leaned back in his chair. "You make some amazing meals. How about a movie after dinner? I mean, if you can stay awake for one."

"Ha! Maybe if you didn't pick such boring pieces of drivel, I would actually want to watch the whole thing," Kama countered.

"Sweetheart, you have never made it past the twenty-minute mark," Jack teased back. "How about you pick this time? I'll do the dishes."

"Done," Kama said and put dessert in front of them.

She gave Jack a suspicious look as he crooked a finger and motioned for her to walk over to him. Still, she complied, and he put both hands around her waist and gently pulled her onto his lap. Jack kissed her throat, and Kama tilted her head back with a sensual sigh. She leaned against his chest and stayed in his embrace.

"It's going to melt," she said as she looked at the dessert.

"I don't care."

She didn't flinch when Jack tightened the hug and was content just to be held by him. As they cuddled, the silence began to put her on edge, as emotions that she had tried to push away and ignore, came rushing forth. Kama looked over his shoulder and finally gave in to some of the panic.

"I thought I had lost you," she whispered, as she curled her fingers gently around his, needing to touch.

"But you haven't. I am here for you, always," he said. "We will get through this, Kama."

"Just don't ever let me go," she said.

"You are my Mate," Jack said.

Kama nodded, and hopped off his lap, and returned to serving up dessert. He had said "mate" a few times, but she still had a hard time with it. If they couldn't tell anyone, what was the point? She hoped in six weeks it would be a different story; however, she suspected that after she turned eighteen, there would be more talks about how their relationship would progress.

Yeah, I am interested to find out how the Pack will take the news. Some of the women will be upset to learn he and I are dating, but no one else has made any moves. I mean, if Lorna wanted him, wouldn't she have taken him already? I don't know if I am completely ready to be the Alpha alongside him. I'm not quite sure anyone will listen to me just yet. But I do have friends here, and they will support me. Maybe I should have my own crew? If we are going to live a life where we can go fight mutant thingies, I don't think saying I am dating the Alpha should be too bad. Yes, Wolf-girl, he is staring and laughing at us.

"Get it figured out?" he asked.

"Yeah, for now," Kama said and smiled. "Don't forget to scrub the plates before you put them in the dishwasher."

"Isn't this why I have a dishwasher?" Jack asked. "What is the point of having a cleaning machine, if it doesn't actually wash the damn things?"

Kama rolled her eyes at him.

"Did you actually eat here before I started coming over?"

"Sometimes…"

"Take-out doesn't count," she said and then laughed, pointing to the dishwasher. "This little home model acts more like a sanitizer. If you put in nasty, crusty dishes, they will come out the same way. Don't worry. It will probably take me a long time to find a decent movie."

She sauntered out of the kitchen to him muttering under his breath about useless equipment. Kama walked back into the living room, picked up the blankets off the floor, and tossed them back on the couch. She walked over to the rack holding the DVD movies and started to browse.

"Is it really possible this man doesn't have even one musical?" she grumbled.

She spent twenty more minutes looking through the offerings before she heard him come in.

"Victorious?" she asked.

"Getting a new machine," he said. "There has to be one out there that actually cleans the dishes."

"I am very curious about something, Mr. Twist," she said. "I found an oddity in your collection."

"Yes, Ms. DeKosse?" he asked. "What has your sleuthing uncovered?"

She refused to give in to his snarky tone. At least, she tried. Instead, she rolled her eyes and then asked her question.

"You have no American musicals, yet you manage to have a Jackie Chan opera I have never heard of? And who is Chris Tucker? Is he new to opera?"

After a few moments of silence, Kama looked up at Jack, who was giving her an incredulous look. She couldn't quite understand it, but it felt like he was waiting for the punchline to a joke. One she didn't know she had told. Kama finally broke the silence in exasperation.

"What?"

"You aren't teasing, are you?"

"What would I be teasing about, Jack?" she asked.

"Kama, honey—"

"Okay, you just wait," she interrupted.

"What?"

"You only call me Kama-honey when you are going to speak to me like I am slow or ignorant or something."

"I most certainly do not," Jack countered.

"Okay, then. What where you going to say?" she demanded.

"Jackie Chan is a well-rounded entertainer. He does comedy, martial arts and even a bit of directing, but he doesn't sing opera."

Kama gawped a few moments trying to figure out what to say in return.

What? Did the man really just try to tell me *all about Jackie Chan? Right?! Like he has spent his life preparing to be an Opera Diva. Was he born under a rock or something? Seriously...*

"Clearly, he does, Jack-*honey*. You have a copy of it right here," Kama said, waving the DVD at him.

She watched his face contort as he tried to keep his laughter under control. Kama resisted the urge to whap him on the head with the case. She waited calmly for him to get it together before he spoke to her.

"Kama, it's a video."

"I can see what it is, Jack."

"No. I mean, it's an action-adventure movie. Chris Tucker is an American actor and comedian," he said. "It's been out for five years."

"Jackie Chan doesn't make movies," she scoffed.

"Yes, Kama-*honey*. You're holding a copy right in your hand."

"Nice, Jack, throw my own words at me," she huffed. "You have never heard Jackie Chan sing? How is it even possible? He has a marvelous voice."

"Well, until I met you, I didn't listen to opera," Jack said. "But on a good note, you did pick an actual movie to watch."

Kama shrugged and handed him the case. She curled up on the couch and wondered if she should get snacks.

"Does it at least have music?" she asked.

"Ummm, yes," he said.

Kama furrowed her brow.

"Have you actually ever seen this movie?" she asked.

"Ummm, no," he said. "But all movies have soundtracks and thus, music."

She rolled her eyes at the ceiling but smiled as Jack put the movie in the player.

To be honest, it's not too bad. The kid is cute. I wonder what role she is really going to play. Wow, Chris Tucker, what a voice. Lessons could fix his pitch problem.

Kama stirred, feeling Jack slide his arms around her and cuddle her against his side.

"Did I fall asleep?" she murmured.

"You made your predictable twenty minutes," he chuckled. "It's nearly midnight. Maybe you should just go to bed."

"If it had been an opera I would have stayed awake for the whole thing," she said with a loud yawn.

"We will watch an opera tomorrow," he promised.

Kama smiled, snuggled into his shoulder, and fell back asleep.

CHAPTER Nine

Kama grumbled and squinted angrily at the stream of sunlight bathing her face in sleep-disrupting light. It took only seconds for her to remember what had transpired the night before. As she lay on his chest, she grinned at the soft rumble of Jack's snoring underneath her head. She slowly sat up and looked down at Jack. He slept like the dead, but she smiled knowing he needed his sleep after she had kept him up. She shook her head, because he had been correct after all.

I know I fell asleep during the blasted movie, but the important thing is I stayed asleep the rest of the night. And now, I am starving, and since the man is going to sleep for a while, I think I will make breakfast. I know I saw buttermilk down there, so pancakes, here we come. Yes, we saw sausage, you greedy thing. Huh. I wonder if calling myself names is just acknowledging balance, or maybe my head is a bit loose. Stop snorting. It's your head, too. More's the pity that you can't cook. I would like to snuggle a bit more.

She watched him sleep for a few more minutes, and then hopped out of bed and headed downstairs to make breakfast. Kama took about three steps out of the bedroom door before the chill drove her back to grab robe. She heard muffled noises and found Jack tossing around and clearly reaching out for her. Sitting on the side of the bed she caressed his cheek softly until he settled.

I wonder if his nightmares are plagued by the war we just went through, or if it's a kickback to his being a Marine. It doesn't seem fair to have to relive the trauma after experiencing it the first time, anyhow. Maybe this is just a side effect of his Spirit Quest?

She still didn't really understand the whole thing. It sounded rather impossible to her. Of course, being a werewolf had sounded fantastical, yet she was one. So she figured the possibilities were endless. With a grin at her rambling thoughts, she again headed toward the kitchen, dressed in one of his long, flannel shirts to cover herself, since a robe was nowhere to be found.

Things to accomplish sometime this week: bring some of my clothes here and convince him to let me stock this kitchen. While it is nice to wear his shirt, I would actually like some slippers or something. Yes, I guess we are planning on moving in. No, I don't think he will mind at all. Well, he might, but since we made up, we have been here at least three nights a week. Although, I do like having my own place. Either way, we're ready for food.

Kama went to work and got breakfast sizzling in the pans. She hummed the music to *Grow* as she flipped the pancakes. She still had a hard time believing Jack had never heard of Jackie Chan's opera career. While she made some good, strong coffee, she compiled a list of her favorite songs to introduce him to. She put the delicious array of food on a tray and went back to the room, setting it on his bedside table. Smiling, she reveled in feeling so at home in his place.

"Are you awake?" Kama asked, nibbling his lips until he woke. "Breakfast is ready, if you are."

She smiled as Jack cracked one eye open and caressed her cheek before sitting up. Kama couldn't help herself and started to poke him while he stretched. She didn't expect him to move so fluidly, since he had just woken. She giggled when he pulled her into his lap, kissing her breathless.

"How did you sleep?"

"What sleep?" he smirked.

Kama reached over to the tray and grabbed a sausage link, despite the heat. She gave him a haughty look and ate it, offering him none. She pushed off his lap and handed him a plate filled with pancakes, fruit, eggs benedict, and plenty of sausage.

"Coffee?" she asked with a huge grin. "As for sleep, I think I managed a few good hours of rest, in between all the snoring. I mean, you claim I hog the entire bed, but wow, do you make some noise."

"I would love some coffee," he said.

Kama waited for a return quip but got none. She figured he was only half awake, handed him a mug, grabbed her own food, and sat on the edge of the bed. They ate in quiet, and she appreciated how he didn't fill the time with idle chatter. She took a deep drink of her coffee.

This is so good. I think I could get used to waking up with him. Okay, we should plan what we are doing for the day. We don't have training until this afternoon with Juan. I guess I could check out Tina's class. Sheesh, I am really doing this. My life is becoming all about being Loup. Finding some kind of balance is going to be key. Being a warrior is all well and good, but I don't want to be wrapped up with only Pack things. I don't know what else to do, though. Maybe I can talk Beth into taking a class with me. Of course, I would have to figure out what kind of class— oh, I know. We could take a painting class. Though I really don't think I have ever painted anything. Then again, that might be the reason to try it. He is grinning at us…

"How is your food?" she asked, snatching a strawberry from his plate.

"It's good," he said. "It's the first time I've been served breakfast in bed."

"Well, it's the first time I have served anyone breakfast in bed," Kama said.

"Lucky me," Jack said. "I enjoy having you here."

She winked at Jack, and they fell into general prattle as they fed each other bits and pieces, purely enjoying the company and relaxed atmosphere. She wiggled her toes and tried to figure out her new life's goals. Having the same dream for so many years had stifled all other prospects. With everything suddenly open again, Kama wasn't sure what to try first.

Then again, we might not have to give up singing completely. Of course, the reason we decided to end our studies at Julliard was because we couldn't figure out how being a Warrior and being a Diva would be possible. Wow, this is too much for early morning and one cup of coffee. I wonder if Jack…really?

"What?" she asked, blushing.

"I asked you, twice in fact, what you wanted to do with our day," he said with an easy grin.

"We can try to watch the movie again," she said. "It didn't seem too bad."

"Maybe this time you can make it to the part that has music."

"I made it to the karaoke scene," Kama announced haughtily.

"An opera diva knows what karaoke is?"

She rolled her eyes at Jack, who openly laughed at her.

"I only have a few hours anyhow," she said. "Everyone who is not the Alpha has a training schedule."

"Well, I could give you private lessons," Jack said.

"Yeah, favoritism is the way to keep our relationship quiet," she snorted and then swatted at him while he shrugged. "Besides, even though you beat me yesterday, you still wouldn't be hard enough if you were training me. You like me too much."

"I do like you a lot, but I would still make you earn every blow you landed. You are a decent fighter, though," he admitted.

"I have worked hard to get there. The Arms Master pushes me pretty hard. I used to think he hated me, but honestly, he is no worse than any other teachers I have had. In fact, he rarely insults me. Aside from the bruises and screaming muscles. It also gives me something to do."

Kama watched him gather the plates and pile them on the tray. She took advantage of his going to the kitchen to freshen up in the bathroom. She grimaced at her reflection. Her hair had managed to create some kind of gravity-defying abstract art.

Great. Why did this man not suggest I use a brush? Oh, right. He doesn't have to think much about hair. Maybe I should cut it. Although, it would be another change and I don't think I need any more of those right now. Okay, now that I don't look like Medusa on crack, I can show my face again.

Kama walked out of the bathroom to find Jack leaning against the door frame, giving her an appreciative look.

"What time do you have training?" he asked.

"Three," she said.

"Good. We have time."

She took the hand he offered and knew all her hair brushing efforts were going to be for nothing.

Kama forced herself to walk down the stairs. Her excitement over the upcoming pizza delivery made her want to skip, but she refused to look childish. She paused for one moment on the landing and wondered if she ought to put on a pair of sweats to cover her legs. She looked down, barely able see her knees under Jack's flannel shirt and figured she would be okay. She had dresses that were shorter than what she currently wore.

Only a few minutes left, and we get them for free. Didn't they get rid of the offer because of all the car accidents? It's probably delivered by bike, anyhow. I should have ordered an extra one, but six should be enough. Oh, man. I really should have ordered one with pineapple. Ahhh, there it is, the knock I have been waiting for.

All pretenses of decorum went out the window. Kama skipped down the hallway and into the foyer. She took a breath to compose herself and opened the front door, proudly resisting the urge to grab the pizza from the delivery boy. Instead of seeing the treat she longed for, Kama looked up into familiar, brown eyes. She took an involuntary step back.

"Cade…" she breathed.

She looked over her shoulder, hoping Jack had stayed upstairs in bed. There were no scenarios she had ever run in her head where the two men would meet. She couldn't image anything good could come from Cade being there. When she looked back, she found he had followed her into the foyer. He gave her a smile that broke her heart.

"What are you doing here?"

"Looking for you," he said, sounding happy. "We need to talk."

"No. We don't need to do anything. I already told you; we're not dating anymore."

"Kama, you aren't being fair. You got to say everything and be done, but you never let me…"

"You have never heard the cliché about life not being fair?" Kama interrupted. "This is not going to happen. I am not going to have this talk here with you."

She met his eyes and met his determination to express himself. She didn't want to flinch, but he wouldn't release eye contact. Kama almost wished they had something else to talk about. A conversation which didn't involve telling him to go away, but nothing else made sense.

"Why won't you even talk to me?" he asked. "We were friends before we dated."

"Because you never go back to just being friends, Cade," she said. "I am sorry it didn't work out, but we can't go back to when we just had lunch and made each other laugh. Now, will you please leave?"

"You keep pushing me away, but you forget how much I care about you," he said. "I am always here to help with anything. Even with all the crazy you have in your life with your furry obligations. I like spending time with you even if you are just a whole bundle of complexities."

Kama chewed her lower lip as she watched a lazy grin accompany the wink he gave her. She knew she couldn't give in to his charm, but it would be hard. Cade had been nothing but nice to her; breaking up with him the first time had been hard. But she had broken up with him and made it clear. His being there made no sense.

Why the hell is he here? More importantly, how *is he here? He shouldn't know that Jack even exists, let alone where his home is. Did he follow me? Wow, I sure suck at being Loup if I didn't even notice him stalking us. He needs to go.*

She tilted her head and looked at him.

"Again, how did you end up at this place?"

"Lady Luck is always on my side. You should remember at least that much about me," Cade said. "After you changed your phone number, I stopped by your house and your mother let me know you moved. Honestly, Kama, you acted like I was going to come and hurt you."

Kama felt a flutter of panic.

"Actually, Cade, I acted like you weren't going to take the breakup well. Which apparently, you haven't. You have no right to just show up and demand anything from me."

"I thought we were in it together? And then you get to make all the decisions to just be done?" Cade asked. "Did I mean anything to you?"

Guilt spiked through her at his words. She knew he had the right to be upset, but it didn't make it any easier to hear. Kama heard Jack moving through the house. She knew he had heard the conversation with Cade escalate.

He probably figures I am shaking down the pizza guy. Okay, let's get Cade out of here now before… crap too late. Damn, Jack moves fast. Move, Kama.

"Just give me ten minutes to talk to you."

Kama looked at Cade and forced her face to be passive and calm.

"Unfortunately for you, all the talking in the world is not going to change things," she said. "You need to leave, and please never come back. It's over, and I don't want to see you again."

She pushed him toward the door firmly. Cade didn't quite fight back, but he resisted much more than she had expected him to. Kama's heart sank when she heard the foyer door open. She met Jack's inquisitive look and gave him a reassuring smile. She started to walk toward him when Cade grabbed her arm.

"Kama, just hear me out."

She watched Jack's eyes narrow and his lip curl back. He took a step forward and she held up her hand to stall him.

Right. There is no way Jack doesn't know this is Cade. He is reacting like I am being mauled in front of him. Apparently we never grow out of jealousy. I wish I could go back in time and stop myself from ever being such as ass and throwing my dating Cade in his face.

Kama tried to shake Cade's hand off her arm, but he held on tight. She shot him a heated look and frowned at him. She heard a low warning tone from Jack.

Crap, too late. He shouldn't have touched me. What can we do to fix this situation?

"Take your hands off of her, now." She heard Jack growl the words and noticed Cade's eyes narrow. He pulled at her arm again in attempt to turn her toward him.

"Just give me…"

Cade's words cut off with a squeak. Kama watched helplessly as Jack moved from behind her and pressed Cade up against the wall with a hand around his throat.

Isn't this where time is supposed to slow down or something? Then again, it can't slow down with Jack choking him. This is bad. Why did he show up here? How did he even know where here was? Okay, get Jack to stop choking him and get Cade gone.

"Don't ever touch her again."

As the words left Jack's mouth, he was propelled backwards and stayed pinned to the wall. His eyes rounded in surprise and then an amber color started to take over.

"Cade," she hissed. "What the hell just happened?"

"My power," he said, sounding panicked.

"You flip coins," she said.

"And other nifty tricks," Cade said, meeting her eyes.

"Let him go," Kama said sternly. Jack dropped to the floor with a thud, and as Kama turned to face Cade, she noted the space in the foyer began to look much smaller.

Oh gods, he is going to kill him.

She looked back and forth between the men, pushed the panic back and squared her shoulders. She knew she had to take control before the situation spiraled into the worse category.

"Enough."

The word vibrated through the air with enough power to make the men pause. Kama stood taller and commanded their attention. She grabbed control with both hands and focused her gaze on her Mate.

"Jack. I've got this," she said and only had to wait a few seconds for his posture to relax.

She met his heated look with an uncompromising one of her own until he turned and walked back into the house. Kama looked at Cade. She took a deep breath, grabbed him by the arm, and then escorted him back away from the foyer and out onto the stoop. She walked back into the house before she turned to face him.

"You need to leave," she said. "Do not ever come back. While I think you are a nice guy, Cade. It is over."

He opened his mouth and she stared at him, with the hardest face she could summon.

"He will kill you," she said. "I won't be able to stop it next time."

She felt a stab of guilt as dejection covered his frame. She watched him process the reality of her words.

"Kama…"

"Good-bye Cade."

She shut the door before the tears would fall and crack her mask of indifference. She held her breath until she heard him walk down the steps. Kama shook her head and took a moment to calm her emotions before going to face Jack. She prepared herself to go talk to him when a knock sounded at the door.

"Does he have some kind of death wish? What the bloody hell..." she snapped as she walked over and yanked the door open.

"Pizza?"

Kama quickly replaced the scowl with a wide, welcoming smile at the terrified pizza guy. She took the slip and scrawled a signature. She added a hefty tip for being surly.

"Thank you. Perfect timing," she said. "Could you please shut the door behind you?"

The pizza smelled like a hot cheesy nirvana to her, and she paused in the kitchen long enough to grab napkins. Kama walked through the house with a tiny bit of dread; she tried her best not to let her roaming imagination undermine the joy the pizza had brought Step by step passed, and she heard no sounds. Finally, she paused; the weight of her own thoughts crashing down on her until she just stopped walking. She hefted the boxes and tried to make things right in her mind. Her strong attitude faltered.

How can I possibly explain to him what just happened? Apparently he's never heard of magic workers in all the lands of the paranormal. Then again, it's not like we have some kind of guide telling us who is out there and what kind of magical creatures there are; though it would be really handy.

She imagined Jack was sitting in the house, stewing over the encounter. The sounds of her own breathing were harsh and guttural. She took a deep breath, and then another, trying to force herself to be calm. She walked into the living room and found Jack standing and waiting for her. Kama held out the boxes with a tentative smile.

"Pizza?"

Relief washed over her as he nodded and they sat on the couch. She busied herself with eating half a pizza before she looked up and met his gaze. She easily read the curiosity, irritation and intensity in his face.

"Yes, the man at the door was Cade. No, I have no idea how he knew to come here," she said.

"What pack is he from?"

The softly growled words were as surprising as a smack to the head would have been.

"What are you talking about?" she asked.

"A little human boy, as scrawny as that, couldn't have possibly tossed me," Jack said. "Where is his pack?"

Kama held out a slice of pizza to him and waited until he took it.

"In case you missed the part where he held you against the wall with his will," she said and then floundered for the right words. "He's not Loup, Jack. He's... other, for lack of a better title? A magician is the closest I can think of."

"A magician? Like a juggler or card flipper?"

"No, although up until an hour ago I thought he could only flip coins," Kama said. "In all fairness, I don't really know much about his ability. He only showed me how he could make a pyramid of coins."

"Oh," Jack said sarcastically.

"It's done, Jack," she said. "I handled it; he won't be coming back."

She looked at him until he met her eyes. She held the gaze until Jack took a breath and nodded.

"This is not exactly how I imagined spending the rest of our time together this morning," she said around a mouthful of pizza.

"Is he dangerous?"

Kama put her food down and looked at Jack.

"I would like to say no, but honestly, today taught me I don't know as much about him as I thought I did. He's been nothing but nice to me, so no, I don't think he is dangerous. I don't plan to have anything more to do with him. I'm done with school, so there is no reason I should run into him again," she said.

"Okay," he said.

"Just like that?"

"I trust you, Kama," he said.

She nodded and went back to her food.

When the heck do things get back to calm? I don't even need normal, but calm would be great. Okay, let's at least enjoy the last few hours we have together.

Kama smiled at Jack and put the movie on again, determined to watch it with him. Jackie Chan was pretty funny and she enjoyed the film. And to her embarrassment, she fell asleep before they got to the karaoke scene. She woke with Jack nuzzling her neck.

"Sorry, sleepyhead, but you have training in thirty."

She grumbled but made her way upstairs to change.

Good thing I can use his driver. Practice is going to be rough today because I am just damn tired. Of course Mr. Twist had a lot to do with me being awake so much last night. I hope Juan plans to go easy on me this morning, but if he sniffs out I am exhausted or even a bit off my game, he is going to work me harder than ever.

To her surprise and relief, Kama made it through practice just fine. She hadn't been Juan's target and managed to stay unnoticed the entire two hours. After a quick wash up, she headed back toward the southern end of the park to see if she could find any of her friends. She smiled at the thought.

Friends. I know we have always been private, except just a few. That all changed with Cynthia moved to California right before senior year. Then poor Giana didn't like being out of my secrets and we just stopped talking all together. Seriously, how could I have even begun to tell her about all of this stuff? It probably would have gotten her killed or something. I wonder how it works — letting other people know about the Loup. I mean Ajani kind of had the bad luck to learn about it, but can we tell other people? I'm not sure if I would have wanted G to know anyhow. But now I have Beth and Olivia, not to mention Dan and Mary and their crew. Funny to think, it took me becoming a werewolf to have a real group of friends.

Kama made it to the Lounge after a slow walk through the park. She looked around and saw Dan and Lani sitting in the back. Waving to them, she made her way over to the coffee tables. Even though she had been there for five months, it still amazed her to see the rows of coffee makers and microwaves. While she waited for her turn, she idly wondered just how much of a fire hazard the tables posed.

"Milk Explode!"

The words were all the warning Kama received before being pushed into the table by a packmate she didn't know. She turned her head to see who almost ran her over. Instead, she changed plans and tried to jump back but had no room as another young man tried to tackle the first. There wasn't room for her to get out of the way before the two scuffled.

The taller dark haired boy cuffed the shorter of the two, who turned, smiled, and attempted to foot sweep the taller boy. The taller one backed up and returned the grin.

"Get him Trent," someone called from behind her.

Trent nodded and jumped over the clumsy motion. As Kama watched, growing increasingly irritated as their antics delayed her having coffee, Trent rushed toward the smaller boy and attempted a mid-air kick. He landed hard and the other gasped as he received a kick in the ribs.

"Don't be a punk, Corey, kick his ass."

Okay so we have Trent the tall jerk and Corey the short jerk. Can they get done with their pissing contest so I can have my coffee? Why did I have to get caught up in the testosterone contest today?

Kama jumped up to avoid the tangle of bodies, but they rumbled past and pushed her off balance. She wobbled, but managed not to fall into the microwave closest to her. Despite wanting to kick them both in the back of the knees and make them face plant into the cement, she scowled and tried to move as far away from them as possible. Unfortunately for her, the boys became more rambunctious as their friends egged on the fight and she couldn't get away before Trent grabbed for Corey's leg and tripped him hard. As Corey fell to the ground, he reached out to stop his motion and connected with the side of the table.

Why?!?!

The table buckled and tipped towards her. Kama caught the edge but couldn't stop the coffee pot from sliding at her and splashing hot coffee down the front of her pants and onto her boots. She grunted but didn't cry out as the liquid made contact with her skin.

And those two jackasses didn't even stop wrestling. Someone owes me for a dry cleaning bill.

Kama righted the table, carefully avoiding the small stream of coffee that still poured over the side. She sighed and brushed at the liquid on her pants. She turned and walked toward her friends, who were waiting, and was bumped again.

"Dammit," she snapped.

She turned and faced the two boys who were still tussling. She grabbed Trent by the shoulder and pulled him away from Corey.

"Okay, stop it," she said.

"Oh, chill out, we are just having fun," Corey said.

"You just spilled hot coffee all over me."

"Sorry," Trent muttered and seemed to calm down.

"Yeah, sorry," Corey said and began to walk away.

Kama shook her head and rolled her eyes.

And I thought I left high school when I graduated. Great. Loup Central seems to be no different. Wait, where the hell are those two going?

As she watched, the two started to walk out of the Lounge.

"Umm, Trent?" she called. "Corey?"

"What?" Corey called back.

"Come clean up the mess," she said.

"You can get it, right?" Trent called over his shoulder, then turned and winked at her.

Kama moved towards him before she realized her own intentions. She put her hand on Trent's shoulder and turned him to face her.

"You made the mess. Go clean it before someone slips on it," she said.

"Well, Corey here is the real culprit, so it's his job," Trent smirked.

"Is not, you jerk. You're the one who thought you could take me."

To Kama's irritation, Corey swatted at Trent, and the two began roughhousing all over again. She side stepped their play and scowled at them. She grabbed them each by an arm and marched them back to where the coffee lay spilled on the ground.

"Get the mess cleaned up," she said calmly.

Trent walked over, grabbed a tall lanky boy with white blonde hair, and pulled him over.

"Clean this up."

Kama stopped and stared at Trent. She really had no desire to get in a fight, but she wasn't about to let Trent walk all over another kid just to avoid cleaning up a mess he made. She turned and faced Trent and Corey with a scowl.

"I don't care which one of you does it, but it needs to be done. No one else needs to clean up after you."

She resisted the urge to call them toddlers and settled for looking them up and down and raised her eyebrows in question. Kama could see the assessments they gave her. For a moment, she was certain they would try to jump her, and she mentally sighed. She narrowed her eyes even further and held the stare until they looked away.

"Fine," Trent said with a scowl back. "Get the mop, Corey."

"Good boys."

Kama gave them an overly bright smile and got her coffee. She passed Mary as she walked toward the table where the rest of her friends sat.

"Who does she think she is?" she heard Corey mutter.

"For starters, she is the one who saved my damn life," Mary said. "She is good enough for Aturus to put on the war team. Be happy she didn't beat your tail."

"Yeah, like that could have happened," Trent laughed derisively.

"She took down Raye," Mary said. "I'm pretty sure you two knuckleheads would have been easy. You might just want to pay attention, she's only been here since Halloween and already been sent on more missions than either of you."

"She's the one who throat punched Raye?" Corey asked.

She nodded at him but didn't appreciate the smirk he gave her.

"I thought you would be hairier."

Kama wanted to laugh where she sat but instead turned to face Dan.

"She does have a flair for the dramatic, huh?"

"Oh please, Diva, she is talking you up because everyone has at least heard of you at this point," he said.

"I just wanted them to clean up their mess," she sighed. "I didn't think it would have turned into a big challenge."

"With those two, maybe not, but get ready. There are some who want to know what you are made of."

She smiled and took a drink of her coffee. After all the hassle it didn't taste as good as she wanted it to.

"Thanks, Mary," Kama said.

"You should have knocked their heads together," Mary said as she sat.

"I don't see how fighting every person is a benefit?"

"Just rising up the ranks," Mary said with a shrug of her shoulders. "Not like you need much help there, but it's good for the others to know you have people who have your back."

Kama nodded and took another sip, watching the boys go from cleaning up the mess to fighting with the mops used as impromptu swords. She shook her head and then met eyes with the people at the table where they all burst into laughter.

Yes, I do enjoy having friends. It's a lot easier to accept this new life knowing that I don't have to do it on my own.

CHAPTER Ten

Kama took a deep breath and tried out a smile. The guilt and depression seemed to come in waves. Unstoppable, unpredictable waves to disrupt an otherwise lovely day. She didn't like the breakup end of a relationship and couldn't imagine enduring the pain more than a few times. The whole idea of dating bunches of different people made no sense to her, and she frowned at her reflection in the mirror. While she understood it would be natural to have an emotional response to all the stress, she didn't have to like it. She held another, brighter smile until she relaxed into it, damned determined to make her day work out well.

What the hell could Cade possibly have thought? He just showed up. He is so lucky Jack didn't kill him. Okay, it's done. He won't be back, ever. Dammit, I am going to miss his friendship. Okay, Kama, stop even thinking about it. We can't have it anymore. Our decision is to be with Jack, so stop feeling guilty. We broke up with him before we knew about the whole misunderstanding with Jack, so it's not like we dumped one for the other. Okay, stop the rambling mess. We have errands to run today.

She stuck her tongue out at herself, then laughed and smoothed her sweater. The red and silver took some of the sallow color from her face. She pulled her hair up into a high ponytail and let the bangs fall down the side of her face, giving her what she considered to be a mysterious air. She knew she had to look good even if she felt like crap.

Fake it 'til we make it.

She made her way to the kitchen and poured her drink into a travel mug. Other than a few, self-imposed errands to run, she had nothing else to do. Kama learned the unexpected downside of an early graduation was all of the free time she suddenly had. As she walked toward her door, she could hear her brother's door slam close. She hurried to catch him, so she would have someone to talk with for a moment.

Funny how I have become closer to Ajani because of all of these changes. I mean, we can talk to Jack, but everything we discuss with him has been so heavy lately. I never thought my First Change would have such lingering effects; I mean, I barely remember it happening. In my brain, I know those two, drug-dealing scum bags meant to murder me, but I can't remember shifting or anything else. Of course, it's not like I switch forms often. I wonder if it's discouraged here.. Maybe we just don't know enough about it, so it's not as common.

Kama made a quick, mental note to call her cousin, Nula, and have a talk about shifting. During her stay in northern Michigan with her family, she had watched a First Change. Contrary to her own experience, the shift had been fairly easy and trauma free. She assumed it had a lot to do with already knowing the Loup nature, but there had also been a guide to help the young girl through her first time.

Maybe Nula will give me a few hints, and we can start to change how things happen around here. At least then I would have something to talk about, besides my misunderstanding with Jack. I just want to have a conversation about something mundane or silly. Oh well, back to real life. I bet Olivia needs to go shopping for some. more food. I doubt she has any left, and so far, the idea of going to a store scares her silly. Maybe I can ramble about all of these different ideas to her. She will have a different perspective on all my crazy. Hmm. I don't like the sound of my own thinking right now.

She opened the door and caught Ajani kissing Beth. She waited a few more minutes while they said their good-byes. A snarky thought had started to develop, but it evaporated. She smiled as the two finally parted.

I am glad they found each other. They seem to be happy and enjoy spending time together. Although, my enhanced hearing isn't always a good thing, but I am learning how to ignore the extra sounds. One would think the more expensive apartments would have better insulation. I know. We can put up tapestries on the wall. Oh, stop it. Tapestries are not only for castles. You know, for being a part of me, you sure have some convoluted ideas about things. I mean, if you really are the instinctual part of my brain, I have to say, I'm a bit disturbed that my instinct is so snobby and condescending. Anyhow, Beth and Ajani are good for each other. Yes, I saw how he looks at her, and I hope they continue to date. But I can't possibly promise him she will come home at night. We no longer have the luxury of believing we are safer just because we have claws. And back to the somber thoughts..

"See you later, Kama," Ajani said. "I will let you ladies walk your fourteen flights of steps. This sane and normal man is going to take the elevator."

"Bye, Ajani," she said. "The exercise wouldn't kill you."

"Maybe not, but I prefer other forms of exercise."

She ignored the lewd waggle of his eyebrows and waited patiently while her brother and best friend said their good-byes again. When it became clear their displays of affection were a show designed to make her gag, Kama walked to the elevator and pushed the button to hurry the good-bye along. She waved to Ajani as he got in and the doors closed. Beth finally turned to her with a wide smile.

"He is pretty amazing."

"He's not so bad," Kama agreed as she pushed the door to the stairwell open. "At least since he's been dating you. He seems a lot more settled. Ready to go?"

"Wait a minute," Beth said. "I need more coffee."

Kama watched with amusement as Beth walked back into her brother's apartment and then emerged with mug in hand.

"Ajani says I drink it too much and all the caffeine is bad for me, so he's cut me off after two mugs. I've wanted more for at least an hour, but I never learned how to use the latte machine," Beth said. "Of course, it is because he tells me that I am too pretty. Who am I to argue when the man offers me a compliment?"

"You're too pretty to make coffee?"

"Yes. This is your brother's gentle way of telling me to stay out of his kitchen and leave his fancy equipment alone."

Kama laughed and opened the door to her home. She used the percolating time to make toast and some more eggs for a snack. She poured steaming drinks for Beth and herself, and they sat on the couch.

"Has he banned you from the kitchen altogether?" Kama asked. "Though, I do guess it's your free pass never to cook."

"So far, it's the coffee machine and his skillets. I have very successfully used the toaster and microwave," Beth said. "The true breakdown came when he learned I made scrambled eggs with it. He did eat the eggs but told me many times how easy they were to make in a pan."

"He's right," Kama said. "I can't believe I just said that."

She started to laugh, and Beth joined in.

"Today, we need to go shopping for Olivia and get her some new things. According to Jack, she doesn't have anything. I mean, nothing," Kama said. "Do you know, when I went in there last time, she told me she slept on the floor? Shifted, mind you, but still on the hard, cold floor. I had to get Karl and some of the guys to find her some mattresses. I think she needs more clothes, plus other things to make her space feel comfy. I already boxed up stuff from around here I'm sure I won't need. My mother apparently thought moving downstairs meant moving to Siberia and I would have access to nothing. If we end up missing anything, I'll just let Jack know, and he can arrange for her to get it."

She sighed happily into the depths of her mug, enjoying her moment, until she looked up and found Beth giving her a skeptical look. She met her friend's eyes and raised her eyebrow in return.

"Kama…"

"No. You don't get to ruin the good start to my morning with a censuring tone. I had more than enough drama for forever, yesterday, Beth."

"I thought you were upset with the Alpha, and now you're calling him by his first name again."

"Can't a girl finish her morning snacks before all this explaining of messes?" Kama muttered. "Okay, short notes: I broke up with Cade before Christmas. It went poorly, and Ajani had to step in at graduation. Jack and I had a huge fight after he asked me to watch out for Olivia. I then found out he had never broken up with me. I made assumptions because of all the drugs and acted on those instead of realizing he could never walk out on me. We are working things out. And yes, I call him Jack."

"But, Kama, we've had this discussion about what can happen," Beth said. "It can get you killed."

"He is my Mate."

Kama doubted striking Beth with a cast-iron skillet would have stunned her less. The wide-eyed look and open mouth had the potential to be comical. She also realized using the term "Mate" felt natural. She rolled the term around her mind a few more times, satisfied.

"Do you know what you are saying?"

"Yes. I do," Kama said and took another, longer sip. "Can we go back to figuring out how to help Olivia?"

Silence filled the space between the two women, and Kama stood with a sigh. She didn't want to have to justify her relationship with Jack to Beth, again. She already knew Beth thought it was reckless and dangerous. Understanding where the concern came from didn't make it any easier to tolerate. After all, the tension around the topic of the two men already had her mind on edge, and Kama couldn't allow herself to get back into that space.

"I didn't judge you when you decided to date my brother," Kama started.

"You threw me under the bus, Kama," Beth scoffed. "You used my being Loup as a way to help him acknowledge we were real. It was actually a pretty crap thing to do, even though it got all the weird stuff out."

"I knew he liked you and figured it might be a good way to show him that being Loup wasn't a bad thing," Kama said.

"Even still, it should have been my choice when and how to tell him I am Loup," Beth said. "Not yours."

Kama looked at her friend and didn't dare smile. While she doubted she could take all the credit, she had noticed Beth had come out of her shell. Especially with her, even though Kama clearly had the stronger personality.

"I mean, you really could have found another way to tell him. Not like your mom didn't grow up in a Den," Beth said.

"Okay," Kama said. "You are right. I am sorry I told him your secret. Honestly, with everything that had just happened, I didn't know how else to deal with it right then. I should have found a better way to let him know."

"You are forgiven. If anything, you really owe me for getting him to clean up his act. You two get along much better, from what he says," Beth said. "I do want you to be careful, Kama. Aside from your scary mom, dating Ajani is not going to kill me."

Kama put her mug down, hard. While she could appreciate Beth growing more of a spine, she didn't like it being used against her. She immediately checked to see if it cracked and then looked up at her friend.

"I know you are concerned, but somehow I doubt there are going to be scores of women at the Park who are going to try to attack me just to date Jack. I've only been around for a few months; they could have made their move ages ago. There might be some grumbling about us dating, and they will just have to get over it. I can't help the way I feel."

"Are you even sure you know how you feel? Not to be mean, but you have only dated two, whole people."

Kama was torn between being surprised and being irritated with her friend. She carefully thought about the words to say. She had enough drama, and fighting with Beth didn't appear on her list of things to do. She took a deep breath.

"You know, I may not have dated a whole bunch of people, but I do know what real emotions are. For instance, I understood the panic and terror I felt when Cade showed up at Jack's house yesterday."

She met her friend's horrified stare.

"Yeah, I answered the door, thinking the pizza guy would be standing there, but to my surprise and abject horror, there stood Cade. And then Jack came to the door. Then things went downhill fast, with all the magic-working, shifting, and death threats in larger-than-life glory. So, yes, I do understand what is at stake here."

She stood and took her mug to the kitchen. She took some deep breaths to calm herself.

I know she is trying to help us, but it's just not easy. She can date Ajani, and no one will think anything of it. I have a few more weeks of this hide-and-seek stuff, and then we can start to change things. It might take more time than I want, but eventually I can be open with whom I am dating. Sheesh, so formal in my head—stinking, private school education.

She walked back into her living room and found Beth waiting for her. Their eyes locked, and they stared for a few moments. Just when Kama thought she would have to re-start the conversation, Beth spoke.

"You know what? You are my best friend, one I thought I would never have. Date who you want and know I have your back, as Ajani would say. I might not be the best fighter in the world, but I will always stand up for you and support you. If the Alpha is your Mate, then I guess I get the perks of being friends with the Alpha's girlfriend."

Kama surprised herself by tearing up and pulled her friend into a hug.

"Thanks, Beth. I know what it means for you to say this to me. Trust me when I say, no one is going to mess with us. Anyhow, before we both start crying and looking a mess, let's go shop."

"Sure thing, but one more cup of coffee first."

"Okay, pretty one. I now understand why my brother cut you off," Kama laughed. "We will never make it to the Park if you drink more."

Kama waved as Beth left Olivia's platform to go off for her rounds. Looking around at the space, she began to calculate where things should go. She smiled at the younger girl while Karl and his friends put down the rest of the packages. There were a few grunts as the last of the mattresses were placed into the space, and she handed each of them a few bills for their help. She planned to spend some time helping Olivia get everything into place. Shopping had only taken four hours, and she had nothing else to do with her day. One look at Olivia changed her plans.

Okay, she looks like she is going to have a small, and probably very quiet, freak-out. Maybe she just wants to organize her room by herself? I doubt it. She looked totally shocked when we started bringing down all of her new stuff. It's still odd to think she sleeps in shifted form. Hey, let's go get some training in. Hopefully the practice room is empty. I wonder if I can take on more duties or something, because this much free time will either drive us crazy or get us into trouble. Maybe I should take Olivia and have her practice with me. She keeps looking from bag to bag; this has got to be too much for her. Okay, first, give her something else to do , and then we can come back and tackle getting this place to feel like her own.

"Olivia, how about we go and spar for a bit?" Kama said and watched relief cover the girl's face.

"That sounds fine," Olivia said.

"Maybe we can teach each other some new tricks."

"I'm sorry, Kama, but I don't know any tricks," Olivia said.

"Actually, I meant new styles of fighting. Maybe something we are sure the other hasn't tried before," Kama said. "I'm sure there is a move you do really well, and I would love to learn it."

She considered integrating the girl into her group of friends. They were a fun group, and it would help her. They walked toward the northern end of the park in silence, and she didn't break it. She had noticed Olivia never filled the silence with idle chit-chat. Kama had the feeling it probably wasn't allowed in the place where Olivia came from, but she didn't ask, for fear the answer would haunt her dreams.

Every time I talk with her, I learn something that makes my stomach churn. I don't know how this poor girl even managed to survive, let alone have some semblance of normalcy. It amazes me how she has been able to adapt to this new situation. Essentially, she went from prison to unfettered freedom, after going through a war. Maybe she needs some counseling. I wonder if we even have Loup shrinks. Okay, practice room, here we are. Maybe just a short spar, because I am hungry. And of course, it's occupied. Aturus and Juan and all their instruments of pain strewn around the room—we should leave. Aw, dammit. They saw us. This is not going to end well for me. He is going to make me participate in some kind of body-breaking way.

Kama nodded and walked into the room as Aturus waved for her and Olivia to enter. He and Juan stood in the center of the room, holding rattan sticks. She and Olivia took a seat against the wall and watched as the two men faced off.

Aturus raised the rattan and began to go through a series of motions she was completely unfamiliar with. His movements were easily fluid, as if each move were an extension of the last, and caused her to pause for a moment and watch, fascinated. He never took his eyes off of Juan, but instead, slowly melted into a defensive stance. Kama held her breath in anticipation. She flinched against the wall as Aturus brought his stick down against Juan's, swept with his left leg, and tripped the other man, throwing him off balance.

Juan countered and brought his own weapon across the back of Aturus's neck, not bothering to stop as the wood snapped against the man's skin with a sharp sound Kama figured would result in a bruise. He jumped back, but impressively didn't make a sound. Aturus grinned, as if to say he had expected this attack. He then pivoted, reversed his grip on his stick to cover his forearm, and thrust out with the palm of his other hand, striking the center of Juan's stick, which drove it up with force and smacked him on the end of nose.

Oh, damn, that had to have hurt. His eyes are really watering. I would be bawling or cursing if I got hit so hard in my face. I can't believe Juan is just shaking it off. Aturus is all relaxed and smug, while Juan's face looks like a big ole' peony. It is going to suck for him tomorrow when the swelling on his nose goes down.

"What did he do wrong?"

"He shouldn't have shifted his balance when he struck out with the stick, then he would have been firmly planted and ready to get out of the way," Kama said.

"Diva, don't you have anything better to do with your time than be in the salle? Aren't you supposed to be off primping or something?" Juan scoffed. "Maybe a manicure to go to?"

"Quit being an ass because the Diva saw you get busted up. You were off balance," Aturus said. "He did bring up a good question, though. Why are you here? Don't you have the day off?"

"I'm sorry, Arms Master," she said. "I figured I would get in some practice before the room got taken for a class."

"We give you downtime for a reason," Aturus said. "Do you think you can follow orders enough to take a break now and again?"

Kama tried her best not to look frustrated.

The man just asked for an answer, and when I gave him one, he scoffed at me. Sheesh. Maybe Olivia can be talked into getting a snack topside. If I call Michael ahead of time, we can come in through the back and sneak upstairs to eat…Why is he looking at me? Oh, wait, I guess he wanted the question answered.

"I can find something else to do," she said. "Practicing these new skills makes sense. I am used to working on my skills daily, not matter how good I think I am."

"Don't you have some singing or something to do?"

Kama swallowed the hurt feelings and schooled her face to be calm. She then looked over at Juan and answered his snarky question.

"No. I can't be an Opera Diva and a Loup warrior in the same life, so one of those options had to go," she said.

A towel was thrown into Juan's face. Kama looked over to see Aturus. He jerked his head at Juan and toward the door. Juan left with incoherent grumbling. Aturus walked closer to her, and met her eyes when she dared to meet his gaze. She suddenly found the pattern on the tiles to be most fascinating. Kama stood there, avoiding looking back up at him, until his boots appeared under her fixed gaze at the floor. She slowly dragged her eyes up to his and found a scrutinizing look on his face.

"We all have lives outside of the Park, Kamaria."

Why does he have to call me by my full name? Can't he just call me Diva? Every time he says Kamaria, *I feel like I really screwed up.*

"I'm sure I will find something new to do, but I can't seem to figure out how to reconcile the me who is Loup and the me who had everything in order before she became Loup," she said. "Right now, I am working on being the best warrior possible. It seems the best way to stay sane."

"Fine. You can work for an hour," Aturus said. "I do want you to come up with a hobby. You can tell me what it is tomorrow after class.

Kama breathed a quiet sigh as her Arms Master walked out the door, bellowing at Juan to ante up the beer he owed him. Her brain tripped over itself trying to figure out some kind of new hobby. She wasn't sure what she would tell him. Maybe she could come up with a hobby so boring he wouldn't want to hear about it. Or maybe, she could claim Olivia was her new hobby. She got up and shut the door. With smile, she looked at Olivia.

"Ready to spar?"

The younger girl stood up and away from the wall.

"What tricks do you want me to show you?" Olivia asked.

"I don't know," Kama said, walking into the training area. "Surprise me. We can just have a friendly match until one of us is on the ground. Nothing too rough. Let's just learn something new."

Kama slowly advanced on her opponent, but to her surprise, Olivia struck out at her chest. She reached under Olivia's arm and pinioned it between her own, before dragging the girl to the ground. The move was quick and not painful, so Kama waited for her to stand up

"Try the move more slowly, and I'll show you another option," Kama said.

Olivia nodded, got to her feet, and without hesitation, punched out toward Kama. Using her arms in an exaggerated motion, Kama trapped the girl's arms, reached out, tapped her sternum with the palm of her right hand, and pressed up against her chin with the left.

Olivia looked slightly startled but only nodded.

"Can you show me that again, slower?"

The girls had a good time working together on hand-to-hand moves. To Kama's surprise, Olivia actually broke into giggles a few times. They were always quickly suppressed, but Kama felt it a major victory when they broke through. They each took their time, sharing good hints or tips to help the other learn. After a long water break, she prepared to try out some of the new techniques.

"Okay, let's put all this practice to the test," Kama said.

She waited for Olivia to climb back to her feet and get into a defensive stance. Kama pushed closer to the girl with a series of light and easy jabs.She extended her hand forward and struck the girl's chest, expecting the block they had worked on, but it wasn't thrown. Taking a few, small steps back, she rushed back in with the same move, but ducked under Olivia's arm and tapped her between the shoulder blades. She then nearly tripped as a surprise sweep of her legs made her wobble. She managed to right herself and get to a ready position.

"Nice," she said with a grin. "I sure didn't see it coming."

She took advantage of Olivia's thinking they were done to return the leg sweep, and as the girl toppled, Kama gave her a light shove and let momentum carry her forward and to the floor. As she knelt down, she cupped her hand and pressed her thumb and ring finger onto Olivia's lymph nodes.

"Yield?"

"Sure," Olivia said easily.

"Sloppy balance, but it was an interesting combination, Diva."

Kama whirled around, heart pounding in her throat, and found Aturus leaning casually against the door frame. She exhaled a thin stream of air and looked at him.

"Your hour is up," he said.

"But…we just got done with practice, and we were going to spar a few rounds to put it into real use," Kama stammered.

"Round one?" Aturus asked.

"Yes."

"Best two of three, then," he said. "Diva, round one to you."

Kama nodded and smiled at Olivia.

"Ready?"

"Yes."

She wasn't sure what tone she heard in the other girl's voice, but it sounded like competition. Kama moved carefully in, unlike the first time. She punched out a few times, and the girl ducked. The next few moments passed in what Kama could only describe as being in a fugue state. Olivia had ducked under her arm, and before Kama could turn and face her, she found herself enveloped in large, fur-covered arms.

Holy crap, I didn't even hear her shift. Did she just really go all-out for the fight? I guess she is out for the win.

Her thoughts stopped rambling as she tried to figure out how to gain the advantage on an opponent standing six feet tall and heavily muscled. She twisted and tried to push her way out of the embrace. As soon as it became clear the move was pointless, Kama relaxed and let her weight hang. The redistribution of her weight allowed her to loosen up Olivia's grip, and she pulled free. It took her precious second to reconcile with her brain the sight before her.

Okay, I know we shift into warrior form, but—damn! At least some part of me is irritated at how wrong the movies get it. They tend to make us look like an odd mash-up of person and wolf that snarls and drools all the time. She is amazing in her warrior form. Oh, hell. A form advancing on us and ready to win round two. Move, Wolf-girl.

She narrowly missed being propelled across the room as Olivia swung at her with her arm. The next few seconds were spent with Kama ducking and avoiding the flurry of punches and kicks thrown at her. She did manage to get a well-placed kick in, on the side of Olivia's knee, and stepped backwards to breathe and come up with a plan. To her dismay, the girl shook off the kick quickly. Kama decided to rush and jump on her back, hoping to maybe choke her to the floor from behind.

She moved fast and leapt, only to be met with the side of the girl's body as Olivia turned. Kama bounced against the tight muscles, and then let out a hard *oof* as she fell to the ground. In a swift movement, one meaty pound pinned her to the ground on her stomach and claws lay across her neck.

"Round two to Olivia."

Kama took her place on the floor across from Olivia and looked at her opponent. Then quickly looked at the floor, because the girl stood comfortably naked, waiting to start the next round.

Talk about embarrassing yourself in the biggest way possible. I bounced right off of her and onto my butt. Of course, the Arms Master is watching because, why wouldn't he? He gives me this great speech about not giving up my entire life just to be a warrior, and I give him the performance of me fighting like an idiot. Apparently, I am going to need to think these things through a bit more. Maybe there is a better way to balance these life things. Okay, we can muse about this later. Right now, I need to show everyone I can fight. Now to remember how to tap the power Nula told me about when I was in Michigan. I should be able to shift mid-leap and tackle Olivia to the ground.

She smiled as the plan formed in her head. It would be a glorious ending to the fight, and later she could show Olivia her trick.

"Ready?" Kama asked.

"Yes," Olivia responded.

Kama sprang into action and began to run towards her, intending to make short work of the confrontation. She figured their newly acquired audience wanted to see the best they had to give, and she planned to wow them. There was little space to work up real speed, but it didn't matter. She met the younger girl's eyes and locked her gaze. She pushed against the ground with the balls of her feet and lifted into the air. A triumphant feeling coursed through her, and she readied herself for the shift.

Okay, we got this. She is expecting us to try what we just spectacularly failed at. Once we leap at her, we should expect her to raise her arms to fend off a blow to the face and neck. All right, instead of going into warrior form, we are going to shift to wolf form and tackle her to the ground. Easier to shift our whole body than just our arm or leg. All righty, we are in the air. Now, shift! What do you mean 'no'? We can do this; we have done this before. Oh, crap, this feels wrong. You really could have warned us about this being a bad idea. We can't breathe. Help.

Kama's last thoughts muted as the world around her faded to black.

CHAPTER Eleven

Jack walked into the Marionette's Theater in Central Park and smiled. He and Carla had just gotten off a conference call about a merger that looked like it would go through. As he passed the threshold, the world fluxed a moment for him. While he had been experiencing odd feelings over the past few weeks, he had chalked it up to being overtired and stressed. However, his schedule had slowed down after the end of the holiday season and he felt much better. Things just seemed to fall into the place, like they were meant to be. Instead of being the mix of pictures and messages he had been receiving, this time, a stomach rumble sounded and he moved toward the tunnels entrance with a shake of his head.

Did we actually eat today? Yea, we had the lunch Carla brought in. Some kind of gourmet, pizza dish with fancy toppings and dips. There is nothing wrong with a standard pepperoni and cheese. And while I am musing about the topic of food, there should probably be a better way for members to have food accessible. I think we need to do something about the Lounge. Having the coffee machines and microwaves is great, but I think we can do more for the Pack down there. Not like catering in food every day, which would cost a fortune, since those people can seriously eat. Maybe we can put a kitchen proper down in a lower level. At least I would know where to find Kama at any given point.

His ramblings had carried him down to the Lounge and, to his surprise, he was greeted enthusiastically by his Pack members. Ever since the memorial, he had been having more conversations and been approached by people as they needed him. His invitation had been well received, and he realized the benefit it would have to his group. It wouldn't be like one, big, happy family; he expected there to be squabbles and fights, but overall they seemed to feel more connected for the moment. Jack had to admit to himself, it felt good to go in to the gathering area and be invited to sit and chat. It had started with Karl asking him to come and chat. Once the others saw he had meant what he said about interacting with him, they had tried it as well.

Slowly but surely, the group found a new normal to live with, now their friends were gone. He and the Betas were working hard to help those who had come back deal with the survivor's guilt, as well as those who still didn't really understand all that had happened. After a short stay, Jack walked back toward his office and shook his head as he ruminated.

Somehow, it didn't occur to me that being Alpha would be so much more than being a commander. Sure, I have to lead them, teach them, and guide them. But there is so much more. It seems like the last decade was the warm-up period for the real job of keeping this Pack together and working well. I suppose it helps how much we have grown as a group, but what a lot of work. Despite the military model, it's clear to me it is time to change and rework our structure to better fit us as we continue.

His mind churned over the possible changes he could make to help the Pack. He walked past his office, nodding at Shellye and Simon, the guards The Judge had insisted on installing in his office corridor. Jack had no idea why, all of a sudden, he needed security, but they kept the area around his office nice and quiet. After a few moments of pacing in the suddenly too small space, he decided the conference room would be better space to detail his ideas. The large room had a huge table which easily sat him and the Betas. There had been many growing moments there.

As Jack sat back in his seat, he felt a tingle, and his eyes widened. He recognized it and knew it would be encompassing. He leaned his head back and took a deep breath. The fluctuating feeling seemed to be the precursor to the visions he'd been experiencing. He had come to see value in the lucid, waking dreams where he still interacted with the Goddess. Even when they came unannounced. The room around morphed into a landscape, and he stood looking around him.

"I guess it's time to explore," he said.

So far, none of the visions had done anything harmful to him. After a quick survey of the scenery, he walked up a long, dirt driveway, toward a rustic-looking house made of bricks. On the left side, the low roof had wide, bracketed, projecting eaves. A side porch had arch-heads between the columns. An arched doorway on the first floor led up to decorative stones covering the head windows. The tall, square tower had round,, windows around the cupola. On the right, the single-level structure boasted many rectangular, windows. One final, rounded structure sat at the very end and had bowed bay windows.

Jack wasn't surprised when all of a sudden, She walked with him.

"Amazing, isn't it?" She asked.

"Nice," he said. "It would be even better if I knew where we were and what this is."

"Italy. And it's a standard, Italian villa, with cornice structures, glazed doors, pedimented windows, and balustrades," She said with a pleased nod.

"And here I am without Carla to interpret for me," he said wryly. Then a thought struck him. "You and Carla are two different beings, right? I mean, she does some pretty miraculous things."

Her laughter sounded like a gentle, pouring rain, mixed with the tinkle of wind chimes and the rustle of leaves in a gentle breeze.

"No, Carla is quite mortal," She said.

"Back to the Italian villa," Jack said. "Why am I here?"

"I wanted to show you something."

They walked into the house, exploring. Children ran around, teasing, laughing, and playing with each other. In the next room, he watched a small girl contentedly stringing poppies into a necklace. The bright red petals fell to the floor around her, but she continued her task diligently. He watched them with longing, remembering the missed opportunity with Melissa. There were at least two dozen children he could count. Squeals of delight, petty bickering, and shouts of excitement created a cacophony that filled him with joy.

"Who are they?" he asked.

"Your progeny," She said with a simple shrug.

"Why are you showing me them?"

"Once upon a time, you wished and dreamed for this," She said. "I am showing you your dreams will be realized."

Jack stood mesmerized as the children played. He pretended he could make out features that might have come from him on each one. She cleared her throat, and as he looked over at Her, She started to fade.

"Where are you going? I have so many more questions," he said.

"Someone else needs a response from you. He never was a patient person."

She became a cloud, which made him choke. As Jack began to cough, he recognized it as a plume of real smoke which belonged to the amused-looking Judge.

"You wanted my attention?" he asked.

The Judge walked further into the room and sat in the seat he usually occupied. Jack took the hint but made it a point to grab a bottle of scotch and two glasses before he took his own seat. He wasn't sure what the talk could possibly be about, since his old friend generally preferred the silence.

"I need to thank you again, for keeping the group together," Jack said. "You have been a great mentor to me, as well."

The Judge nodded and released another plume of smoke.

"She must have showed you some pretty amazing things. You've changed. It's been for the better. Making you stronger and all. Guess you learned a few, important things as well."

"Yes, I had some things clarified for me," Jack said. "But I still don't understand it all. Can you offer me some insight or your wisdom?"

The Judge sat forward and looked at him for a moment. Jack maintained eye contact and tried not to breathe too loudly. He had never asked for help before, from anyone. Despite relying heavily on his Betas to run the Pack, Jack had kept his distance. He knew about them and even some details of their personal lives. He, however, didn't share with them. He tried to keep his personal life, business dealings and Pack business separate. Jack realized it had been a mistake, and hoped he would be able to rectify the situation in the years to come. He took a breath.

"What's on your mind, son?"

He hoped he masked his surprise. Often, The Judge called him "boy" and every once in a while by his first name, but he had never called him "son."

"I don't mean to sound crazy. Hell, I can't even say that I might not be going crazy," Jack said. He then admitted, "I am having hallucinations. Ever since I have been back from my Spirit Quest, I find myself having episodes. I will have these things, like waking dreams. It's sometimes like déjà vu because, after the vision, I have an interaction of the same type. Or I get a whole bunch of images, and there are all sorts of messages, once I figured out what they mean. Or I hear things, usually laughter, when I am the only one around."

The Judge inhaled deeply and exhaled a thick cloud of smoke.

"Maybe Lorna would have advice, since she has been the one to take the Quests."

"Don't be an ass, Jack," The Judge said. "Your Betas see you as the ultimate strength and stability of the Pack. Don't shake their belief in you. Spirit Quests are almost religious in nature. They sure test your notion of faith. You will figure it out as time goes by."

"I shouldn't have come to you?"

Smoke blown in his face betrayed The Judge's displeasure.

"Since you're going to be an ass anyhow, I will use small words to explain things to you. Of course you needed to come to me. Who else would explain it to you? You were blessed to have had an interaction with our Goddess. These aren't hallucinations you are having. These are memories of the conversation you have already had with her."

"But, one of the memories was of an event, and it just happened today."

"You believe in the notion of a Spirit Quest and a Goddess, but you can't come to grips with nonlinear timelines? Do you really think your tiny, little mind could absorb and understand everything in just a few weeks?"

Jack thought about the information as he stood and poured two jiggers of scotch. He knew he shouldn't be surprised the Spirit Quest still affected his life. The Goddess had shown him answers. Though, he realized, more questions had surfaced ever since his contact.

"These events being memories make sense," he said. "But what some of them show me just doesn't make sense. For example, I saw a field of flowers. Later, I learned they are the birth flower for August. I know this because Curt sent Lorna a bouquet, and she is not a flower person. When I saw a lime green gem, I found out it's called a peridot. Other than the belief it protects against nightmares, it again relates to August. Apparently, August is going to be important for the Pack, but I have no idea how. Maybe motherhood will make Lorna calm?"

The raspy, smoker's hack caught him off guard.

"Are you choking to death?" Jack asked dryly. "Or are you actually laughing."

"You have a better chance of seeing the gal without a gun than her not being high strung," The Judge said. "Listen, I'm going to have a serious moment here. I don't want to have to interrupt myself to insult you, so let me talk a minute, okay?"

"Sure. Actually, wait. I'll get another drink. This way I won't be able to say anything."

Jack got his drink and then sat at the table across from The Judge.

"As you are learning, She works in Her own way. You are being given help because you asked for it. For thirteen years, you have run this Park and Pack with great aplomb. However, being a great leader means you know how to get the help you need. Your world is changing. Each time you access a memory, something important will happen. She has decided to directly intervene with you and this Pack. Take the help She offers to you," The Judge said. "You know I have been around a long time, probably longer than you can actually guess. No, I'm not telling you how old. My point is, embrace the changes and move ahead."

The Judge held out his glass for a refill, and they took a silent sip.

"Be grateful, son. She doesn't do this for everyone."

"I try to be, but it still is confusing. I see these scenes or picture or images. Usually I figure out what it means as the event happens. I suppose if it were easy I wouldn't have accepted it either," Jack said. "You have dealt with Her before?"

"Sure, but that is a story for another time. Right now, we are going to enjoy some scotch before I have to beat someone with my bat for doing something stupid up there. Maybe the next time you see Her, you can ask for the next batch of new cubs to be smarter."

Jack had the perfect retort on his lips, but he looked up in shock as the door to the meeting room slammed open. Karl stood there, red-faced and panting. Immediately, worry sprang into Jack's mind. Loup in their human form were about as fast as any Olympic runner. Twenty-five miles an hour was the fastest they had ever clocked one of their own running. For Karl to have pushed himself to run hard enough to lose his breath meant an emergency. He willed himself to talk in a low, quiet voice. Flustering the young man wouldn't get the information any faster.

"What's wrong, Karl?"

"Alpha-Dude," he wheezed. "Aturus sent me to get you. Olivia and Kama were having a big spar. Then something happened, and Dudette passed out."

"Which one, Karl?" Jack asked with a calm he didn't feel.

"Kama. Aturus took her to Doc's. I'm not sure being there is any better than being out cold, 'cause the scary lady will stick her with a million needles."

Jack stood and looked back and forth between Karl and The Judge. Panic made him pause, for the first time in a long while.

"Go, Jack," The Judge said. "Loup don't pass out."

The panic he refused to show welled up inside him. Jack began running down the tunnels. He pushed himself and felt his wolf merge with him. The walls flew by with their ground-eating pace.

Please let her be okay.

The wolf howled the mantra in his mind as he ran.

He walked the last hundred feet to the medical bay. He needed to calm his racing heart and steeled himself for the worst outcome. The room stood eerily quiet and empty. The blood pounded through his veins as he saw Doc standing over an inert figure on a bed. Jack forced himself to move closer.

"Hi," Doc said without looking up from her clipboard.

"Why is she so still?" he asked.

"She got hysterical. I gave her a mild sedative so she wouldn't harm herself."

"Tell me what happened," Jack demanded.

"Aturus brought her in, semi-lucid. She passed out during a training session. I checked her, and, when I told her of her pregnancy, she got extremely agitated," Doc said. "Obviously, these abstinence-only programs aren't working. I'll be right back. I need to get her a vitamin booster. With how she overreacts to everything, it will be easier to put it in her IV."

Jack stared down at Kama. She lay quietly, but he could see the even rise and fall of her chest.

Pregnant.

The thought sucked the breath from him.

"How far along is she?" he asked when Doc came back in with the shot.

"Three months. The baby is due in August, unless it is prone to rushing things like its mother. Maybe inform your Pack that there are twelve months in a year. Not all of them have to give birth at the same time."

He watched Doc give her the vitamins and then sat, not sure how long Kama would sleep. The thought of her sleeping with another man dominated his thoughts. Anger rose up he clenched his fists at the betrayal from her.

Even if she thought I had left her, this is an extreme reaction. And apparently she didn't bother to waste any time with finding someone else. How can she be my Mate and be with another? It makes no sense. How am I supposed to deal with this? Look like some kind of idiot and take her back? Hell, no one even knew we were dating. Dammit, I love this woman. Do we just ignore it and move past it? Or is this the sign that this was never meant to be?

Jack leaned forward and put his head in his hands. As his thoughts tumbled over in his mind a rush of memories flooded his mind. Lorna scoffing as she received yet another bouquet of gladioli from her Mate. His conversation with the Goddess about his need and desire for a family echoed in his head as he watched a small group of children play around under an arch of swords. Another group sat making dolls out of corn husks as poppy petals fell to the ground around them and dissolved. A burst of love for her and pride swelled up with in him, rushing over and consuming him. A lion's roar echoed through space and time, slowly changing into the wail of an infant.

He looked down at his Mate and smiled.

Jack heard Kama shift and move. He sat still waiting for her eyes to flutter open. It took her a minute to come to full consciousness. He continued to pay attention while she blinked groggily, trying to focus in the dim light. He put a hand on her arm as she tried to sit up.

"Lay still, Kama," he said quietly.

He relaxed when she lay back down. He stood up and readjusted the blanket covering her. Jack knew she didn't recall the last few events; she was too calm.

"What happened to me?

"You and Olivia were having a sparring practice. After an intense bout, you passed out. Aturus brought you here," he said.

"Okay," she said and then fell quiet.

He recognized her processing face as she tried to remember what had happened and still couldn't come to a reasonable conclusion.

"When Doc gave you the diagnosis, you got hysterical," he said. "She gave you a tranquilizer to calm you down. You've been out about a half hour."

"I have never passed out before," she said.

Jack knew the exact moment Kama remembered everything. Her eyes went wide, and she lay back down and stared at the ceiling. He watched her internal struggle play across her face. He wanted to reach out to her, but, she turned her head to look at the wall. He placed a hand on her shoulder hoping to offer some comfort to her. Instead she began to sob noisily and his heart broke for her.

"Oh, my god. I am so sorry, Jack. I can't even believe this. I am sorry."

Her crying intensified and he patted her back. He gently rolled her over to face him. Jack met her eyes and gave her a gentle smile.

"Take a deep breath," he suggested. "Calm down. You are going to pass out again. Or worse, Doc will come back."

He breathed deeply as an example, and soon enough she took some deep breaths of her own. Her face turned gray, and he grabbed the bucket Doc insisted she would need "sooner or later." Jack held it for her as she emptied her stomach, carefully gathering her hair and pulling it away from her face. He pressed a glass of water into her hand. He helped her lay back down and wiped her face with a cool cloth. Jack felt bad when she looked up at him, so pale and terrified.

"I'm sorry. You can go. You don't have to be around me anymore," she whispered.

"Are you telling me to walk away? Why would I even want to?" Jack asked, shaking his head.

"I'm pregnant."

"Yes, you are."

"You're not mad?" Kama asked.

"Well it certainly is a bombshell, but I have it on very good authority it will all work out."

"I don't know what to expect, Jack. This isn't something that will go away. I am going to have a baby and not yours," Kama said, wringing her hands.

Jack held her hands in his. He wished that the Goddess had given his Mate some of the same assurances he had gotten. Granted it had taken him most of the time she slept, to figure out the pregnancy was a good thing.

"Kamaria, it's how it works with our kind. To be honest, I didn't imagine we would start our family so soon, but we would have always had to find a third," he said, lifting her chin so she would have to meet his eyes. "Don't ever forget, I love you."

Jack cringed as Kama started crying again. His heart hurt to see her so distressed.

She doesn't realize I had a lot of help to understand all this. I know learning some of the particulars via a Goddess vision led to processing the huge shock much easier on my part. Of course, I have the advantage here in being older and having a hell of a lot more life experience. I can't imagine how much this is distressing her. And on top of it all, she thinks this is going to put us back into a really bad place.

"Even after all this?" she asked.

"Yes, even after all this," he said with a smile. "You are giving me a child. How can I be upset with such a gift?"

The room fell silent again. As she struggled to sit up, Jack assisted her and resisted pulling her into his arms.

If there was any question this woman is my Mate, it is gone now. I feel helpless, watching her sit there with her arms wrapped around her knees. She is pulling away from me, trying to put some distance between us. We have to convince her this is the real thing.

"Well, now what?" Kama asked. "Actually, don't answer. I don't know how much else I can take today."

"Now, we start planning for a new future. We know we still have to figure out how to work with all of the snags. But we will be fine."

Jack patted her knee as her tears fell. Sitting back in his chair, he stared at her and waited for her to calm down again. When he caught her looking at him, he smiled again.

"How long have you been here?" Kama asked.

"Maybe forty minutes," he said with a dismissive shrug.

He reached over and put a soft hand on her shoulder. He noticed how she relaxed under his touch.

"I don't know what I am going to do. I never even imagined this as a possibility in my life.. I can't deal with this, because I never planned for it. I never thought about it. I don't even know if I can handle it," she said between sobs. "I wanted to be an Opera Diva."

Jack sighed with a long, escaping breath and carefully weighed his words before speaking.

"You aren't going to deal with it alone," he said and then tilted her chin up to look her in the eyes. "We may have some hurdles and some bumps to deal with, like so many others. I know there is the whole aspect of letting the Pack know we are Mated. I know you will have to tell your parents and it will be scary. I also know I don't want you to deal with it alone. I want to be with you, by your side, for it all."

He watched her nod and then rub her thumbs against each other. Her nervous release method gave him hope things were getting better.

"I would imagine hearing 'I'm sorry' begins to lose its impact after hearing it repeatedly, but I do not know what else to say," she offered.

"I love you?" he offered.

He met her eyes and refused to look away.

"Can you just hold me?" she asked.

"I thought you would never ask," Jack said, sitting on the bed next to her. He slipped an arm around her and pulled her into a hug. "All I want to do is hold and protect you."

They sat in the medical room for another half hour. He spent the time telling her about more of his Spirit Quest and sharing the information the Goddess had given him. She nodded against his chest at the thought of having a long, family line. By the time Doc came back in, Kama held her stomach in laughter at his retelling of his first interactions with Karl.

"Glad to see you are no longer hysterical. So much easier to do these things when you are cooperative," Doc said. "Okay, Alpha. Get off my bed so I can examine her."

Jack unwrapped himself from around Kama and stepped down, ignoring her look of surprise. Doc opened the door, and a couple of guys wheeled in some equipment. He looked it over, trying to recognize what it might be, and heard a light chuckle. He turned to face the woman and raised an eyebrow.

"This would be part of the reason you spent twenty thousand dollars on a medical budget two years ago," she said. "Don't worry. The next list will be on your desk in about two weeks."

He gave her a mock look of despair, and Doc laughed at his theatrics. Over the last ten years, she had changed little. Not that Jack tended to focus on her looks, even though they hadn't changed much, either. She had a diamond-shaped face and smooth skin. Dark brown eyes held a hint of understanding complex ideas with ease, and her lips formed in a semi-smile that could quickly turn into a smirk. Her chestnut hair was usually pulled up out of the way, but Jack knew it reached her waist.

Jack had met her when she tried to escape from being dragged to prison. Doc had been an up-and-coming, concierge doctor in the city. She had worked for wealthy families and built up a strong following. Until the moment she took her Hippocratic Oath as a guideline instead of a rule. A young patron had drugged a date, and despite Doc's best efforts, the girl died as aa result of an overdose. She had called the police, and, instead of the young man going to jail, he fought against the cops, resulting in a bullet lodged in his leg. The Chief of Police came to the house to explain how the responding officer made a mistake. She had been taken aside and warned. If she wanted to keep her job, she would not only treat the wound but also make sure no one ever learned what had happened. As she treated his leg, the smug bastard gave her a knowing grin and let her know he would need her services the next weekend.

Doc went back to check the wound later that night. In a moment of despair, she filled the syringe full of morphine and pushed it into his artery. It wouldn't be the pain-filled death he deserved. She watched him dispassionately as she packed to leave. She knew it would only be a matter of time before the police came to pick her up. As she made it downstairs to meet them, reality of what she had done set in. Despite knowing she deserved to go to jail for killing the potential serial killer, Doc panicked. She recalled the reaction from the Police Chief and how easily the girl's death had been dismissed. She couldn't count on fair treatment from the system, so she fled. She made it to the northern end of the Park before cruisers started racing up the streets. Her plan had been to get out of the city and go through upstate New York, all the way into Canada. Instead, she veered into the Park. As the sirens grew louder, she squeezed through the barred door at the Blockhouse. Shouts sounded from the policemen trying to find her in the Park, she chanced going down into the old structure.

Jack met her as she cowered in the corner, hoping the police wouldn't find her there. She told him the whole story, and he made her the remarkable offer to come and work for him and the Pack. Doc accepted and had been there ever since. He doubted she had actually been topside in the past decade. Then again, she had all the lab equipment her heart desired. She also had to continually modify treatments, since there weren't many medical journals on how to treat werewolves. Not to mention, with seventy some Loup to take care of, she was busy all the time. They never came in for scratches and bumps, either. Those who visited always had serious injuries.

He met her eyes as his jaunt down memory lane ended, and she raised an eyebrow.

"Ready for the sonogram? Let me get some gel," Doc said and exited the room.

"Did she say sonogram? With both of us here? Won't that be you showing preference for me? Did you watch with Lorna?" she asked, turning to him. "I have done nothing but cause a mess for you."

"Kama, this is our baby," Jack said. "I am excited to experience these firsts with you. Doc understands our need for privacy. She did just see us hugging. I will be at each and every appointment with you."

"Really?" she asked. "It will make it easier to have you there. You tend to keep me calm."

"When I said I would support you, it wasn't lip service," he said. "As much as possible, I will be by your side. I do have the misfortune of letting you know the bad news, which is that the act of giving birth is something I cannot partake in, because I don't think there is a way to help there."

"If it's anything at all like my mother retells the story, it should be easy," Kama said with a giggle. "Despite having all us kids, she didn't exactly enjoy her pregnancies and, according to my father, got rather nasty through them. However, the births were easy, and she reclaimed her pleasant disposition soon after. I always had to laugh, because my mother is never *not* intense. I could never imagine worse."

Jack laughed, too. His wolf smugly reminded him of the image they had had months before of Kama being pregnant.

"My father had agreed with her that four kids was the perfect number, two boys and two girls. And then I showed up. She had been so calm and quiet through her time with me, he didn't believe her until he saw the ultrasound," Kama said, loosening up even more. "Then it got worse. My mother had hellacious headaches for the first two months and couldn't stand to be around sound. Mind you, she is a chef, and chopping and banging is her way of life. The next four months were smell aversions—again, she cooks for a living. The last three months, she just hated everything and everyone. However, once she had me—and tied her tubes—she said everything had been worth it."

"Here is hoping you have the most serene and beautiful pregnancy ever," Jack said. "This will be our best adventure yet."

"Thank you."

He saw the question in her eyes and figured he would have to reassure her for a time while she worked through it all.

"Love, you are not alone," he said.

He reached out and held her hand. Doc came back in, and, with a few flips of switches, the machines bleeped to life. Jack wondered about the feel of the gel, because Kama flinched when it was squeezed onto her belly. The monitor lit up, and his attention never wavered from it. He sat transfixed, looking at the small, gray, lima-bean-looking object, and heard a soft exclamation from Kama when the doctor pointed out the tiny blip of the heartbeat. Jack stared at the screen for an long time, not blinking. After a long moment, he realized he held his breath as he looked. He sighed and continued to stare in wonderment, both at the screen and at the woman he had grown to love. Doc answered a few questions, but he stood quietly, still watching. Kama reached out and touched the screen where the little heart continued to blip. His hand joined hers, and she looked up at him.

"Beautiful," Jack whispered.

"I agree," Kama said, looking up at him with joy on her face.

"What are you going to call her? Or him, if it's a boy?" he asked.

"I don't know, yet, but we have time to figure out what to name her," she said pausing and then grinning at him. "And she will be a girl."

"You sound pretty sure," he said. "Mother's intuition?"

"No, I want a girl," Kama stated and turned back to watch the monitor.

Doc snorted loudly, but Kama chose to ignore her and stare at the little fuzzy bean that would become her daughter.

"This isn't a restaurant. You can't just order up a gender."

"Yes, I can," Kama said.

"Pregnancy delusions usually come in later months," Doc said with a smirk at him. "Have fun with this one. I imagine you will need a lot of patience."

She placed some papers on the table beside the monitor. She shot him a questioning look, and he nodded towards the door. Doc left without hesitation. Jack watched Kama stare at the monitor for a few more moments before turning to face him. She smiled at him and held her hand out for his.

"Do you want to touch her and say 'Hi'?" she asked.

"Are you sure?" he asked.

He was already extending a slightly shaking hand. Kama took it and placed it over her still very flat abdomen. It felt warm to the touch, and to his disappointment, he didn't feel anything.

"Of course I am sure," she said. "This is our baby. The start to our family."

Jack's whole face lit up as he gently caressed her stomach while looking at the monitor. They stayed in the spell of the moment until Kama's stomach gurgled. She looked up at him and winked.

"I think our daughter wants some food," she said.

"Let's go, then," he said. "We can pick up some on the way home."

Jack glanced back at the monitor for a moment but looked over as a sob filled the air. Kama held the papers Doc had left. His heart sank in a moment of panic, until she turned the page around and showed him the small, grainy picture with a red heart drawn over what appeared to be a fuzzy minnow. As he looked closer, he could make out nothing besides the blurry image. He hugged her close and smiled, remembering the many faces from the villa.

I wonder how many more surprises are in store for me. I have the feeling this is just the beginning.

He waited and wasn't disappointed to hear a giggle designed to lift the spirits and evaporate all vestiges of pain. It sounded like a bright future lingered in the air around him.

Jack walked with Kama out of Central Park, and they met his driver waiting at the Blockhouse. He smiled at her as they climbed into the car. The ride to his house was silent. He didn't know what she thought about, but his mind raced as he made plans to redecorate the small room on the second floor into a nursery.

CHAPTER Twelve

Kama woke up in the dark. It took her a moment to get her bearings, but a soft rumble next to her helped. She grinned and snuggled closer to Jack's warm body. She put her cold hand against his chest and didn't remove it when he flinched. She yawned and was in the middle of a full-body stretch when she remembered the news.

Oh, gods. I am pregnant. I am going to have a baby. And Jack is thrilled. I never would have imagined he would be calm about it, let alone excited about starting a family. I mean, he wouldn't let me go home alone and try to process the news by myself. Perhaps I underestimated him? Maybe I just don't know him as well as I like to think I do. But he called us his Mate and told us he loved us. Let's just go with this.

"Good morning, Kama," Jack said, nuzzling her neck. "Did you sleep well? How are you?"

"I remembered I am pregnant," she blurted out. "It's still odd. Yet, I don't feel too different. Except when I say it."

She sat up and looked down at him. She laughed as he winked at her and then propped his head up on his arm.

"Are you coming back for dinner tonight? I know you have rounds and training today. I figure it will be a nice, quiet way to spend the evening. Unless you already had plans. I noticed you have been hanging out with Beth and some of the others more. And you also are still helping Olivia."

"No plans. And I will come back only if you let me cook," Kama said. "It will be a stress release. Not to mention, it is the most normal activity I can do."

"My Love, you always cook. Seems to me we already had a conversation about cooking not being my strong suit. I can't believe you already forgot, especially since you spent most of the time laughing and making rude remarks about it. I can't believe you could mock me like that," he said. "So, my beautiful chef, get out of bed and make me a coffee, then write down a list. I will get the shopping done. What are you still waiting for, Diva? I gave you an order."

Kama pressed her lips together to stop the snarky remark. She gave him a brief nod and went to the kitchen. While the coffee brewed, she made a light breakfast of scrambled eggs, sausage, and toast. Kama carried the food back upstairs and presented Jack his mug with a bow.

"Your coffee, Alpha," she said.

She sat on the edge of the bed and proceeded to eat her breakfast, steadfastly ignoring him. She shrugged her shoulders as he peered over them but gave in to the giggles as he inhaled deeply then kissed her nape.

"I guess I need to be clearer with my orders," he said.

"Oh, they were clear, and I did what you asked. Did the coffee displease?" she asked brightly.

"No, the coffee was delicious. However, I would have liked some breakfast, too."

"Hmm," she said. "Yet, you didn't ask for any. I would have shared with you, but I am already sharing."

"Aren't you worried about getting fat?"

Kama laughed at his bait.She found the question preposterous and made a show of eating her last sausage link.

"With this metabolism? Not at all. Besides, it's not fat. I can't believe you would be so mean already. I have just barely come to terms with it all."

"Seems to me you are adapting well," Jack said with a grin. "What do you want me to bring home tonight?"

"Anything is fine. I really don't have a preference," she said.

"How about a smoked turkey breast? I have been known to peel a potato or two," Jack said.

Kama knew he was going out of his way to make her feel comfortable and normal. She tried hard to imagine what her day would have been like without the news of the baby spinning around her head.

I think I am still in shock. Of course, not as much shock as waking up with Doc standing over me instead of Olivia.

Kama had come into awareness with each eyelid being lifted and a stabbing, pinpoint of light bore though her corneas into her brain. She tried to lurch into a sitting position. After a volley of questions from Doc, she lay back down. Many scratched notes later, Doc looked back at her.

"You are pregnant."

"No, I'm not," she had said. "I'm probably just overly stressed with all the changes. You're wrong."

"I am never wrong. You missed a period, you've had sex— not to mention you're young and fertile. Pregnant."

Kama had started shaking uncontrollably and hyperventilating. A few seconds later, she felt a sharp poke as a needle entered her arm, and the world faded out. When she had come back around, Jack sat next to her, looking calm and collected.

And all he did is sit there and look at me and get excited about what would be happening. Then he talked about our family and plans for our future. He processed all this much quicker than I did. What we had better do, and quickly, is adapt to this new reality. First, plan how to tell Mom. Thankfully, Dad is in Italy for the next few weeks on his annual, family reunion/business trip. Second, we have a lot of work to do to get ready for this baby. Children were not a part of my life-plan well, maybe I might have had them later. But not until my world tour and many albums were done —much later, so we are going to need to figure out what needs to be done. What? Oh. He is waiting for us to give him an answer.

"How about some homemade pasta? I know it might sound odd, seeing as I love food, but turkey just isn't my thing."

"Ah. Well, lasagna would be great. What time are you going to come over?" he asked. "Other than the tasks you assign me, I plan to have some wine and watch the fireplace while you work away in the kitchen."

Kama looked down at Jack, amazed that he had managed to stay so calm with all the new changes. Apparently, he had warmed to the idea of parenthood much more quickly than while she had fretted and planned about impending motherhood, he wanted dinner.

"I'm not going to tell Cade," she blurted out. She knew Jack's raised eyebrow meant he waited for more information.

"How can I? I can't tell him. The last time you two were in the same room, he threw you into a wall using magic and you almost shifted on him. I can't imagine the next meeting wouldn't go sideways and crazy. I had always thought his magical abilities were simple, but I have no idea now," Kama said. with an urgent insistence. "I can't imagine I could tell him about this baby and he would stay out of the picture. What if I tell him, and he wants the baby? He could grab her and just disappear."

"Kama," Jack started. "How about we talk about this in three or four months? Nothing has to be decided just yet. You only found out about this pregnancy, and it's all new. I want you to just focus on you and the baby. Get settled with it and worry about your health. Let's wait on the making of big decisions. I don't want you to do anything that you will regret later in life."

She sat for a few more moments, letting his advice sink in.

"However, we can make a small change. No more wine for you," he said. "Not like you're old enough for it, anyhow."

Kama laughed and scooted to the side of the bed.

"Whatever. I've got rounds. Good-bye, Alpha."

Kama burst out in laughter at the haughty look he gave her and felt the tension in her melt away. She stood up and walked to the bathroom. She took a brief, hot shower and pulled her hair up in to a ponytail that had become her new, go-to style. She stared at herself in the mirror and tried to bolster her courage. She went down to the kitchen and in twenty minutes had a pot of sauce on simmer for the day. She only hoped it would be ready by the time she got back. She grabbed her coat and took a deep breath.

Just one, small thing to do before rounds.

Kama walked up the stairs, fifteen floors worth to be exact, and stood before her parents' door. She knocked. It sounded louder than anything she had ever heard before. Except the beating of her heart, which had increased to a frantic pace.

Why did I do this now? I could have told her after my rounds. Maybe she is already at the catering hall, or perhaps she went to the restaurant. Nope. I can hear her in the kitchen. Oh, and the coffee smells divine. I wonder what kinds of food restrictions we will have. Can we even have caffeine? She's here.

Brenna opened the door, and Kama gave her a hug. She avoided the questioning look and took her mother's mug with a smile. She released a sigh of contentment as she took a deep drink.

"Good morning, my darling daughter," her mother said. "I'm surprised to see you this morning. I'm finishing up a small breakfast. Come help me prepare."

Kama sniffed the delightful aromas hanging in the air and smiled. She knew she could cook well but nothing like her mother. She wandered slowly into the kitchen and looked at the cooktop. She began to laugh loudly.

"Mama, you are cooking enough for six people," she said.

"Of course I am. Old habits die hard," Brenna said with a wink. "You can take the leftovers with you to your friends."

Kama nodded as she tied on an apron. She grabbed the peaches on the counter and began to chop them. She figured her mother would be baking them in oatmeal. As she worked, her mind spun. The original speech she had prepared didn't seem like it would be a good idea. She had arguments lined up for why it would be okay and what plans she had for her future. Her mother's questions broke into her reverie.

"Have you recovered from everything? You looked like you were on the verge of a major collapse. I don't pretend to know how things are run down here, but I am hoping you will have some quiet for a while," Brenna said and gave her a scrutinizing look. "How are you feeling, dear?"

"Pregnant."

Oh, shit. Did we really just blurt out major news? Don't cry. Take a breath and keep it together. Damn, that was stupid of us. Mom is going to need a moment to adapt. She just moved through the "this must be a joke" and now she is moving into the "disbelief" look. She is staring at us. I can't recognize the look she is giving us. What the hell does the look mean?

Kama began to giggle nervously. She tried to keep it quiet but had a hard time. She snuck a glance at her mother.

This is what prey feels like. Okay, she is ready to speak to us. Think, Kama. We have to have a damn good answer after blurting out life-changing news.

"I would think there might have been a better way to make an announcement of that caliber, Kamaria."

"Well, what did you want me to say, Mama? Pass the scones, and, by the way, I'm having a baby."

And yet I managed to come up with a worse and not better response. In fact, she might actually think I am being glib. She's just standing there. Maybe it would have been better to cry. She isn't saying much. She's mad, I know it. Crap. Brenna DeKosse is never without words. Say. Something.

Kama stared at her mother and drew in a slow breath. She had a moment of surprise as her mother held her arms out open wide. She paused for a moment but went into her embrace and melted into the hug. The soft, rhythmic patting on her back loosed a small sob from her throat.

"I am sorry," she said. "Please don't be too mad at me."

"Oh, darlin', I am surprised, aye," Brenna said, the brogue thick on her tongue. "How could I be mad at you?"

"For ruining my life? I'm not supposed to be having a baby. Hell, I don't even know what future I have right now," Kama said and then gave her mother a watery half-smile as she pulled out of the embrace.

Please don't ask about the father...

"I don't think having a child ruins anything. I managed to have five and still be successful," her mother said. "It might not have been in your plans, but it doesn't mean your life is over. I expected Dante and Jill to have a baby first, but you have always been full of surprises. Don't think of this as a punishment. It's a great responsibility, but you are one of the most responsible young women I know."

They went back to preparing breakfast, and Kama's mouth watered, as if she hadn't had breakfast an hour before. As she cleaned the counter, a random thought bubbled up.

"How could you have thought Daddy was gay?"

She met her mother's surprised expression.

"How on earth did you hear about that? Oh, I know who told you. I haven't thought about it in years."

"Grandpa tells a great story." Kama grinned.

"He does," her mother said wryly. "Why would he tell you that particular story?"

"I asked what you were like when you were my age. After being in your old room, I realized there is a lot about you I don't know. I mean, I could have had years mocking you for having no idea about boys."

"Seems to me we are quite alike," Brenna said. "I might not have known how to read flirtations, but apparently I knew a bit more about how babies were made."

Did she really? Oh, yes, Wolf-girl, she is taking pot shots not two minutes after I told her I'm pregnant. I'm glad to see she is taking it so well.

"Yea, I had no choice but to learn," Kama shot back. "You and dad made sure we knew with each, sick joke you subjected us to."

"Speaking of choices," Brenna said, getting serious. "There is more than one right choice when it comes to this baby."

Kama stared at her mother in shock. For a person who had taught her daughter to be so family oriented, she stood amazed her mother gave her the option to not have the baby. She had understood from the beginning the different options available to her, but she didn't expect her mother would be open to all of them.

"I am having this baby. There is no other option for me," Kama said. "Somehow, I expected you to take it worse. I also need to tell Daddy, and I think he is going to lose his mind. Do you think I should call and tell him?"

"Probably not. He still thinks of you as a young child."

"You were awfully cheerful when you said that," she said. "What do I do?"

"I think the best course of action is just to wait. Your father is already up to his neck in family and the family business. Knowing your grandpa Giovanni, they are conducting their affairs with bottles of wine from his vineyard," Brenna said with a laugh. "You will still be pregnant when your father gets home. And in a few weeks, it might not feel so odd to talk about it."

They finished breakfast with idle chit-chat. Kama gladly filled her plate with eggs Benedict and a vegetable scramble.

"At least I graduated first."

"Aye, it means you won't have to waddle across the stage."

Kama gave her mother a baleful stare and then had to sit through Brenna's laughing at her. More. She shook her head. The people she feared would be the most upset seemed to accept her being pregnant as just an event. She had expected more...well, just more.

Seriously? Now she makes a fat joke at us? Maybe she should have been a bit more upset. In about ten minutes, the baked peaches and oatmeal will be done. No, I do not think there will be a lot of leftovers to share with my friends. Besides, Beth has Ajani cooking for her...Oh, damn. I need to tell her. This might not be a fun time. She wasn't particularly receptive when I let her know about me and Jack being together again. Maybe I just won't see her today. Really? Did we just think about avoiding Beth? Get it together, Kama. The Pack will find out anyhow. Let's go do this.

Kama smiled at Jack when he opened the door. She leaned in for a soft kiss as they stepped into the foyer. She allowed him to help her out of her coat and gave him a wink.

"Good afternoon?" he asked.

"Hi," she said. "Yes, my afternoon was pretty good. Much less exciting than my morning. Before I went to the Park, I went home and told my mom."

She kissed away the worried look on his face.

"She is being supportive. I expected a lot more anger and disappointment. It's almost harder to adapt to being pregnant. Though I have made the decision to wait a few weeks until I let anyone else know about my condition. "

"Is there are reason why? You do know the Pack is your family, too. Most people will want to help you through this," Jack said. "Interestingly enough, most Loup are pretty excited when it comes to a Packmate having a child. Most of us really do love children."

"I am still a warrior, Jack. I don't want them to think any less of me. Even worse, I don't want them to think they can pick on me because I won't be able to fight back."

"Attacking a pregnant woman is forbidden," he said in a low voice. "No one would be stupid enough to try. Any violence towards you would end up with the offending party being brought up in front of the Tribunal. It's our court system, where each person has a say in front of me and the Betas. If found guilty, the person would be held accountable, not only for the offense against you, but also for attacking the baby. The punishment would be severe."

She nodded and made her way into the kitchen. The tone of his voice spoke volumes about just what kind of punishment would be meted out. Along with the groceries, a new, bright, and shiny pasta roller sat on the counter. She knew Jack meant well, but she had never used a roller in her life. Kama decided that she would have to get her own set of kitchen knives there as soon as possible. She needed the proper tools to work in his kitchen.

Does this mean he is thinking about us living here? I just got my own space. I don't know if I want to move yet. Sure, it's been great to be able to spend the night here, and I am comfortable here. Okay, Kama, get to making dinner. He didn't ask us to move in, so don't get all worked up over something that hasn't been discussed yet.

She busied herself making her pasta dough to stop the spiraling thoughts. She started to quietly sing *Arlecchin! Colombina!* Though short, it still remained one of her favorite opera pieces. She continued her impromptu concert with "Habanera" and found herself giving way to full-bodied vocals. She added flourishes with her hands and looked up to see Jack leaning against the doorframe sipping a glass of wine and smiling.

"Bored of the fireplace already?"

"How could I be content sitting alone in front of a fire, when you are in here giving a performance?" he asked.

"This is just singing for fun," she said. "My days of performing are long gone."

"Kama—" he started.

"Jack, the only pregnant opera divas are those who became singers first. I am perfectly happy singing as I make dinner."

She tasted the sauce and nodded to herself. Kama looked up and met a surprised look on his face.

"You left the stove on all day? Isn't that a fire hazard?"

"If so, my mother should have burned the city down a few times," she said. And she then conceded, "Perhaps you need to get a few, good crockpots for me to cook with. Then you won't have to worry about my burning your house down."

Kama walked over to him and refilled his wine glass. She didn't resist as he pulled her into a kiss. After a few moments she broke the kiss and leaned back with a grin.

"Let me get this tray into the oven, then you will have a full forty minutes of me to yourself," she said.

"I'll wait in the living room and not disturb you," he winked.

"Good."

She heard him snort as he walked away, and she rolled her eyes. Despite the past few months making her feel like her life had been in a blender without a lid, she had started to settle. She felt more in control, even if she had no idea what she would do.

Well, that's not true anymore, now, is it? I'll be preparing to have this baby. I'm sure the idea of free time will evaporate.

She poured herself a glass of water and went to the living room. Jack sat on the couch in front of the fire. She walked around and sat in front of him, with her head resting on the cushion, watching the flames dance around. She looked back at him and noticed how the fire reflected off his face, giving it a haunted look. She returned the smile he gave her.

"I love watching fire. It's alive in a dance of intrigue. If you pay attention long enough, you think you just might be able to figure out the pattern," she said.

Kama yawned and stretched out. She leaned back against the couch, letting her head tip back onto the cushion, and blew Jack a kiss but ducked the real thing when he leaned over. She sat up straight, pulling her knees into her chest, and wrapped her arms around them.

"Are you cold? I can grab a blanket," he said.

"I think this is the first year I didn't get to make Christmas cookies with my mother," Kama said. "The thought kind of caught up with me. The last six months have been weird. Being Loup has changed everything for me."

"Tell me about your cookie tradition," Jack said.

"Every year, we do the big Cookie Fest. We go to the catering hall so we have plenty of room, and we make all of our favorite kinds of cookies. Sometimes, Ajani or Twin would join us, but lately it has been just me and Mom. Once we got done baking and decorating, we would put together baskets and deliver them to whoever was on her list. This is the first time since I can remember that we didn't," she said. She blinked fast as unexpected tears came to her eyes and swallowed them. "Maybe I'm getting to old for it anyhow. It just used to be our tradition."

She looked up and found Jack looking at her.

"I'm sorry you didn't do it this year. I don't think you are ever too old for family traditions," he said. "Maybe next year you can go back to making cookies with her. And in a few years, you can bring our daughter and teach her how to make them."

"Our daughter? So you believe me now?" Kama asked with a watery smile.

"I sure do," he said. "Ever since I have met you, I have been constantly surprised and amazed at you. After all, who else takes a Rite after six weeks? When you say the baby will be a girl, I believe it."

"Funny, I thought taking my Rite would allow me to keep the life I knew. I figured being an adult would make it possible," she said. "Instead, I learned my life would change and nothing could stop it. The tighter I tried to hold on, the more it slipped through my fingers. Someday, maybe I will get to go on a Spirit Quest and figure out why this path made the most sense."

She looked up again and found Jack giving her a soft smile.

"Okay. What?"

"I don't even know if you can go on a Spirit Quest," he said. "I went because Lorna wasn't able. Although, I honestly don't know. Maybe it's something we should explore. Funny just how little we know about our own nature. Every time I think I understand what it is to be Loup, another surprise pops up."

"I can ask my cousin and see if she is any help," Kama said.

"She would tell you?" Jack asked in surprise.

Kama spent the next couple of hours telling him about her trip up north to Michigan. She tried to remember all of the details. She retold the story of her first hunt with great flourish and even laughed at herself while talking about biting the deer's hindquarter. She told him about sparring with her cousin and the fallout. She left out what she had learned about her mother, figuring it wasn't her story to tell, but did boast about the room with the handmade furniture. As she spoke, Kama realized just how much she missed Nula and her grandfather.

"Wow. It sounds like an amazing place," he said, once she took a breath.

"We can go up and visit sometime," Kama said. "Though, I do suppose you should meet my family here first. That will be interesting."

Kama closed her eyes, drinking in the warmth of the fire. She wondered how and when they would tell her family. The baby would be big enough news, but to then let them know she had a boyfriend again and was serious about him would be monumental. Another thought struck her.

"What about your family?"

"My family is a bit complicated," Jack said, and she watched him gaze into the fire. "I grew up in an orphanage."

"What happened to your parents?" Kama whispered.

She couldn't imagine a life without her parents in it. She didn't press as he stared ahead.

"I don't know," he said. "But, when I was ten, I went to live with the Thomas's, my foster family. I had loving parents, an older brother, and an older sister. And I had Melissa, who came in a few days before me. They had to move the year I turned sixteen, but they hadn't adopted us. Melissa and I couldn't go because we weren't eighteen, yet."

"I'm sorry, Jack. It sounds like a rough time."

"Being with my foster family was one of the best things that ever happened to me. I found love and support that I had never had. And I met Melissa. She became my world. We got married once we aged out of the system. She died two years later. I went into the military to escape, and then came here. And the rest you know."

"You married your sister?"

"Not at all. Melissa and I may have lived in the same house, but she never felt like my sister," Jack said frankly. "Does it bother you?"

"Not really."

Kama was surprised to find she meant it. She knew Jack had to have had other relationships before her. Marriage actually made sense, as she couldn't imagine someone not being in love with him.

"How did she die?"

She cringed to see the raw look of pain pass over his face. The only other time Kama had seen that pure of emotion coming from him, was when they had learned about her pregnancy.

"An aneurism," Jack said quietly. "It was sudden, and I lost a part of myself when she left me. I didn't know how to cope, so I didn't. I buried my feelings and ran. Part of my Spirit Quest allowed me to come to terms with this tragedy. Family is important, and it's something I needed to remember."

Silence fell between them. She knew he had opened up to her in a way he never had before.

"Have you tried to find your parents since you have been back?" Kama asked.

"No. There were misunderstandings about the lack of communication. The orphanage kept their letters from me because they thought I would hang onto the hope of being reunited. I thought that my parents had abandoned me and Melissa. I was angry for a long time," he said. "But it is a new year, and I think it might be time to see if I can find them. My Quest helped me understand a lot. It would be good to see them again."

She sat still, gazing into the fire, not sure if she should get up and sit next to him. Before she had time to obsess about her choices, her stomach rumbled loudly and the kitchen timer went off. She looked up and saw Jack grinning.

"Guess it's time for dinner?"

Kama went to the kitchen and pulled out the tray of lasagna. As it cooled, she put together a large salad and added a vinaigrette dressing. She frowned as she looked around the kitchen. She wanted something more but couldn't identify just what she wanted to eat. Her eyes landed on a bowl of fruit, and she nodded. She grabbed a pineapple, cut off the leafy top, and trimmed off the bottom inch of the spiky fruit. She stood the fruit up and peeled off the skin in strips. Finally, she removed the eyes and ate a wedge for her effort.

"Do you want to eat in the dining room or here?" she called out.

"Is your cooking pride going to be damaged if we eat in there?"

Kama snorted and ate another piece of pineapple.

"We eat in the kitchen a lot, Jack. I think we have used the dining room three times," she scoffed.

"Yea, but I know you take dinners seriously," he said, walking into the kitchen.

Kama met his eyes and gave him a smile. A plan began to form. She wanted to laugh at him, because his returned smile started to fade the longer she held hers.

"What plans are going on in that pretty head of yours?"

"When you find your family, I will cook, and then we can use the dining room."

Kama filled plates and set them at the kitchen table. She sniffed appreciatively. Taking a huge mouthful of lasagna resulted in a slightly burnt tongue, but she enjoyed every, hot bite.

"I might not be able to find them," he said after a few moments.

"Only if you never look," she said. "You're pretty good at what you do."

When they were almost through dinner, her eyes widened. Her face lit up, and she sat up straight.

"Jack."

"Yes, Kama," he chuckled.

"Jack, I almost forgot. I have something for you," she exclaimed.

She walked out of the kitchen and found her coat. After fumbling in the pockets, she found the small, black, cardboard box with a purple and gold ribbon.

"Merry Christmas, Jack. I know it's past the holidays, but we weren't really talking at the time. Anyhow, this is for you."

Kama watched curiosity play over his face. He began to carefully untie the ribbon. She got antsy as he slowly opened the gift, hoping he would love it.

Right? Can't he just open the darn thing? Come on, Jack. Who would have thought this man would be so prissy? Just rip it. There, the box is open.

Kama watched him stare at the box before a smile covered his face. She knew it contained a platinum money clip. On the plate sat a wolf carved out of onyx with a ruby for its eye. It howled under an embossed full moon. After they had made up in September, she had begged her sisters to make it. In typical, Twin fashion, they kept her on edge. They refused to even mention any progress until they finished the project. Despite their constant badgering, she had refused to tell them who it had been made for. She waited until he looked up at her.

"Do you like it?"

"This is exquisite," he said, his voice thick with emotion. "Thank you."

"You're welcome. I am glad you like it. You told me once that you liked onyx, and your birthstone is ruby."

"I guess it's my turn," he said.

"For what?"

"It's a good thing you are beautiful," he said and kissed her on top of her head.

She watched him walk out of the kitchen and, with a shrug, grabbed an apple from the fruit bowl.

Yea, I know. He's got jokes. I am smarter than he knows. And yes, this is some kind of crap. Isn't pregnancy supposed to give you a eat whatever you want free-for-all? And being Loup? I should be able to eat like a whole chocolate cake and ask for more. Instead, all I want is fresh fruit. Well, a suckling pig sounds good, too. Maybe we can convince Mom to roast one? You're right. It might be a bad idea. She is on a roll with her jokes...

Kama looked up as Jack came back into the kitchen with a long, rectangular box. It had a long, red, velvet ribbon around it.

"Merry Christmas, Kama," he said.

"What is it?"

She tilted her head and frowned at him as he laughed openly at her.

"Open the box," he said.

Kama rolled her eyes and slowly pulled the ribbon apart.

It sure does make us a hypocrite. Although, it's a gorgeous ribbon. Very funny. We are not going to wear it across our body like the movie we saw. I can't even...,ooh, my.

Kama pulled tissue paper back to reveal a free-flowing, pearl gray, wool, wrap-style coat. It had a long scarf with fringes attached to the neckline, which would hang over her right shoulder. As she fingered the soft material, she noticed on the left, up the side of the coat, were three, beautiful, wooden buttons. They were oversized at five inches each and shaped like crescent moons. She stared closer and noticed the Pack Claw symbol carved into the center of each.

"Jack, this is beautiful."

She stood and pulled the coat out of the box. Jack held out his hand and assisted her in putting it on. It fell from her shoulders to just below her knees. Kama pulled each button through a loop and turned to face him.

"Want to know the secret?" he asked.

Her mind raced furiously but came up with nothing. She nodded and kept her eyes locked on his.

"The buttons are made from the tree of your First Kill."

Kama burst into tears, surprising herself.

"Oh, love. I don't want you to be upset," Jack said, wrapping her in a hug.

She cried and sniffled against him until she could form words.

"When I found out Ristori was a vampire and my test, I knew it would be the literal, as well as metaphorical, death of my singing career. I still have nightmares about doing it, but I know, at the end of the day, I did the right thing," she said. "This beautiful coat reminds me that good things can come from a bad situation. Now I get to carry a bit of my Kuba with me always."

She kissed him and stayed in his embrace a few minutes. Jack helped her back out of the coat, and they retired into the living room, on the couch, to watch the fire some more. Their conversations were sporadic, and during a pause, she played idly with her hair until a yawn caught her.

"How about a movie?" she said as she shifted on the couch, trying to find a comfortable position.

She made a face as Jack laughed at her.

"Any suggestions?" she pressed. "Why don't you just pick. You make whining noises when I suggest musicals. Which is what I would pick."

She caught the pillows Jack tossed at her. While she pushed them into the perfect support position, he put a disc in the player. She waited for him, and then leaned against him after he sat.

"Good night, beautiful," he said.

"Whatever. The only reason I would fall asleep is because you chose a boring movie," she said haughtily.

She felt him kiss the top of her head as he laughed. Kama watched about the first fifteen minutes of the movie. She found herself snuggling closer into his side. She knew he would mock her in the morning and didn't care. She smiled contentedly as she drifted off to sleep.

CHAPTER Thirteen

Two days later, Kama climbed down the tunnel, holding a small box carefully against her. She moved fast but not so rushed that she would tempt dropping the box and spilling the contents. She found the rungs she looked for against a damp and dank wall. They led into inky blackness, which was what she wanted. Once on the platform beneath, she used her small flashlight and navigated to her secret space. She had found it months back when exploring the bizarre layout of the tunnel system. Contrary to commonly held beliefs, the tunnels were not constructed on just one layer. Instead, the Motor Transit system had dug deep for the original lines, but as water levels shifted and changed, they backfilled the swampy mess and built on top of them for greater stability.

As she had poked around, she had found an old office space at the end of a platform. Kama had spent a few weeks cleaning out the clutter. A few broken chairs, filing cabinets, and piles of papers had been pushed over onto the unused tracks, so she wouldn't trip. She enjoyed having a space in the Park to herself. She hadn't even told Beth about it yet. While she didn't anticipate ever living at the park, like some of her friends, having her own room would work fine.

One hundred more feet and we will be there. We can make it. Don't worry about the smells. They will pass. It's only another few months. Women do this all the time. I suppose the world should be happy there are less Loup around. Of course, it might help if the population was culled anyhow. I sure am cranky today. Then again, this is why we are sneaking into the depths. It's probably safer to be alone with our funk. I would probably have Challenged at least half the pack by now.

Her current state of unhappiness had started with the inability to tie her shoes without wanting to puke. Her stomach had no baby bump, so it never occurred to her being upside down might have effects. The grumpy day had moved forward as her mother insisted upon seeing the results of the tests she'd had. One, quick look and a haughty proclamation of Doc just not being good enough had digressed into a squabble about the mongrel pack's lack of knowledge on pregnancies. Kama had dissolved into tears, and, in apology, Brenna had insisted on bonding time while they prepared all the favorites for her lunch. She carried the precious food in the box, away from her packmates who would surely want to share.

And then I would be in trouble for trying to kill them. Heck, with the mood I am in, I would probably succeed. A few more feet and then through the door. Next trip down here, I need to remember to bring a chair. The blanket is nice, but who knows how long I have before getting off the floor is impossible?? Maybe some kind of space heater......no, there isn't electricity. Who the hell...?

Light spilled out as Kama nudged the door open. She searched the room and found a couple of huge, pillar candles had been lit, making the space much cozier than her flashlight would have. She found Lorna's eyes looking back at her. They were red rimmed and puffy, too. Apparently, it had not been a good day for the pregnant members of Central Park.

"Kama, did someone send you for me? How did they even know where to find me?" Lorna questioned.

"No one sent me," Kama said, walking in and closing the door. "I thought I was the only one who knew about this place. I came to be alone.

"Your eyes look like mine. We must be on the same timetable for crying," Lorna sighed.

"You know I'm pregnant?"

"Betas tend to get told the important news," Lorna said. "Once you start to tell people, the news will spread fast. This Pack gossips worse than any old biddy I know. This will be your place of peace and quiet."

"Seems the pregnant minds think along the same lines: Hide from the rest," Kama said as Lorna cracked a smile at her.

"And here I thought the luck fairy had come to me. I found this place a week ago. Isolated, clean and dry—a godsend, a place to be alone. I brought a few things down today. I hope you don't mind if we share for the moment, and then I will find another hidey hole to escape to."

"It's fine. I really don't mind."

"Never give up your space, Kama," Lorna said. "I know it might seem insignificant, considering how big the park is; but our wolves are territorial, and it drives us. Once you claim something, hold on to it."

"Yea, it seems like Challenges are all around lately. Or maybe I just didn't notice it before."

"They were never aimed at you before. When Roseanne died and you stepped up, you effectively took her place. Which was a pretty big jump forward in the pecking order," the Beta said. Her voice lowered and the tone got serious. "People are now testing to see if you are as good as the rumors make you out to be. Here's a piece of advice I want you to seriously consider: After you have the baby, go after the first Challenge given to you hard. You are going to need to beat someone's ass pretty good to make the rest of them back down. It's the only way to secure your place, without a bunch of petty squabbles every other day."

As she digested the information, Kama sighed mentally. It made sense to her, and she appreciated the advice. She plopped down on one of the two, large, bean bag chairs recently added to the space. She noticed a blanket on the far wall and under it, a small table. As her stomach rumbled, she put the box down. She realized it would be rude not to offer her Beta some of the food.

"I fought with my mother about seeing a doula from my grandfather's pack. She said our doctor didn't know anything about Loup births. When I defended Doc, she told me someone familiar with the Loup would have known immediately what my symptoms meant, without any tests. Loup women can't shift after a certain point in their pregnancy. I took it as a slight," Kama said. "She made me lunch to apologize. Though now, I don't understand what I was so upset about. She's probably right. The whole pack up in Michigan has known about our kind for hundreds of years, instead of ten. I'm sure it's a good idea. I hate it when that woman is right."

She opened the box and placed the containers on the table there. The aromas made her mouth water, and for once, she appreciated how her mother always packed enough to feed a small army. She spread out the containers and gestured for Lorna to take a plate and plastic ware.

"Curt, my partner, offered to get me a housekeeper," Lorna confessed. "In the moment, I took it to mean he thought I left the house a mess and burst into tears. He then tried to explain to me how I deserved to work less, since I already had the full-time job of growing a life. I interpreted that as him thinking me incapable because of the baby. The poor man just stood there while I stomped out. I'm not sure he is going to survive until August."

Kama laughed as she took a huge piece of warm soda bread and slathered it with fresh butter. She nodded at Lorna to help herself. Taking a large bite, she sighed around the mouthful of bread.

"I'm due in August, too," Kama said. "Maybe I should let the doula come. This way Doc doesn't have to multitask, although I'm pretty certain she would just knock me out until my turn."

The soft giggles coming from the Beta surprised her. Lorna was a strong person with a loud voice, so the light, airy sound didn't make the association with the personality Kama had constructed for her.

"If you can convince one to come, I will happily use her. As you said, they have been doing this for years," Lorna said. "Oh, my god, what is this little piece of heaven?"

"Those are my mother's famous, fried mac and cheese with bourbon-soaked bacon bits. We also have fresh soda bread, lasagna, fresh peach cobbler, ,feta-stuffed tomatoes, and a green bean casserole," Kama said with a grin. "I left before the potato cheese soup was done, because one of her assistants told me congratulations, and as I cried, I made the largest snot bubble possible."

She embraced the quiet as the two of them ate. They tried to have a conversation, but talking behind their hands, because their mouths were full of food, became comical. They lapsed into an easy pace of light chat between refilling their plates. The food didn't last long, and the two women cleaned up. Lorna took out a small bag and placed it on the floor.

"This is pretty great," Kama said. "Not to be weird or pushy, but I would like to spend more time around someone who understands all this."

Lorna giggled again, and Kama smiled at her.

"I'm not sure I would say I can understand all of this," she said, gesturing at her belly. "One moment, I feel normal. The next, I am watching a movie and sobbing over everything. Then I pick fights with Curt over stupid things. And this is only three months in."

"Well, so far, I have managed to cry every day and fight with my mom. So I think we might be normal."

The women shared a laugh. Kama felt better than she had in days.

"If nothing else, I would appreciate the company during check-ups," Kama said. "Doc is proficient but somehow she manages to have the most condescending and sometimes scary bedsides manners I've ever encountered."

"Right? And I swear, if she threatens to sedate me, one more time…"

Kama laughed. "How about the scoffing? Aren't doctors supposed to make you feel comfortable?"

"I don't think she learned that."

"Well, I would be happy to share appointments," Kama said. "We can get fancy and maybe even grab lunch afterwards."

"As long as we are sharing, would you like a cleansing?" Lorna asked.

"I don't know. I've never had one," Kama admitted. "What is it?"

"You've heard of chakras, yes? Awesome. Well, many cultures believe they house our mental and emotional strengths through energy and balance. When we undergo a physical change, such as pregnancy, it creates ripples that come out in our behavior. The aches, pains, and stiffness, along with the emotional outbursts, are common with having blocked chakras. Once we clear the energy, it helps us gain balance in all aspects of our lives."

She watched Lorna take out several, small stones and crystals. Each crystal was set carefully, placed to create a circle around them, and the Beta sat across from her. Lorna placed a wooden bowl between them. Water lapped at the side as it moved. As she closed her eyes, Kama followed suit. A soft chanting gave way to a melodious energy, which flowed around her, and Kama found herself joining the humming. It drew to a natural conclusion, and she sat and enjoyed the feeling of peace and calm. A splash in the bowl made her open her eyes, and she found Lorna dipping her fingers into the water. A few, softly spoken words accompanied the gesture.

"Do you feel better?"

"I really do," Kama said. "This is amazing. I haven't felt this in control for months now."

"It is powerful. I try to do this at least once a month, but now that I am pregnant, I think a weekly cleansing might be necessary, for Curt's sake. Next time we meet up, I will tell you the story of how we met."

She burst into the giggles again, and Kama laughed with her.

I don't know if we can get used to such a laugh from her. It sounds like something that would come from a beauty queen, not, not from someone who happily totes a gun and, at least according to the rumors, enjoys using it. Oh, well. She is interesting. And she made us feel better. We could set up lunch dates for this. And she is right. We probably do want the doula here. Why is my mother always right?

"Can we set up a time to do this again?" Kama asked. "I will be happy to provide a mom-made feast, if you don't mind doing another cleansing. Not to mention, it's nice to be with another woman going through this. My mother has been reliving her four pregnancies through a very fond lens of perfection."

"I would love to," Lorna said. "Your mom should really think about cooking professionally. I'm serious. She made some amazing dishes. Why are you looking at me like that?"

"She owns a restaurant and a catering hall," Kama laughed.

She laughed even harder as Lorna's eyebrows went up into her hairline. The sound stopped short as pain pulled across her right ribcage, eliciting a groan. But still, she grinned at her new friend.

"Why does this surprise you?"

"I guess I figured she was a stay-home trophy wife," Lorna said ruefully. "I mean, you are a Diva and all. I guess I didn't think she would be the working type. Yeah, you can stop snickering at me any time."

"Can't. Breathe," Kama gasped out. It took a few more moments for her to compose herself. "I am going to have fun telling her this story. She will be amused. And before you make me laugh more, let me clue you in. My family is mixed race. She is white and proudly embraces her Irish heritage. My dad is Italian, but he is black. This way, when you meet her, you won't have your mouth open in surprise."

She relaxed as Lorna joined her in laughter, but became confused when it stopped abruptly.

"Why would I be meeting your mom?"

"Because she is an excellent cook, and despite having this great hidey hole to come down to, I generally eat at the restaurant or with her in the catering kitchen. I kind of figured you would want food sometimes, too."

"That is a generous offer, but I wouldn't impose."

"Ha," Kama scoffed. "You haven't met Brenna DeKosse. She lives to feed people. And here you are, another poor, pregnant, Loup woman who has no idea how to be proper, so she must step in and make sure you and the baby are getting enough nutrition. Only, she won't be quite as condescending to you when she says it."

They lapsed into silence, not quite tense but enough to remind them the friendship was new and they didn't really know enough about each other.

"Did you have your first sonogram yet?" Lorna asked.

"Oh, yes! A few days ago. I can't believe I saw her heart beating. I will have to go and buy a naming book tomorrow, so I can start looking for the perfect name," Kama said excitedly.

"Her? Mine looked like a fuzzy *mamón*. How do you know you are having a girl?" Lorna asked.

"I want a girl, so I am putting the power of positive thinking into play."

Kama waited for Lorna to laugh again or snort at her idea, but instead she got a thoughtful nod of her head.

"Well, it does make sense. Well then, I would like a healthy boy," Lorna said. "I remember being a girl and being pretty evil. So we will try the other."

They laughed as they gathered the trash and walked back out of their hidey hole. Plans were made to meet up the next week. Kama had a feeling she would enjoy her time with Lorna.

I might even be able to use our time to ask some of these questions I have about being Loup. I wonder how she got to be Beta, anyhow. The others look so old, and she only appears to be a few years older than me. Either way, I have training to get to.

A few weeks later, Kama strolled through the park with Olivia, trying to come up with words that would make sense to the younger girl. The shock and anxiety over the loudness and vast crowds forced her to take it slow; something she was not used to. Ever since she had passed out during their spar, Olivia had tried to avoid her. Kama had just redoubled her efforts to spend time with the young woman.

Yeah, the poor girl had been certain Aturus would punish her. Even when he explained how she held no blame, she still expected it. No wonder she didn't want to see me. It's like she doesn't know what to make of me since I told her that I am pregnant.

Kama had bitten the bullet and told her friends about her news. She had asked them to meet her at what had become *their* table in the Lounge. She brought along a box full of soup and sandwiches. She had hoped stress cooking would help.

I sure didn't expect to be this nervous telling my friends.

She handed out the food, and her friends thanked her before digging in.

"I'm pregnant."

Someday, we will learn to not just blurt out news.

Mary and Lani stared at her with big eyes and then began to squeal. Olivia nodded her head, already having heard the information. Damien and Dan gave her the thumbs up and continued to eat. Kama felt the heat from Beth's stare and slowly met her eyes. The look spoke volumes, but Beth put a smile on her face and moved to give Kama a hug.

"What? When did you find out? Who are you even dating? How far along are you?"

Mary and Lani pelted her with questions and enveloped her in hugs and more squealing.

"I think you have everyone's attention," Damien said with a rumbling laugh.

"You should do voice-overs with that deep voice," Kama said. "And I don't want attention.. I wanted to tell my friends the happy news."

"Well, I think we should celebrate," Mary said. "We're going to do a spa day."

"I know the perfect spot," Kama said excitedly. "It's up on 5th and..."

She stopped when Lani burst into giggles. As the infectious sound died down, Mary and Lani shared a look, and it started all over again.

"Come on, share," Kama said. "All I mentioned was I knew a good place."

"Sometimes it's hard to remember you have only been here for a short time," Lani said. "Mary is an esthetician in her other life. She has been nagging me to let her do a makeover."

"Can we come, too?" Dan said eagerly.

"Sure, love," Mary said. "I didn't realize you were up for a waxing."

From the pale color Dan's face adopted, Kama guessed he had experienced it at least once. He quickly stammered an excuse and, with a pointed look at Damien, stood up. Kama stared as Dan kissed Mary, and then Damien did the same. She still had a hard time understanding how they worked. Lani explained it as a "Love V." Each man dated Mary, but they weren't romantically involved with each other.

Whatever works for them. They are happy enough. Okay. Beth is still sitting there quiet. Wow, I think she might even be glaring, or at least her idea of a stern look. Yeah, I agree. She wants to talk to us in private.

"Hey, Beth, want to go topside and grab some hot chocolate with me?" she offered. "I forgot a drink, and I've had enough coffee already."

Beth nodded. Silence surrounded their walk up and out of the tunnels. While she thought of a million conversation starters, Kama didn't say anything. Her attention turned to her stomach when she saw the local, Vietnamese food truck. Hot chocolate forgotten, she ordered four, healthy-sized, *bánh mì* sandwiches, and they walked the few, short feet back into the park. Determined to enjoy at least one sandwich, Kama ate it before speaking.

"What's on your mind?"

"I don't know what to think, Kama," Beth said. "Does *he* know?"

"Jack? Yes, of course he does. And he's happy about it."

"And your parents?"

"Shocked, but okay with it. Well, my mom is. Dad's still in Italy," Kama said. "As you know, I haven't told my siblings yet, else you probably would have heard about it from Ajani and not me."

She watched Beth put down her food and pace.

"Kama, you are my best friend. You are like a sister to me. And right now, I feel like I am watching you on a collision course with disaster. I know you think you know what you are doing, but you have been Loup for less than six months. Everything you have done has been done with caution tossed to the wind. I get it. Having your life turned around is scary, but slow down."

Kama put her food down, appetite gone.

"Slow down? I haven't been given a chance. Every time I try to find a new normal, I'm thrown on a mission or tossed in a new class or expected to be an Ambassador," Kama said.

"You can say 'no,' " Beth said. "You don't have to be so careless."

"*Allora.* What do you mean—careless? I try my best to stay out of stuff, and people keep drawing me in. I didn't provoke Raye; she came after me. I didn't deliberately get pregnant. Trust me, I was more surprised than anyone," she said.

"You aren't ready to claim him, Kama," Beth said. "You can't get into a fight. There are two of you to think about now."

"They can't touch me. Jack said anyone attacking a pregnant woman would have to answer to him," Kama said.

"Oh," her friend said. "I'm just scared for you. I think you are rushing into…everything."

Kama walked the few spaces between them and pulled Beth into a hug.

"It will be fine. I'm not rushing, and I have no plan to make a claim anytime soon. If anything, I just want my life to settle down," Kama said.

"Have you ever had a calm life?" Beth snorted.

"No, but I am trying," she said.

"Yeah, I can see that. Might I suggest you start by getting rid of your extra classes?"

"Look, I have a week until my birthday. How about I promise to keep my head down until then?" she asked.

The answer was for Beth to roll her eyes and then pick up their garbage. Kama walked up to her and linked arms. They walked back toward the tunnels.

"You are coming to spa day, yes?" Kama asked.

"I have rounds," Beth said.

"We haven't set a date yet."

"I'm sure I will have rounds," Beth said.

"Oh, come on. It will be fun," she implored. "They are your friends, too. You have to be present."

"Fine," Beth grumbled. "Only if you promise to bring some of the Devil Cub cakes."

"Done," she said.

"I am happy for you," Beth said.

"Thanks. I needed to hear that," Kama said pulling her into a hug.

Since Lorna and her friends knew, Kama figured she needed to let everyone know. She looked to Beth for the best method.

"Let's go tell Karl the good news," her friend said with a laugh.

She knew Karl didn't gossip per se, but he also didn't stop to think before he spoke. She had counted on him spreading the news around the park fast. Kama hadn't expected him to pick her up and spin her around.

"Dudette, that is awesome," Karl said. "You want to be pregnant, right? I don't want to celebrate if you're sad."

"Yes, this is a good thing."

"Well then, congrats. We should go for a drink or something. Oh wait, you're too young to drink. Well, we can go get a hotdog. But you have to promise not to ram my face into the table," he said with a grin.

"Don't touch my food and we will be fine."

Kama grinned at her patrol partner and nodded. He hugged her again and finally set her down.

Within a few days, the news had been spread. She made it a point to talk about it with her friends. To her surprise, not much else had really been said to her. A few people had offered congratulations, but most didn't treat her any differently. Except Aturus, who informed her that her training schedule would change immediately. Kama expected to be moved back into the beginner class, but instead she found she would have private lessons with him to accommodate the pregnancy. To be fair, he did offer to open the class up to everyone. He had just made it clear they were to wear an empathy belly during the training.

Aturus knows about fake bellies? What in the world just happened? It almost makes him human. I wonder if he has a family. There is still so much to learn about this new life, you know. Despite. Despite all the weirdness, Wolf-Girl, this is our place. We have friends to hang out with. There is this job we have, and of course, Jack. Even though I never imagined being pregnant, I have Lorna to commiserate with. I think things are going to be okay.

Kama walked down the tunnels, giddy. She had gotten an invitation a few days before for the spa day extravaganza. When she walked onto the platform, a wide smile lit up her face. Mary had transformed the space into a temporary spa. There were tables set up for massages, chairs for manicures and pedicures, and recliners with huge lamps. Along with Lani, Beth and Olivia were there to complete the party. To Kama's surprise, Mary introduced her to four of their packmates, who would be their attendants that day.

"I've been training them," Mary told her. "Someday, I want to open my own place, and I figured having some of the pack with me would be good. Let's get down to the fun and relaxing part of today."

"I think you should just set up permanently here," Kama said, looking around. "I know I would be here at least once a week."

She smiled at her friend and then grabbed Olivia's hand and led her off towards the massage tables. After an hour of pampering, they put on robes and sat in chairs for the next phase. Thick, warm mud was smoothed onto her face, and she sighed. She hadn't felt so relaxed in months.

"Did you enjoy your massage?" Kama asked.

"They rubbed my body with oil," Olivia said. "Overall, I'm not sure what they were testing for, but it didn't hurt."

"Oh, honey, a massage is to relax your muscles, and it's supposed to feel good," she said.

"Okay, but why do we have mud on our faces?" the younger girl asked.

Kama heard the long pause and wondered if Olivia had expected something different. She realized the young woman probably had no idea what they were doing. Going to the spa was routine for her, but she tried to see it from Olivia's point of view.

"The mud is to help clean our pores," Kama said.

"Doesn't mud make us dirty?" Olivia asked.

"Not this mud," Kama laughed.

"Oh. I thought maybe we were being observed to see if we could handle the discomfort."

She stared at the young woman lying back in the chair.

"Why did you think they were testing you?"

"We got tested every day to see how we were progressing," the girl said matter-of-factly. "Janus sometimes ordered extras to see what we could endure. Most of the time, they just took blood or samples, but sometimes, they hurt a lot more."

Kama didn't know what to say to the girl. She wanted to ask a thousand more questions about the place Olivia had been raised in and all of her experiences there, but she knew overwhelming the girl was not the way to get the answers her brain desired. Not to mention, it would not be fair to force her to relive the horrors she had seen there just for the sake of curiosity.

"We don't test much here, unless we get very ill or injured. Then Doc comes and tries to figure out how to best help us," Kama said.

"Ah, much like when Janus introduced venom into my system. At first, I thought he needed to document and test my endurance, to see how I would react while being sick from the poison. Later, I realized he used the exams to build my resistance to it," Olivia said with a nod of her head.

Kama felt the mud on her face crack with her surprise.

"Not quite the same type of thing," Kama said. "We usually only see Doc when we are sick or hurt. Olivia, we will not subject you to tests just to see how you preform."

"But we train every day," the girl said. "Is that not a test?"

Dammit, brain, work. Yes, I suppose it is a kind of test. Well, don't we look stupid. Do we have an answer to give her? No? That's just great. I thought only pregnant females got pregnancy brain. You're the instinct, Wolf-Girl. Fine. Yes. Yes, we are both pregnant. Whatever.

"I guess you are correct. It is a test of sorts, but I had never thought about it that way," Kama said. "Do you feel better?"

"I didn't feel bad before."

Of course you didn't. Moving on.

She could hear the sigh of relief from her friends around the platform. She didn't see a problem with Mary setting up permanently.

"Can I ask a question?"

Olivia's voice broke into Kama's wandering thoughts.

"Sure."

"How do you take it day after day," the girl asked. "It is so loud and bright and chaotic. There seems to be no schedule or reason. I have so much time to do nothing. Most days, I am restless, because I'm not sure what to do."

"It's always been like this for me," Kama said. "Maybe someday it won't feel so scary to you. Though I can help you find new things to do. We can figure out what you like. Maybe we can try cooking tomorrow. Does that sound good to you?"

"I can try. I am finding my biggest change is always being in this form. It's small and weak," Olivia said. "Although, I do find I need to eat less."

"Were you always in shifted form?"

"This is shifted for me," Olivia said wryly. "But yes, we were in what you know as warrior form. We were born that way, obviously much smaller. We didn't start transitioning until we were five."

"Wait a minute," Kama interrupted. "How old are you? When is your birthday?"

"August 29th. When is yours?"

"Next week, on the 24th. Why?" Kama asked.

"Well, you asked me. I was making polite conversation," Olivia said.

Kama smiled at the girl, already planning for a birthday party. Then she remembered the conversation they were having. She dug a little deeper.

"So, you're five then, but really sixteen?"

"Yes and no. Janus explained it to me, but all the pieces still don't fit together. We were birthed in the lab five years ago. Then we grew at an accelerated rate. He had no way to explain why and how it was possible. We aged 3.2 times faster per year than an average person, which, which is odd, because wolves age about 2.2 times the rate of a human. Regardless, he approximated my age of holding to be about sixteen."

"Age of holding?"

"Yes. After I shifted to girl form, the aging slowed to the general, human rate."

Kama blamed the pregnancy for her head spinning with all the information. She knew it wouldn't have made sense to her anyhow. The idea of creating a being, and one that could shift, made her head want to pop.

Obviously, it is possible, because—hello—Loup. This girl has been through things I can't even imagine. If I can help her understand or make it easier for her, then so be it.

"There is still so much to learn about you," Kama said with a smile.

"And you," Olivia agreed. "I am starting to like being here. You all seem nice."

Their friends came back to clean the mud from their faces, so the conversation stopped. Kama enjoyed the attention and sighed contentedly.

CHAPTER Fourteen

Kama sat in front of the vanity mirror, trying on earrings. She carefully held a piece of paper over the right half of her face so she could see the chandelier-style earring on her left ear. She grimaced, switched the paper to the left, and carefully regarded the diamond solitaire in her right ear. She sighed. Neither of them was really the look she had wanted. She felt sassy and, for the moment, her hormones were behaving, so she wanted her outfit to reflect her mood.

Right. Just. Just be a good DeKosse and wear the damn diamond. I doubt Jack is going to care, and if we don't get a move on, we will be late for our reservation. Why am I so nervous, anyhow? We have had plenty of conversations and dates. Granted, yes, we are actually going out to dinner. In public. Before my birthday. Okay, this is why we are nervous. It will be fine.

She stood and smoothed the navy, wool dress. Her hand paused at her midsection even though her stomach remained flat and undisturbed. For once, Kama wished for stronger Loup hearing. Ever since experiencing the view on the monitor with Jack, she had immediately been enthralled hearing her baby's heartbeat and longed to experience the sounds again.

Nope. Nothing. Nothing at all to show the world I am going to have a baby in August. It still doesn't feel real, yet I spend more time thinking about being pregnant than not. After watching the little heart blip on the screen with Jack, I am still amazed.

Kama took one more, quick look in the mirror and decided to live on the wild side and the chandelier earrings would do. She brushed her teeth, humming along to more of her favorite Jackie Chan music, when she heard a knock at the door. After a hasty spit, she yelled out for her visitor to wait a moment. She had expected Beth to drop by and borrow her purple sweater for date night with Ajani. She grabbed the sweater from her closet and walked out to find her mother setting down a basket on her dining room table.

"Mom? What are you doing here?" she asked.

"Well, I figured we could sit down and have dinner together. Your father is gone, and I know you have been having a rough time," her mother said as she unpacked two mugs and a teapot. "We can have a nice quiet girls' night."

Kama's stomach rumbled as the scents wafted through her nose and landed with a whisper of a taste on her tongue. A gentle, herbal aroma called to her. For a moment, she wondered if she would have enough time to sit down and have a quick chat with her mother before leaving to make their reservation. She doubted it but hoped she might have a full cup of tea before she left the house.

Oh, crud-puppies. She brought her own equipment, so we're in for a long conversation. Wait. Why is she staring at us? I'm pretty sure I didn't make a face at her. No, she is looking at our clothes.

"I'm rather surprised to see you were planning to go out this evening."

"I don't see any reason to sit in my house alone all the time," Kama said. "I'm just joining a friend for dinner."

"A friend?" Brenna asked.

Kama nodded and didn't explain anything else. She went back to the bathroom and grabbed the rest of the supplies she would need to finish getting ready. As she walked back out, she found her mother had turned back to the basket and pulled out a small plate of cookies. Kama almost regretted revealing she had a date. The spread contained her favorites. Her mouth watered, and she sat at the table.

"Who is this friend? Why have I never heard of them?"

"Yes, Mama. A friend," she said and smiled. "I do have them. You haven't heard of them because I haven't told you yet."

Kama wanted to keep the tone light and casual. She didn't want to tell her mother about meeting Jack for dinner, but a very thorough look over had been given and there would be no denying being dressed up to go on a date. Instead, she focused on smoothing lotion on her hands and arms.

"Are you meeting Cade to have the talk?"

"No," she said. "I already told you, we aren't dating anymore and have decided not to see each other again."

"Are you going on a date?" Brenna asked.

"I'm really not going to stand here and play Twenty Questions, mother. I have plans to go to dinner," Kama said.

Her mother nodded and continued to unpack napkins and other accessories, which gave Kama a very nervous feeling. Somehow, she knew the odds of her making it to dinner with Jack were diminishing by the second. She pulled her phone out of her purse, anticipating the need to call him before this conversation got into full swing.

"So, who is this man?"

Kama's mind spun at a rapid pace, trying to remember if Nula had mentioned any rules about pack members dating the Alpha from her grandfather's pack. She couldn't recall any taboos, and considering the Alpha position passed along through the family line, she doubted they had ever encountered that particular problem. Even still, she wasn't sure she wanted to have such a serious talk with her mother, considering how Brenna felt about mongrel Loup.

"He's from my Pack. No one you know," Kama said, trying to end the conversation.

Damn. She really could do this later. It's nice to have brought us tea, but we need to leave. I don't want to talk to her about Jack right now. Hmmm. She is staring at us.

"The man is from your pack, then," Brenna said and sat down.

"Yes, he is, and yes, we are going on a date," Kama said and pulled out her phone. "If you will excuse me, I think I should let him know I will be late because of this little heart-to-heart."

She typed up the quick text and sent it. The idle thought of begging him for help had crossed her mind, but she didn't act on it. The last thing she wanted was for Jack and her mother to meet under the current circumstance. Kama watched her mother prepare the tea for her and one for herself.

No doubt, she planned to have a quiet and relaxed evening with me. I know we haven't spent as much time together as we used to. I never imagined my life would be so busy. Patrols only take up a few hours, but there is training and then being with my friends and Jack. I don't think I would change it.

Kama enjoyed the hot tang of hibiscus and chamomile on her tongue, almost forgetting the tension, until her mother cleared her throat. She watched her mother flounder for words to say.

"Darling, I think it might be too early for you to start dating again," Brenna said in a soft and calm voice.

"What?"

"I know this must seem pretty exciting, having young men ask you out on dates. However, given that you and Cade have yet to work things out, it might be best to wait," her mother said. "You just found out you are pregnant. I think you should take a break and get ready to have the baby."

Kama bought herself some thinking time by eating a handful of cookies. She then drank her tea and tried to make a good speech in her mind as her mother poured another cup.

"Mom, you know Cade and I are broken up," she said. "There is nothing to work out. Having a baby doesn't change things between us. Cade is a really nice guy, but he just doesn't belong in my world. He can't be involved with this child. I know you disagree, but it's my choice. Does it make me a horrible person? Maybe. I do know it's the best decision I can make right now."

"Sweetheart, you just need some time," Brenna said. "He is the father, and you may find that you will want him around later."

Kama opted to drink again. Keeping her mouth full seemed to be the best and easiest way to keep from yelling at her mom. They sat without speaking.

You know, for once, she is letting us just be here in the silence. Should I worry about this? I wonder what she is thinking about. I know she said she would support my decisions. Why did she bring up working things out with Cade? She met him all of three times, maybe.

"So, about this young man from your little group," Brenna started.

"My Pack, you mean," Kama said and met her mother's eyes. "There are seventy of us. I don't consider our group too small. Unless you meant it as a derogatory term because you think less of us Mongrels."

"My mistake. Sorry, darlin'," Brenna said quickly. "I didn't mean to offend you. I will work at learning more about your Pack. Most of what I have ever heard about Mongrels has been negative, but as you remind me—you are Mongrel. And a damn fine one."

"Yes, I am," Kama said with a smile. "Really, most of the people are just normal, everyday people. Except Karl. But he is a story for another day. I mean, you have met Beth, and she is perfectly lovely."

"Speaking of her," Brenna said. "Has she actually moved in with Ajani, yet? I accidentally scared her a few days ago. Your brother had asked me if I still had his sugar supplies from years ago and asked me to drop them off. I found the box and decided to stop by before work. I put it on the table, when I heard the shower running. I knew Ajani would be at Four Leaf, since he has a cake to finish. Well, I figured your brother had lost some of his new vigor and had woken late. So, I burst into the bathroom, prepared to give him what-for. I pulled back the curtain and found Beth. The poor lass sang along so loudly with the radio she hadn't heard me enter. Well, she shrieked, and I shrieked and then apologized."

Kama burst out in laughter at the mental image.

"Then, I went and made things worse. Being embarrassed about walking in on her while she showered, I started making her breakfast to apologize. She must have thought I had left and called your brother to tell him about the incident. Beth came out, wearing nothing but a towel, talking into the phone, and explaining how I had caught her. She shrieked again when she saw me, and, as she turned to flee, the towel fell," Brenna said between gasps of laughter.

Kama wiped away the tears streaming from her eyes. She felt a miniscule pang of guilt about laughing at her best friend's encounter with her mother.

Nope, I guess I don't feel too bad about it. It's pretty funny. Beth. Naked. In front of Mom. Twice. At least she got a decent breakfast out of it. Although, I am sure "mortified" doesn't begin to cover it. I can't wait to talk to her.

"I finished the breakfast and left it on a plate for her," her mother said. "I let myself out and went to work. Your brother came to find me and started to offer up an explanation. He couldn't get over the embarrassment and stuttered, until I told him the story of me walking in on Dante and Jill in an intimate encounter."

Milk spewed out of Kama's nose as she choked.

"You walked in on what?" she gasped out. "What? How? When did that happen?"

Her mother grabbed her steaming mug and sat back in the chair.

Storytelling mode…

Kama relaxed as her mother gave all the sordid details about ruining Dante's big night. Much like Kama and Ajani, he had taken advantage of living in his apartment below his parents. Unlike the younger set, he had moved out at sixteen because he had been eager to have his own place. Dante had also been the stereotypical, responsible, elder child, and his parents had no reason to object. Flash forward to when he was twenty-four, still living in his place, but dating Jill. He had set up the perfect romantic scene to propose to Jill. She had said yes, and they had celebrated. Brenna hadn't known about the proposal plans and had stopped by with a care package of food from the catering hall.

"As I entered, I heard a strange noise coming from the back of the apartment. I rushed to the room, thinking he had become ill or had otherwise hurt himself." Brenna cackled with glee. "Instead, I found him and Jill celebrating their engagement. On his desk. At least she still married him after the whole debacle."

Kama had done her best not to choke on food as she heard about the mass embarrassments. She stood to stretch, hoping her mother would take the hint. She sighed as her mother gave her a pointed look from her seated position.

"Tell me about your friend from the park," Brenna said. "Have you known him long?"

"For a while, I guess," Kama said. "Since about September."

"Is he the one you patrol with?"

"Karl? Oh, no," Kama said with a grin. "I couldn't date him. He is a nice guy, but so not my type."

"What is your type? Tell me something about this young man. Where were you all having dinner tonight?" Brenna asked.

Wow, she is trying to be gentle and everything. I know she must be dying to get all of the details. The real question is, how much do we tell her? This might be the right time to introduce the idea of Jack to her. Sure, the age thing is going to be a problem, but we don't have to talk about that now.

"I'm not sure where he had planned to take me," Kama said. "He just said to get dressed to go to dinner."

She noticed her mother's eyes flicked up and down her outfit, the, the look taking place of the dialogue noting "nice, fancy dinner" and "not food from the taco truck."

"So, you just started dating, then?" Brenna asked. "Is he still in the 'impress her' stage? Maybe you could invite him over for some coffee and cake. I would love to meet him and apologize for derailing his plans this evening."

"Actually, we're still meeting for dinner," she said. "Jack just pushed the reservations back. Okay, I need to go. I have to meet him in twenty minutes. The ride will take about that long."

"Jack. And now we have a name," her mother said. "Is he Loup as well, or is he a person in the know?"

"Loup," Kama replied. "I don't actually know how many people in the know we have. I'm still learning about all those things."

"Where did you two meet?"

Los Angeles, but I sure can't tell you. Okay, I agree. Let's get it all out. She is going to want to meet him soon enough.

"On the night I got attacked and Changed for the first time. He came down to meet me," she said. "Jack is the Alpha of the Central Park Pack."

Kama felt like the air had been sucked out of the room. She looked at her mother, who sat perfectly still except the pursing of her lips as she processed the information given to her.

"You cannot possibly be dating that old man, Kamaria," Brenna said. "He's got to be at least six hundred years old."

"What? Who?" Kama asked and then laughed. "The Judge? Of course I am not dating him. Someday, you and Grandpa will believe me when I tell you he is not our Alpha. He is one of the Betas. Jack is only forty-two, not six hundred."

"Forty–two?"

Kama had never heard words strangled out of her mother's mouth in that particular manner, but there they were.

"I think you need to be telling me a lot more about this grown-ass man you are dating," Brenna said. "And why he thinks dating a child is okay."

"I am not a child, mother," she said calmly. "What would you like to know about my Mate?"

I swear, I didn't plan to drop it all on her like this. Her face is kind of purple, and I really hope she isn't having a heart attack right now. Better yet, I hope she doesn't try to strangle me. Oh, damn. She is going to try to kill Jack when she meets him.

"Your Mate?" her mother hissed. "Your Mate is the Alpha. A grown man who thinks being mated to a teenager is okay? You have only been a member in his pack for a few month. Did you have a choice in any of this? Is this how their Pack works?"

"Of course I have a choice. Considering we will live hundreds of years, the age difference is negligible," Kama said. "You can't tell me there aren't similar situations up in Grandpa's Pack. This is part of the reason we wanted to wait to tell you we were dating. It would have been easier after my birthday."

"Like a few weeks of being eighteen is going to make this better?"

Right? We have been saying this… oh, wait. That wasn't agreeing with me. She still doesn't like it.

"Jack is a great person. He owns a steel mill company and runs our Pack. He is smart and funny and…"

"Your Pack knew you were Mated before you told me?"

Seriously, Brenna DeKosse? Are you mad I am dating him or mad someone else might have known first? Heck, Beth knew, and she doesn't like it either.

"No, we are waiting to tell them as well."

"Why?"

"I don't want to have to fight any females who might be upset about us dating. They could Challenge me, and I don't know if I am ready for that yet."

"They would kill you over him?"

Of course she grabbed on to the "me getting killed" detail.

"No. Well, I mean, I hope not. I am a decent fighter," Kama said. "Anyhow, this is why we are taking it slow."

She watched the emotional display run over her mother's face. She was certain a petulant look covered her own face. Neither of them was happy, and Kama sighed. She bit her tongue to stave off offering excuses and explanations. She stood and busied herself with cleaning the table and packing the basket back up.

"I am happy, Mama," she said. "I love him, and he loves me."

She turned around just in time to watch her mother's spine stiffen.

"Did you use Cade to get pregnant?"

Kama's eyes widened in shock.

"What did you say?"

"Did you use that boy to have a baby for your *Mate?*"

She stared at her mother while fury at the unfair insult filled her and pressed her lips together. After a few seconds of processing, she said the only thing she could.

"Get out of my house. I can't talk to you right now."

Kama walked over to the door and opened it. She waited for her mother to walk through and shut it on the excuses that were beginning to form. Taking a shaky breath, she leaned against the door and let the tears flow down her face. A quick text to Jack broke their date, and she promised to explain the next day. She went to bed and was relieved when sleep claimed her quickly.

Kama stepped into her house and threw her purse on the side table in her foyer. It had been a long day at the park; she needed a bath and an early bed time. She sighed as her cell phone rang, forcing her to dig into her coat pocket to find it. She frowned at the display.

Oh, goody. Confrontation time.

"Hello?"

"Kamaria, you need to go upstairs and talk to your mother."

She paused for a moment because she had no reason to yell at the caller, who happened to be her mother's best friend. Though she almost felt like hanging up her phone. She didn't want to hear about her behavior or get advice on how to deal with the situation.

"Meghan, why do I need to go up there?" she asked.

"I know you had an argument. She called me, sobbing incoherently, and I went over to console her. We drank many bottles of whiskey, and I told her to take the next day off," Meghan said. "It's now been two days. She didn't show up for work this morning, and I didn't think twice about it because we don't have an event until Friday evening. However, she hasn't answered my calls all day. So, I am assuming she is upstairs, still wallowing in self-pity."

"What do you expect me to do about it?" Kama huffed.

"I expect you to understand the reality of your mother not being Superwoman. Her husband is overseas for another few weeks. Her two youngest moved out within months of each other, leaving her alone for the first time in thirty years," Meghan said dryly. "In addition, she just had a huge fight with her youngest daughter. You want to be considered an adult? Go up there and act grown. Make sure your mother is okay."

A soft click ended the conversation before she could respond. Kama put her phone down on the counter before she gave in to the urge and chucked it across the foyer and broke it. The wolf heaved a sigh.

I know, and I agree. What she said to us was hurtful and offensive. But Meghan is right. She is our mother, and we still love her. No matter what. We take the higher road and at least look in on her. I'll probably have to help her get showered and cleaned up. Fine. Let's go. I hope she doesn't expect me to be all huggy and gushy. Until she apologizes, I have nothing to say to her.

Kama took a deep breath and squared her shoulders. She mentally prepared herself to be berated. Her mother had made her thoughts about her relationship with Jack clear. She hoped all she would have to do is prod her mother awake and give her a cup of coffee. She had never seen her mother hungover. Then again, she never could have guessed that she would have been accused of using Cade to get pregnant on purpose.

She walked up the stairs and stood before the door a moment to calm herself. Kama fished her key out of her pocket and opened the door. She blinked a few times at the dark, cavern-like nature of her parents' home. She walked in, looked around, and a low growl formed in the back of her throat in surprise.

"You are a terrible daughter. So petty and selfish that you stopped talking with your mother after a silly, little spat."

Kama's eyes widened as recognition of the person standing before her slammed through her brain. The encounter which drove her back to her pack. The library where the woman in front of her tried to force her to kill someone. Kama had refused and ran for safety, only to find that the woman chasing her was a vampire. It was the encounter with this evil being that made her realize just how dangerous the paranormal world could be.

"Stone."

"Aww, I'm honored. You remembered my name," Stone said.

"But you're a vampire. How could you get in here without being invited?" Kama asked, and then panic shook her. "Where is my mother?"

"You watch too much TV, little one," Stone said casually. "We don't need to be invited. Someone invented the idea so you all would sleep better. Thinking there is some kind of magical barrier to keep out the things that go bump in the night lets you feel safe and secure."

Kama rushed at the vampire, swinging. She felt confident in her months of training, and even more so when her fists connected with its chest. She moved back and prepared to launch another volley.

"What is up with you hitting me? Last time we met, you punched me in the face," Stone said.

"After you hit me and tried to make me shoot someone," Kama retorted. "Where is my mother?"

She expected Stone to attack back and stood ready. She tensed and then returned the quick volley of jabs and punches. She wished she had grabbed her Kuba before coming upstairs, but since she didn't have it, she relied on the skills she had been learning. She focused on connecting with the vampire and driving the vile being back. A hand met her chest and pushed her backwards. Kama landed on her rear and slid backward from the foyer into the living room.

What the hell? She looks like she barely touched me. This is going to be harder than I thought. What am I thinking?? I can't fight her. She will kill me and the baby. I am going to have to be smarter than her, since I am not going to take unnecessary risks.

Looking to her right, she saw the very familiar, chairside table, and a plan came to mind. As Stone walked into the living room, she lay still on the floor.

"Your mother is waiting for you—"

"If you hurt her, I will kill you," Kama snarled, cutting into the vampire's speech.

"I forget how stupid young ones are," Stone said casually. "She can't be bait if she's dead. Then again, you only have my word to go on. Now, stop interrupting me and let me talk."

She called us stupid. I really want to kill her and make it hurt. But we have to wait until we know where Mom is. While she is yapping away, we can move over to the chair. Nice and slow. Don't. Don't give her a reason to react.

"When you interrupted my little business back in September, you brought your Pack's existence to my attention and thus to my boss. He decided he wanted you. So, we began watching and learning about you. He sent in a recon team to look for you den in Central Park, and then you all went and blew up his facility. A bit of an overreaction, methinks."

Kama watched as Stone walked over to the cabinet with a top bar and poured herself a drink.

"Yeah, the Irish did always know the good whiskey. Glad to know your mother followed the proud tradition."

The chair and table were directly behind her, so Kama sat up against the chair. She knew she would only have one chance. As the blonde vampire turned to face her, Kama snapped the leg off of the table, leaped forward, and plunged it into the chest area, hoping she had enough momentum to push it in deep enough.

"Ow," Stone snarled.

Kama fell to her knees with the force of the backhand blow, and her ears rang.

"First of all, you ruined my shirt. It's almost two hundred years old and pure silk. Not the weak, mixed blend you all think is real. You can't get beautiful and precise, hand-stitched work like this anymore. Child labor laws and all," Stone said.

The table leg clattered to the floor in front of Kama.

"Secondly, cherry wood? I'm pretty damn offended. You ruined my shirt and tried to kill me with this young piece of crap? This is maybe two hundred years old. Sure, black cherry trees can live to two-hundred and fifty years, but even that is too young for me. You have to have wood with the potential to top my age, which I will not share with you today. And hello, special one, did you fail anatomy or something? You don't know where the heart is? Be very happy the Boss has claimed you. Otherwise, I would take out the cost of this shirt from your ass."

The veneer of a simple human fell away. Fangs had descended—not the tiny tips Kama had seen before, but at least one and a half inches of pointed death. The skin on the face drew back tightly against the skull, making it gaunt. The pale eyes seemed larger and emitted an aura of evil aimed at Kama, stealing her breath. One hand reached down and encircled her neck. She gagged as she choked while being lifted off the ground. The smell of death surrounded her. As she struggled, the fangs descended towards her neck. With a growl, the vampire tossed Kama away, and she hit the wall across the room.

"Be aware of what you are getting into, little girl," Stone hissed. "This is not a game. We kill people all the time. They're just snacks. But you're not people, and you have more value than you know. You're a werewolf. You are the type of thing we use. He will see your full potential realized, whether you like it or not. It's always been like this. You fight against us, and we win."

Kama stood slowly and faced the vampire. She didn't have a plan B or C or D, but she knew she couldn't just lie on the floor and do nothing. If she couldn't take out Stone, there was no way she could even hope to take on the Boss.

"No one is going to save you, because no one knows where he is. By the time they realize you are gone, it will no longer matter."

Fleeing made sense. So, Kama ran. Terror making her blood pump. She quickly ran to the place that had offered her solace and comfort over the years. Her childhood bedroom. Her mind spun.

Of all the myths out there about vampires, not a damn one ever bothered to mention the correlation between their age and the woods? Shit we need to go. What, how, where... Right, the fire escape. My new room is downstairs from my old room. I know my window is open because I left it that way this morning. Speaking of things people never tell you, pregnancy gas? The noxious odor was the most unpleasant thing I have smelled in a while. Well, except this nasty dead thing. I hope this phase passes fast. Okay, go. She won't know where we went.

Kama climbed down the fire escape as quietly and quickly as she could. She pushed open her window and crawled into her apartment. She moved through her home and grabbed her phone off the side table. She quickly dialed Jack and rambled when she got his voicemail.

"Jack, it's me. It's Kama, I mean. You. You know who I am...."

She hoped she gave him enough details to figure everything out as she thought about her plan of attack. First, she would have to find where her mother was being held. Next, she would have to gather a group for an attack.

I can grab Beth and Karl. I'm sure Damien, Mary, and Dan will help me. Maybe I can convince Tina to help, too? Oh, gods. I just need a strong enough group to take whatever this vampire boss thing throws at us.

Kama opened up her front door, ready to run down the stairs and the few blocks to Central Park. Her eyebrows raised and her eyes widened at seeing Stone before her. The snatched phone flew across room and shattered apart upon hitting the floor. She found herself grabbed up by her shirt front.

"Good plan, except where you were super loud. I would suggest stealth lessons, but you aren't going to need them. What you should have done is gone all the way down the fire escape. It's still early evening, and with the sunshine I would have been sluggish," Stone said. "However you did me the favor of staying inside. Let's go. Actually, you probably won't make this easy for me. This might cause a bit of brain damage, good thing you are cute."

Kama felt a hard pressure against her forehead, and the world wobbled and began to fall to the floor. She felt Stone scoop her up, and then things went dark.

CHAPTER Fifteen

Jack sat in his meeting, waiting on edge. Despite all of Carla's careful planning, he had no illusions the meeting would yield the results he wanted without careful negotiations. While he wanted the merger to go through, he wasn't willing to play the run-and-jump games the men from Brazil seemed to crave. He wanted the merger to work for many reasons but not for the reasons the company thought. He had no desire to control it all; he just wanted their community to thrive.

Sure as hell, Garra Shipping was an easier sell, and they wanted nothing to do with me. Well, until I called their Alpha's bluff. Formidable, to be sure, but at least open to suggestion. I am not trying to reunite all the Loup clans of the world, but it makes sense that we close ranks and start to do business with each other. Hell, the more money we keep in our own community the better. Yet here we are, acting like each Alpha is the enemy. I'm pretty sure there are plenty of vampires who would appreciate our skepticism since it means we are then putting all of the money into their hands. We need to be a united front, financially as well as physically.

The conversation grew louder, and he looked across the table. While his command of Portuguese sufficed, he admired the easy nature with which Carla rattled off answers as inquiries were flung at her.

Jack had gained his language skills while in Black Ops. They were more the "drop into the country and learn to survive" speech skills than business discourse. However, once he had gotten back from being a prisoner, he had taken his honorable discharge and went back to the steel mills.

After my time down there, I only wanted to ever hear English again. Probably a bad idea, seeing as New York is filled with many languages and cultures. Good thing I have a running transcript here. It helps.

Jack's meeting table also discreetly housed a laptop. The screen was only visible from his seat. His eyes flicked downward, watching the machine race to process the conversation and keep up. Kincaid had begrudgingly tailored the translation program to keep up with the speed of speech as much as possible. While complaining bitterly about dragging the system down, Kincaid suggested an alternative. He had actually appreciated the challenge of writing the program, but he had choked about getting rid of the dedicated graphics card. Jack knew the man grumbled from habit.. Kincaid loved being able to tinker. Even more than he loved irritating Carla.

Definitely not the type of person that everyone can appreciate. I can't believe managed to get Carla on board to let him to come work for us. Of course she did insist on making him sweat.

Jack had met Kincaid the day the man had tried to infiltrate his company. Actually, he had met him at the end of the day, about ten seconds before Carla had figured out if she were going to call the police or put a hit out on him. With no shame, the man admitted being a black hat hacker. He had been intrigued by Twist Industries, whose intranet offered few online hacking opportunities.

He actually reinforced everything Carla had been telling me about digital security measures and why we had to find more staff. Of course, I doubt she expected to hire him after the stunt he pulled.

As Carla retold it, Kincaid had walked into Twist Industries with the early morning crowd, sporting, sporting a name badge. Since she didn't recognize him, Carla began to discreetly follow him. Never once did Jack doubt that his partner knew every single person who worked for them. Despite having snuck his way into the building, Kincaid only made use of the Jacuzzi, sauna, and the cafeteria. Much to Carla's disgust, he had spent six of his eight hours eating and working on his laptop.

At the end of the day, as he prepared to depart, she pulled him into an office and presented him with a bill amounting to thirty thousand dollars for his food and pool recreation. A few, heated negotiations later, Kincaid had agreed to work for them.

I suppose there is also the fact that he is damn good at what he does. Since he has been on board, I have had no worries about whether or not my system is secure. He is waiting patiently for the hacker who tries to break the system. I wonder what he has lined up for that occasion. I can also count on him to keep our intranet running smoothly, even if he is a callous, condescending ass about it all.

Jack's smile sobered as his thoughts spiraled. For all that Kincaid might be unconventional and quite frankly a pain in the ass, he had earned every penny of his keep during the raid. The man had pulled and secured twenty-three of the twenty-five hard drives that had been available in the server room, not, not to mention the many hours he had already spent decrypting and organizing the information they were finding.

It's baffling to me how many trails we are able to trace, just by following common things like food and medical supplies. Not that I expected for there to be some huge map of the evil infrastructure but maybe some concrete connections showing who some of the partners were and how to trace them. It would be even better if they would just give us the name of the mastermind behind it all. Oh, no. Why did it get silent all of a sudden?

"Gentlemen, I suggest we take a break before tempers get riled."

His attention snapped back to a slightly flushed Carla. She didn't even pretend to hide her frustration; everyone could sense it, anyhow. She leaned forward and braced herself on her knuckles against the table. Her eyes were dilated, and her nostrils flared. There were nods of agreement, and she stood back up.

"There are snacks in the room down the hall, across from the restrooms," she all but snarled.

The other six gentlemen around the table rose, gave a slight bow to her, and left. Because of his angle, Jack had been privy to the smiles a few men wore. He doubted Carla would ever want a Loup husband, but if she did, she had more than a few admirers. He knew she needed her time as she stomped out of the conference room and towards her office. While he had missed what had tweaked her so badly, he knew she would work it out quickly.

I think tonight's best plan would just be to order in. Kama has been exhausted lately. Between. Between the baby and the argument with Brenna, she's been stressed out. Maybe I can even arrange for a masseuse to come to the house for a session or two. It might be just what she needs to relax and calm down. I can't imagine Doc will be happy with all the chaos going on in her life. Even though she did say to carry on with normal activities, I don't think this is what she meant. I wonder how Lorna is doing with it all. Other than her cursing out Curt for getting her too many flowers, I haven't seen much of her. Mental note to check in. Maybe Kama would like some flowers...

Images exploded in front of his face, and this time Jack rode out the pictures until they were done. Despite having had flashback memories from his Spirit Quest for the last few weeks, he couldn't say he enjoyed the delivery method. He had tried to stop them from coming, as if his puny, mortal frame could stop a message from the Goddess. As the stream faded, he sat back and took a breath. While it wasn't painful per se, he honestly had no words to describe it. On the one hand, it felt like ideas were being unpacked from his mind, but they didn't leave any more space. Just questions. On the other hand, he understood on a deep level that the information he had been given would be with him forever. Images that were given could relate to the past, present, or future.

Just as soon as I think everything makes sense, I get flashes of events that change everything. To be sure, I will never forget the birth flower or birthstone of August. I do wonder if there is more about this baby than I remember just yet. Why would the Goddess make sure I had the capacity to understand and accept everything with Kama and the pregnancy situation so smoothly, if this is an everyday event? Then again, I am not the one giving birth. It probably is a lot more complicated than that. Although, seeing that heartbeat...I'm smitten and she's not even here yet. Great, I really have bought into Kama's notion that it will be a girl. Picture clarity time. Now to examine the imagery. Okay. What about a coat? And what the heck is that light about? Granted, I know my job is to figure out everything and work out how it makes sense, but sometimes a user's manual would be a much better route.

A soft tinkle of laughter slowly segued into a gentle clearing of the throat and grabbed his attention.

"I think they are ready, Jack," Carla said. "I overheard a couple of them talking in a regional dialect. Apparently, I wasn't supposed to be able to understand it and thus be amazed about their new ideas on how to work with the merger. Not to mention, the boss's son likes my latest ideas. And he is flirting with me, as if I would ever be that unprofessional. This shouldn't last too much longer."

Of course the Goddess laughed. Just because I happened to ask if they were the same being. I don't doubt She takes on human form to interact with us.

More laughs. Great. Let's just wrap this up so I can go home to my Mate and relax for the night.

The Brazilian Loup came back to the table a few minutes later and negotiations started in earnest. Even though Carla acted as his official mouthpiece, no one treated her with disrespect. The terms that were offered up as a counter seemed fair.

I bet they would be slightly irked to realize that Carla understands it all. She picks up dialects faster than anyone I have ever met. I never would have imagined all her volunteer trips would work so well for us. Even when she is on a break, she finds a way to not be still. And the benefit is that she understands some of the regional slang. Does she ever really take a break? I've only ever known her to work. There has to be more to her life than that, and I should really know about it. I think I understand her drive a bit more Just because I'm having all of these Goddess interventions on how to work with the people around me, doesn't mean I have complete insight to what makes her tick. I hope Carla believes I was completely honest with her when I told her about the Spirit Quest, because the information the Goddess gave me about her was powerful. When this mess is over, we should have a long talk.

For fifteen years, Jack had been content to give Carla her privacy, and she had given him his. They worked together and had a great relationship, but he still knew almost nothing about her. It probably didn't help that she was the one who did background checks and vetted everyone. Through a vision, he learned that not only did she support her father, because disability wasn't enough to survive on, but she also took care of the elderly on the block she grew up on. The biggest recurring theme Jack had been experiencing through the flashbacks was depth and what he didn't know about those around him.

Hell, the only reason Carla knows about the Loup side of my life is because of the accident.

He had hired all six of his packmates to work at Cypress Steel Mills when it first opened. It seemed like a great idea at the time. They had more stamina and strength than human men. They also didn't complain about the long hours.

One benefit of having a total prick for an Alpha. Yes, it happened as I came back from the military and learned about being a werewolf. Having others around who were like me made it easier to come to grips with my new reality. I can't believe I ever followed his rule. Oh, well. I'm Alpha now.

He and the crew had been working full time for months and pushed themselves to the brink of exhaustion each night to meet order demands and deadlines. Carla had marketed the company and sold their ability for fast turnaround times with the product. The night of the accident had been a full moon, and for once the work orders had been filled early. Jack and the men had sat around the break room, having beer and casually talking about what they would do with the bonus money. Carla had interrupted them with a huge, rush order from a major company. They. They needed to pack up the shipment and have it ready for an early morning pickup.

The crew had groaned but clearly understood that being able to handle this kind of rush order could propel the company's success. Jack went to the production floor with the crew and began to stack beams. Up until that point, Carla had been banned from the floor because of working conditions. They had managed to hide the fact that each man could carry a steel beam over his shoulder solo. There was also the lack of protective headgear and eyewear that couldn't be explained. Fortunately, the extreme dirt and swelteringly hot temperatures dissuaded many visits. Carla had no desire or intention to be down there with them. A small lapse of attention caused one worker, Keth, to knock a bar too hard against the furnace. The resulting sparks flew wide and caught some rags in the corner on fire. Another worker ran over and put out the fire but not before the alarm sounded.

Carla came down with a fire extinguisher and watched the comedy of errors that ensued. Sure, Keth stomped on the flames, only to have his jeans catch on fire. He patted at them with his hands and then ripped off the burning material. He threw it down and stomped some more in his naked glory. Of course, as Carla watched, the first- and second-degree burns healed instantly while he stood there, looking irritated. Even better, he had partially shifted his vision to Loup, and his canines protruded from his mouth. To her credit, Carla only sprayed him with the extinguisher to put out the errant flames. Then we had the big talk about the Loup. She had only been relieved that Keth was okay and overjoyed that she wouldn't have to fill out a safety report.

The rest of his introspection quieted as Carla reopened negotiations. His phone buzzed a couple of times and then went silent. He had reached into his pocket to grab it, when one of the men stood up abruptly.

"Not enough. You ask that we exclusively use your shipping agency but offer too little in return."

Jack sat up at attention and met eyes with Carla.

Yes, this is going to take a bit longer than we had planned.

Only an hour later, Jack stood and firmly shook hands with his new business partners. He had been correct about them being eager to merge, but it had not been easy. Each point had been meticulously negotiated and discussed to make sure each party would reap benefits. Carla stood by his side, smiling and bidding them farewell. He could tell she wanted to strangle at least one of them, but he couldn't figure out why. They had done their job as much as she had done hers, but for some reason she bristled with anger.

Maybe it's fatigue. I know I am tired. Or maybe the not-so-subtle flirting unnerved her more than she wants to admit. Either way, I am not going to ask her about it and draw her ire. I am going to pick up Kama and go have dinner. I hope she doesn't mind Samoan food; it's been a while since I have had any.

"Night, Carla," he said. "Go home. We have all the signatures, and they are all notarized. Of course, you could finish up all the filing and other permits tonight, but I am making an executive decision that Twist Enterprises is closed for the evening. Unless you would like your position to be demoted to security, you get to leave before me."

The half twist of a smile on her lips satisfied him. He could see the drawn lines of exhaustion on her face and knew for once she would not argue with the order he gave her.

"Sure thing, boss."

The words were simple, but Jack felt like he had just won a major war. The temptation to tease her hung in the air. She even raised an eyebrow at him while he focused on keeping his face from twitching or breaking into a smile.

"After you," he said, walking to the door and holding it open.

Even though his back faced her, he still dared not laugh. The shaking of his shoulders would give it away, and then she would stab him. And Carla never did anything half-assed, so it would hurt.

"Nice restraint, Jack," she said as she walked through the door. "I do believe the Spirit Quest really has changed you."

Jack resisted the urge to take the bait. He even refused to give her a false prophecy certain that leaving an open avenue for the Goddess and Carla to join forces was an idea far beyond bad. He didn't even need to wait for a tingle or any other sign to know he made the right decision.

"I have been groomed by the best, dear friend," he said.

He watched her eyebrows rise up her forehead.

"Dear. Friend."

"Carla, we have been business partners for fifteen years. You have been by my side through this whole venture. I am ashamed if I have never called you friend before," he said, meeting her eyes. "But, you are correct. I did change with the Quest. Things were settled, ideas were born, and there is still much more for me to understand. I not only value your friendship, I care about you. You have been an integral part of my life, and you should know how important you are, not, not to mention how much I appreciate your dedication to this company."

Jack watched the emotions fly across Carla's face, ranging from surprise to caution and landing on an easy comfort. He knew it would take her time to feel relaxed enough to accept this new change in him, but he knew they would get there. They walked in comfortable silence, and just as he made his mind up to ask her to join him for a quick drink, his phone buzzed again. He had forgotten the earlier call.

"Excuse me," he said and stopped walking to dial his voicemail.

"Jack, it's me. It's Kama.. I mean, you know who I am. He has my mom. Remember that vampire I ran into months ago? The one who attacked me at the library and convinced me to come back to the Park? Anyhow, she was waiting for me and said her big boss has my mom. He's some big, scary vamp. He owned the Facility where Olivia—Crap. She's co—,"

He heard a scuffle, an odd whistling sound, and then a crash. He could only assume the phone had been ripped out of her hands and thrown. Panic rose in his throat, along with sour bile, and his brain spun.

"Jack?" Carla asked. "What is wrong?"

"Kama," he stuttered, and for once in his life, words failed him. "She's been taken. I—"

"Go," Carla said. "She needs you."

The next moments were a blurry haze. He quickly made it down the steps and threw himself into the waiting car. In the miasma of his mind, he noticed Carla, not far behind him, had pulled out her phone.

"Lorna, it's Carla Johnson…"

Surprise flooded him, though he knew it shouldn't.

Of course Carla has Lorna's number. What the hell happened to Kama? Did she really get snatched by a vampire? The Facility…

The mention of the place rang in his head and forced an onslaught of images to flow. The war, the raid in Los Angeles, and the mutants all wound and slid through each other while ideas fought to gain purchase in his mind's eye. As they faded, Jack clearly understood the connection, and his fear skyrocketed. He barely waited for the car to slow, before he jumped out and rushed into the Park. He let his wolf push to the front of his mind and guide him through the entrance and down to the tunnels. He strode quickly along the dark paths and found his way to Lorna's workroom.

"Carla said Kama got kidnapped?" Lorna asked as she met his gaze.

"Kama left me a panicked voicemail, but she said a vampire had taken her. This vampire has been hounding me for months now. Turns out he was behind the problem in L.A. and is the head of the mutant facility we took out," Jack said. "I've got to get to her."

"How do you know all that?"

"The Spirit Quest. It changed me," he said, echoing Carla's words. "After my visit with the Goddess, She talks to me and helps me understand. Conversations that I've had with her, they just keep coming. Images in my head that are meant to help me understand things just like this."

He waved his hand as he floundered. Jack watched as Lorna processed the information but said nothing. He wanted to throw things, just to be able to do something. Instead, he paced until an idea formed.

"Lorna, get your things and set up to scry for her."

"What? I can't do that," she said.

"You did it for her Rite. You're already familiar with her," he said.

"Jack, setting up for a Rite takes hours. Not to mention, I physically marked her. I can't just scry for Kama without knowing where she is. At the very least, it would take me two hours to prepare, but then, the chance of finding her without having touched her is little to none," Lorna said, flustered. "There is a better way to find her. Let us send out trackers."

Jack went through all of the possibilities he could think of for finding Kama. The biggest problem was time. At least an hour, maybe more, had already slipped by. The more time that elapsed, the harder it would be to find her. Throw in the nauseating idea of a vampire having his Mate, and time became much more precious. An half-formed idea surfaced and he went with it.

"I need to Slide to her," he said.

Lorna paused, her lighter mid-air, a few inches away from the sage she had been about to light.

"What? Jack, what are you talking about?"

"I need to Beam Slide to Kama," he said.

He met Lorna's gaze and watched her go through some internal bout. The "be tactful, he's the Alpha" side must have won, because when she spoke, her words were careful.

"Jack, you can't Slide to Kama unless you know where she is. Maybe you can get the computer guy to ping her cell phone or something? Juan is on tonight. He's the best tracker we have, and he is familiar with her. But Sliding to her is a death sentence. A Spirit Quest is one thing, it is all about connecting with Her. The reason you can even Slide to a location, is that it is static, and even then, you have to have an emotional tie to the place. Don't worry. We will find her another way."

Jack paced the room as Lorna picked up her phone and called Juan. He couldn't sit still and listen to her explain the situation. His wolf growled in his head, and he agreed. They refused to do nothing.

This is our Mate. She is in trouble, and we need to get to her. What the hell good is being Alpha if I cannot protect what is most important to me? I know the Goddess's hand is all over this. I doubt I would have thought of this on my own.

His wolf snorted; the situation unnerved them both. They were of the same mindset, and in an odd moment of clarity, Jack realized they had never been closer. They were merging, and he began to process both with his instinct and his intellect. Images flew before their eyes, and he understood them with a new level of cognizance. As Lorna finished her phone call in the background, he turned to face her.

"Lorna. I need to Slide to Kamaria. Now," he said.

He watched her rise and stand tall before him. The words to defy him were forming on her lips, and he Challenged her with a stare. Precious moments ticked by.

"Alpha, it is impossible," she said, averting her gaze. "If I try to push you into a Slide without knowing where you are going to land, you could get lost."

"I can Slide to *her*," he enunciated carefully.

Lorna met his eyes. He waited until he saw her acceptance. Her head tilted to the side, and her eyes widened just a bit. He took a deep breath while she looked around the room.

"All right," she conceded softly and then shook her head. "We need the moonlight."

They rushed into the Quest chamber, and Jack hoped with every fiber of his being that he would be in time. He stood in a pool of moonlight splayed across the wooden floors. With sudden insight, he took off his clothing. Lorna drew a circle around him, lit a bundle of white sage, and began chanting. He felt energy rise. The hair on his arms and back of his neck rippled and undulated against the current. The light he stood in became much brighter and enveloped him. Despite the odd sensations, he focused on Kama and what he felt for her. The air squeezed from his lungs, and his heart hammered as though it would burst.

He felt the merge with his wolf complete as they crossed through the realm of the Goddess, and with ease, they shifted into warrior form. He recognized the feel of the Slide and knew they moved closer to Kama with each second. He braced himself. His sight came back when he crashed through a thick, glass window covered with steel blinds. He rolled through the trappings and moved to the side as his wolf guided. He sprung onto his feet, and his gaze swept the room. He quickly catalogued what he saw. Brenna on the floor, wiping a trail of blood away from her mouth as a large man with two-inch, incisor fangs looked murderously at her, and Kama stood in front of him in defiance, her hands fisted at her side. Fury coursed through him, and Jack rushed toward the vampire. His brain noted the heavy, marble-inlaid, steel desk before he ran into it, and he used it as a battering ram.

He noted with grim satisfaction how far away from Kama he had managed to push the vampire, who landed against the wall, pinned by the desk. He stared at the creature, and began to stalk toward it.

Being sideswiped in a tackle forced his attention away from Kama. He hoped to have bought her enough time so that she could get back to her feet, but he had no time to check. Instead, he found his body lifted up into the air and thrown against the nearby wall. His body rattled with the impact, but he was too furious to care. Jack stood up and faced his assailant.

Assailants. There are two of them. And they are mutants.

The thought train forced a wry laugh out of him. Kama had infiltrated every section of his life, including his speech patterns and vocabulary.

Once we are out of this huge mess, I am going to have to have word with Ms. DeKosse. But much later.

He looked carefully over the two before him. They were larger than he and some kind of gorilla-creature, based on their body structure. They had the noticeably huge stomachs, tight chests, and muscled arms, which were longer than his, even in warrior form. Jack worried for a moment about the massive amounts of strength they possessed and wondered if he could tackle both of them. The next moment, rage returned, and the need to protect his Mate pushed all other thoughts out of his mind. Especially the thought about them being children.

It is stupid to remember they are Olivia's age. Right now, they are standing between me and that vampire.

The gorilla closest to him roared. The bulging head was misshapen and hung much lower over the eyes than normal. While most of the teeth were large and flat, pointed canines showed as the creature opened his mouth.

"I understand you are not here by choice," Jack said. "Just stand aside, and we can help you later."

A meaty arm swung toward his face, and Jack ducked. The other mutant grabbed him from behind, and the fight began in earnest. He and the wolf assessed the situation and decided the best option was to take out the two of them as fast as possible. Jack wanted to be humane, if he could, but the priority was helping Kama.

Okay, they are going to fight. I need to be able to get in and fight hard and get out. How do I press the advantage? These guys are just as big as me and maybe even as fast. With two of them, I can distract them from working together by attacking them one at a time. According to Olivia, they have no healing ability. Must have been a wake-up call for her to learn she was the only one in the Facility who could. So, best course of action is to break the neck of one and then take out the other as soon as possible. I'm not going to have much time to get back to Kama, so the faster the better.

He focused on the smaller of the two mutants and began his attack. Despite the second mutant trying to defend its brother, he began to rain blows down. His wolf pressed against his mind, and he tucked into a rolling motion and knocked the mutant off of his feet and into the other. They went down in a tangle of limbs, and he pressed his advantage with a flurry of punches. While the initial plan had been to snap a neck and quickly end it, he found his best advantage in the exposed throat. He drew his arm back and slashed across the thick neck. Blood geysered out and landed on his face. Jack slashed again, and the wounded gorilla lunged for him with an open mouth full of teeth.

He punched hard into the chest and then raked his claws down to the belly. The creature fell over with a whimper, and Jack knew he would die quickly from all the lost blood. Which left a fairly pissed off brother to deal with. The growl was filled with a pain Jack had not expected to hear, but he braced himself for the attack.

It came in a rain of unrelenting with kicks and punches to his abdomen. He grunted, but his years of service and training, though, were clearly superior to the second gorilla. He landed blow after blow and tried to figure the fastest way to dispatch of this one as well. A hard punch to his head dazed him, and when he looked up, a huge maw descended towards his face.

CHAPTER Sixteen

Kama woke with her face pressed against something cold. She opened her eyes and immediately closed them again. The quick flash of scenery made her queasy. She sat back from the window acting as her makeshift pillow and took a breath to settle her stomach. The car she rode in moved through the dark streets of New York. It pulled into an underground garage, which seemed dark and brooding.

"Just in case you were thinking of doing something stupid, like jumping out and running," Stone said. "We do still have your mother. If you make it difficult, we will deliver her to you one piece at a time."

It smells like corruption in here. And we are stuck in it for who knows how long. Wow, this building is right downtown. Why does no one notice a building only open at night? Because, of course, we are in the city. Everything is open all the time. I have no idea how we are going to escape. Stupid, impenetrable, vampire fortress. Okay, let's go up and save Mom. Please let her be okay.

Kama sat immobile, waiting for Stone to tell her what to do. She used the still moments to make plans. She felt it would be better to have some idea of maybe how to save herself and her mother. Plans could change, but having no clue where to even start at all would only leave her with the option of doing something foolhardy. She noted idly it felt like preparing to go on stage for a performance. She let her training fall into place and slipped into a very calm piece of mind.

"This way," Stone said, opening the car door.

They walked through the garage to an elevator. Kama watched Stone use a key card to access it. They rode up to the twelfth floor, not all the way up as she had expected. She had counted the floors to keep her mind off the ever-closing-in claustrophobic space. It had started to shrink in on her, when the bell sounded and the doors opened. From the elevator, they walked down a long, empty corridor. She had anticipated some kind of security guarding the threshold, but to her surprise, none were present. It only served to make her a lot more nervous, and she ducked behind Stone. They reached a huge, marble door, and Stone knocked.

"Please, enter." The voice sounded richly deep and had a melodic quality.

Kama followed Stone into the room. Her eyes grew wide as she took in the sheer opulence of the office space. The interior was spacious, decorated with sleek, modern, metal and glass furniture. Except the desk, it was marble like the doors and the size of a small car. Huge windows covered the far end of the space. She noted the absolute quiet and felt like she would break into hysterics. She noticed something standing in the corner, only because it moved slightly. She had no idea what it could be, but figure it had to be the security. Kama forced herself to look ahead and try to appear calm.

A silhouette sat behind the desk in front of the windows. It stood as they entered.

"Please come in, Miss DeKosse," the deep voice said. "Constance, I will assume you have already checked our guest and removed any undesirables."

Because she stood next to Stone, Kama could see the flash of utter loathing cross the vampire's face. In all their interactions, the vampire had been seemingly light hearted and glib. The emotional outpouring scared Kama.

Really? Her name brings out this reaction? She didn't look at me like that, and I ruined her best shirt when I staked her. And Constance? She doesn't look like a Connie to me. Hold it together, Kama. We need to be on our game.

Stone had taken her Kuba from her coat pocket during the car ride over. An unnecessarily intrusive pat-down had also occurred. Kama trailed behind the vampire to the end of the room. Her Kuba was handed to the man, and Stone stepped back. He walked back around the desk and sat down.

"Thank you, Constance, dear. You may be excused."

Kama watched Stone exit, not quite at a run but darn close.

"So very nice to meet you, Kamaria. Your mother has told me quite a bit about you. We need to get to know each other."

"Where is my mother?" Kama asked.

The man sitting behind the desk leaned forward, and power emanated from him. She stood in shock as she looked him over. His handsomeness caught her off guard. His skin was a light caramel color, maybe a shade or two lighter than hers. He looked about Jack's age, but she knew he had to be much older. He had beautiful, hazel eyes and a welcoming smile. He wore his hair short, in neat curls, and had no facial hair. Dressed in an impeccable business suit, the being responsible for kidnapping her mother and causing her such panic seemed completely calm.

"Please have a seat, won't you, dear? Your mother will be with us shortly. You can remove your coat and get comfortable. I am Mr. Cordwell. Thanks for coming here tonight."

What the heck? This man could be any of my parents' business associates. He doesn't look like a vampire. Oh, right, Kama, because we look so much like a werewolf. It sure would be easier if he wore a cloak, steepled his fingers, and cackled like an evil fiend.

Kama took her coat off and draped it over the arm of the chair. She sat and tried to calm herself. Hairs stood up on the back of her neck, and she looked around her prison. The room fairly glowed with power. As she watched, he touched a pulsing panel on the top of the desk. Metal shutters slid down across the windows, interlocking and closing tightly. The lights in the room automatically brightened to accommodate for the lack of the city burn.

Cordwell picked up her Kuba and carefully looked it over. He seemed intrigued by the sigils she had etched into it and ran his fingers over each carving. When the inspection was finished, he crushed it in one hand. He brushed the pulverized wooden bits into a pestle, added some oil, and set it on fire. The scent of sandalwood and cypress filled the air. It smelled like desperation to her.

Great. We have just been sealed in. I have no idea how we will get out of here. One door in, and those things in the shadows would jump on me before I could get us out. The windows might be an option, if I can get around the shutters, but Mom wouldn't survive the fall. Why isn't he talking or something? What could he possibly want with me? And now he's smiling at us. I want to throw up.

"By now, you have figured out there is no escape. Good. Now we can get down to our discussion without you being distracted," Cordwell said, his English crisp and flawless. Still, she detected the hint of an accent. "I want you to know that I have been waiting to meet you for a long time. When Constance first mentioned you, I became intrigued. Then your little band of wolves destroyed one of my holdings, and I decided that we had to meet. Not to mention, you are lovely. Your mother's description didn't do you justice."

"Can you please tell me where my mother is?" Kama asked, forcing herself to ask politely.

She watched him raise a small, silver bell and ring it twice. They sat in silence for what felt like an eternity in her mind. The door to the office opened, and Brenna walked in, carrying a tray with a tea service. Kama's heart fluttered in a rapid beat and then sunk. Not once did her mother look at her. She had expected to find her mother in some kind of prison cell or chained to a wall, not acting as a maid.

"Mr. Cordwell, your tea," Brenna said.

"Thank you, Brenna," he said. "Stand by the desk and wait, please."

She watched her mother move to the position and stand calmly. Her mother, who normally moved around endlessly and had a vibrant personality, wasn't present. Instead, the woman before her made no sound and complacently obeyed orders. Panic gripped her, and the reality of her situation finally sunk in. Her mother was a fighter, and watching her stand calmly serving the evil thing before them broke Kama's heart.

"Cream and sugar in your tea?" Cordwell asked.

"No, thank you," Kama whispered. "Mama, are you okay?"

"Come now, Kamaria," he said. "I have not poisoned it. It is a cold, February evening, and a hot drink will make you feel better. Your mother will be able to converse with you once we set the rules. Brenna, fix your daughter's drink for her, please."

She waited until her mother came closer and tried to make eye contact. Kama held her breath, trying to mask her impatience, until the tea had been poured and the cream added.

"Thank you."

She smiled at her mother and saw a slight quirk of her lips in return. It had been a quick flash, but she knew her mother's spirit remained intact, at least a little. Kama realized the vampire had put one, if not more, compulsions on her mother to make her obey. She figured it had to be some kind of magic, since her mother being this calm and complacent didn't make sense to her. As honey slowly poured into her cup, she reached out again.

"Mama, are you okay?" she asked.

Silence filled the air until Cordwell leaned forward.

"You may answer."

"Yes, dear," Brenna said. "Enjoy your tea."

Kama took a sip of the tea to buy precious time. Fury began to rise, but she knew anything rash would get them killed. Her mind did mental gymnastics, trying to figure out how to get out of the situation. She watched her mother pour him a glass of wine.

"How are you enjoying your tea? It's made with a hibiscus flower from my homeland, and I find it tasty," he said. "I would have offered you wine, but in your condition, it is frowned upon. Although, I have to admit I am shocked at this new and rather odd restriction for women who are expecting these days. A daily glass of wine used to be recommended. I can see you are surprised I know your news, but don't be. Your mother and I have had long and delightful conversations during her visit here."

"Visit? So we can leave?" Kama asked.

"Of course not," Cordwell said with a smile. "We both know this arrangement is permanent. However, I have learned that nothing is gained by being rude and hostile. I mean, punishment is another method, but I always try to treat my guests with kindness until they prove unworthy. As you will find, most people are eager to please me and accept my friendship."

The words made a shiver of fear grip her, and she fumbled her mug and just barley caught it. His casual conversation kept her off balance and vulnerable. She had no idea how to cope with her mother being in his thrall, let alone try to figure out what he wanted from her. Kama raised her eyes back to him, and he graced her with a smile. She opted for the direct approach.

"Why did you take my mother?" Kama asked. "Why am I here?"

"Your mother is here to keep you company, my dear. You are here because you will make my life easier. When Constance alerted me about Loup being in the region, I knew in a short time there would have to be a fight. I am still rather new to this area, but as you know, we don't work well in the same spaces. Don't get me wrong, I am a patient man. My plan had been to wait and watch to see what you did. Then you went and attacked my laboratory, unprovoked."

"Unprovoked? You sent mutants to invade our Den and hurt us," Kama said, standing. "We didn't do anything to you first."

"You would do well to remember never to interrupt me again," Cordwell said. "Sit down."

A pinching weight settled on her mind, and Kama sat before she realized her actions. She glanced at her mother, who looked terrified. For her. She sat back and tried not to provoke the man again. Nothing would be gained by making him mad.

"As I was saying, normally I would just wait until your small-minded politics and aggression towards each other caused a fight and you killed each other off. However, we learned you operate as a cohesive unit," he said. "Unusual, but it also created an opportunity. Your pack dynamics mean the right person can be planted as my envoy. After a few years of setup, I could take over control with ease."

He took another slow sip of wine. Kama wanted to slap the glass out of his hand but contented herself by taking a sip of her tea.

I'm pretty sure he will use our next outburst as an excuse to hurt Mom to keep us in place. I know Stone kept blathering on about how media gave us the wrong impression of vampires, so, so what do we actually know? Wood kills them. Yes, we know this from Ristori, but she hinted at more. The tree it comes from has to have the potential of long life. Or at least as long as the vampire has been around. And he burned the shit out of my Kuba so what wood do we have? His modern office makes a lot of sense now. Think, Kama. There are not going to be a lot of chances. We have to be ready.

Kama looked around the office and, when she felt eyes on her, turned to face her host again. Cordwell, as a vampire, didn't make sense to her. He radiated power and authority, even though he was slightly shorter than she. He appeared to be middle aged and, to her dismay, was handsome. She wanted him to be scary and ugly. Although, she knew when she finally saw his true visage, it would be in the midst of the battle for her freedom.

"I'm Egyptian, if that helps you make sense of me. Your curiosity is plain on your face," he said in his smooth voice. "Despite coming from a noble family, I never reached the desired position of pharaoh. Instead, I learned how business works and apparently found my calling. Now, let's continue our talk, if you have calmed down enough."

She tensed as he stood and walked in front of her. Kama refused to flinch when he looked down at her and caressed her cheek with a few fingers. The light contact sent an uncontrolled shudder through her. Kama felt her stomach clench, and she fought down waves of nausea.

"Okay, dear. Let's just talk about the important parts, because you seem eager to know them. When I learned about you, I figured that Constance and I would teach you to be our eyes and ears. It's a tried and true method. Over the course of years, you would strategically rise in rank and help us take over. So I gave Constance the duty of keeping track of you for a few weeks of observation, plans were made to acquire you. I realized the easiest way to get your compliance was to also adopt your mother," Cordwell said.

He walked back to his desk and patted Brenna on the head, like a child. Kama looked at her, and her mother's gaze turned sorrowful. For the first time since the ordeal started, a spark of fury coursed through her. She pulled it in quickly, knowing she would need to use it later.

"Imagine my delight in speaking with her. Not only did I learn that you were Mated to the Alpha of the group but also carrying a child," he said with evident glee. "What I said before about being patient was true. I have waited for entire empires to fall before I moved to secure my power. My businesses have grown for thousands of years to become successful. But you made it easy for me by following your heart and emotions for a man. And then I learned you would gift me a child. It seemed almost like a reward for my persistence."

Kama felt terror course through her. She placed her hand protectively on her abdomen.

"Gift you?" she breathed the question quietly. "What do you plan to do with her? Are you going to make her like you? Are you going to make her kill me?"

"Oh, my dear Kamaria, I am not a monster," Cordwell laughed. "You don't quite understand, do you? You will obey because I will give you no choice. Your will is mine to bend as I see fit. But there will be no need with your child. She will love me because she chooses to. She will serve me willingly out of the desire to please me, because that is how she will be raised. Your child will be the ultimate ambassador for me. Your line will ensure my ultimate power. With your pack under my control, I will have access to the Loup nation in a way they will never see coming. In a short, few hundred years, I will control them all. Thank you, dear."

A loud, metallic thunk caught Kama's attention, and she raised her eyes in time to watch the shutters flip open and start to ascend. She watched the tiny slice of the waxing moon reflect back to her. She met her mother's eyes and saw grim determination there. A bead of sweat running down Brenna's temple betrayed the kind of mental fight she had put up to break the compulsion. Cordwell's eyes narrowed into irritated slits. He raised one hand and knocked Brenna to the ground. Kama sat on pent-up rage while she watched her mother fall to the floor. Because of the earlier command, she couldn't move. A bruise began to blossom, bright red against the paleness of Brenna's face, as her mother lay there. Kama waited for her to get up but quickly realized the one act of defiance had taken all the will her mother had had. She inhaled deeply, feeling unable to do anything. The scent of her burning Kuba and the oil flowed into her nose and opened her mind to an idea.

Mom risked it all to open those blinds for us to escape. She doesn't want my baby to work for Cordwell any more than I do. If my mother has the strength to do what is needed to save her family, so do I. Okay, I just need to let him get close enough—

The window imploded with a shower of glass and a tangle of metal shutters. Cordwell hissed and moved away from the shrapnel. Kama watched a Loup, in full warrior form, come bursting through the open space. It stood and shrugged the debris off its nine-foot form. In a heartbeat, the werewolf assessed the situation, grabbed the marble desk, and shoved it at the vampire.

Jack.

Kama knew without a doubt her Mate stood before her, despite never having seen him in any form but human. The press against her mind lifted. She breathed a sigh of relief, knowing her chances for escape had become much more real. A roar sounded, bringing her back to the situation at hand. Cordwell struggled against the desk pinning him to the wall. She watched a duo of gorilla mutants rush from the shadows to tackle Jack. The flurry of fists and growls moved past them toward the back of the room.

She stood abruptly and rushed to her mother. She bent down to help her stand. Brenna gave her a wide-eyed look of terror but said nothing. Kama tried to reassure her with a soft smile.

"It will be fine, Mama," she promised.

She felt a grip on the nape of her neck and was dropped into the chair.

"I don't believe I gave you permission to leave your chair," Cordwell said tightly. "Just because there is a little excitement going on doesn't excuse bad manners. I had hoped for your transition to be easier. No matter. You will learn quickly enough. It is better and less painful just to please me."

"I don't need your permission for anything," she said. "I'm going to enjoy being the one to fuck you up. Oh, right. You like polite words. Well then, I will happily be the one to escort you to death and the hell you deserve."

Kama grabbed for her coat, her hand surrounding a button before being hoisted up in the air. She felt his hand around her neck, and it started to crush down with pressure slowly.

"Now, now. It appears Constance did not properly explain the situation when she escorted you here. I don't have to kill you to break you, but you might wish I had," he said. "When we have gotten you properly settled, I will let you execute Constance for me. Her defiance, subtle though it may be, is becoming intolerable."

She felt the coat ripped out of her grip and watched it flutter to the floor. She flicked her eyes to where Jack still fought the gorilla mutants. It looked like one of them lay on the ground, unmoving, but Jack and the other were still engaged in fierce battle. Bared claws slashed against skin. Cordwell held her up in front of his face, redirecting her attention. His grip grew tighter, and her breaths were labored. He smiled at her but let his mask of humanity slip and showed her his vampire nature.

His hazel eyes went completely black, losing the spark of life and vitality. The skin around his face tightened unnaturally against his skull. He looked desiccated and ghastly. No aura of humanity remained around him. Three-inch incisors descended from his upper jaw, and he leaned in closer.

She flinched as his teeth penetrated the base of her neck. The touch chilled her to the bone and seemed to cut deep within her soul. Kama felt suddenly drained and lacking in purpose. Her head began throb and her senses became muted as though it was stuffed with cotton, and she found herself losing the ability to hold her thoughts. She could hear her blood rushing into his mouth. Her heart began to beat faster in her panic. Her will seemingly floated away, but she couldn't actually care about it.

We can't shift. We are stuck in this weak form. There is no escape. Wait, we can't hurt him. He already has Mom, so it is hopeless. If we try to hurt him, he will kill her. There is no way to win this. Jack is being mauled over there, and no one knows where we are.

Through all the pain and background noise, she heard a much fainter heartbeat race in distress. The soft sound penetrated the despair fogging her mind. Kama drew on the years of determination and stamina that had made her a professional. Her spine straightened as her willpower returned, spurred by protectiveness.

Oh, Baby. Don't worry. Mama's got you. You come from a strong line of women. There is no way I am giving up now.

Kama remembered the button in her hand. She could hear Nula in her head berating her for compartmentalizing herself. She grabbed onto the thread of hope and began to plan. She opened herself to the possibility that being Loup was a whole, encompassing package. She and the wolf and the warrior were all one and the same. Her body might not be able to change forms, but she still had access to all her abilities. As she dangled in Cordwell's grip, she began to focus.

Kama fed the button, carefully hidden against her palm, between her fingers. Two inches of the crescent protruded from her fist. She adjusted her grip, let the power of her warrior form flow into her arm, and struck. Kama pushed hard and felt the resistance of the three-quarters of an inch of skin between her makeshift weapon and the non-beating heart of evil it sought. She shoved it through the barrier and almost wept as it slid in, unhindered by the ribcage.

Kama began to gag as Cordwell's fist tightened against her throat in response. She met his eyes and cringed under the ferocity. She dropped to the ground in a heap as he released her. She watched him look down at the button protruding from his chest.

"You dare attack me? Punishment it will be. Any last words to your mother?"

"I hope it's old enough."

Kama whispered the words from her bruised throat, meeting Cordwell's eyes in absolute defiance. Green buds sprouted and thin branches developed and grew upward. With a roar, he clawed at his chest but to no avail. Energy filled her, and Kama tilted her head back, letting a melodic howl flow from her throat. The sounds mixed in a minor, discordant key, each tone sounding louder and splintering against each other. She pushed her howling song harder against the sounds coming from Cordwell, his vocal abrasion to the circle of life until it burst into fragments that were absorbed by her pure song. In that moment, she felt invigorated and knew herself to be whole and complete.

The sound of crunching brought her attention back to the large, cypress tree now growing through the ceiling and floor simultaneously. She rushed to her mother and helped her move clear of the blast zone. She looked around the room to find Jack. Never once had she doubted his ability to take care of himself, but she still wanted to see him. He stood looking at aa dead mutant with a tree branch through its head.

"Thanks," he said.

Kama nodded to him while helping her mother to stand and putting an arm around her shoulder. She was certain her mother had a broken rib from the labored breathing. She saw Jack walk over to the phone, sitting on the floor from where it had fallen off the desk, and order a sketch for the building. Quickly, she grabbed her coat and handed it to him. She swallowed the nervous giggles at seeing him naked with her mother in the room. She looked at her mother staring between them.

"Alpha," Kama said with a nod.

"Darlin'. The man just walked the shadows to you. I may not have been happy about the idea of him being your Mate," Brenna said. "However, if he can cross the Goddess's path to get to you, I can accept this relationship with him."

After she closed her mouth from the shock, Kama felt a surge of love for her mother and smiled. Before she could introduce them, her mother stole her thunder.

"Sir," Brenna said.

"Brenna," he said with a polite nod. "Please, call me Jack."

"Of course. We will be family soon enough."

The huge tree creaked and groaned as it shifted and fell down a few more inches.

"Hold her," Kama said.

She walked over to the tree and, after a few moments of careful scrutiny, broke off a branch about as long as her forearm. It looked like the perfect piece.

"I'll need a new Kuba," she said. Then as an afterthought, "And a new button."

"I look forward to hearing the whole story," Jack said with a smile. "Once we are home and safe."

Kama answered with a grin. She sucked in a deep breath and then escorted her mother into the elevator. She didn't know if Brenna could walk down all the stairs. A familiar, black van pulled up as they exited the building. X winked at her.

"Taking out a master vampire? What next, Diva?"

"I think world domination might be on her list," Jack laughed.

She snorted as the two men had a brief discussion. Jack took the offered cell phone and clothes. She gave X a wink as Jack got dressed and then made a few more phone calls. Her mother stood by quietly, trying to absorb it all. Kama rolled her eyes in answer to Jack's raising his eyebrows but had no time to make a snarky comment because a gray car pulled up and Jack's driver got out to open the doors. Kama settled her mother into the front seat. With a sigh, she climbed into the back and didn't complain as Jack pulled her to his side. She rested her head on his shoulder and grinned when he kissed her cheek.

"You're welcome," she said. "For the help. And the coat, but it looks better on me."

"Nice assist," he said, and she felt him kiss the top of her head.

"Assist?" she snorted.

"I had it handled," Jack said, chuckling. "It would have been over soon."

"My tree, my kill," Kama said.

She gave him a smug look and returned his passionate kiss.

CHAPTER Seventeen

Kama walked down the stairs from DeKosse's private dining room and smiled. Her whole family had made it out for her birthday dinner. The joy at seeing them all filled her. After her confrontation with Cordwell, she didn't take their bond for granted anymore. While she had not anticipated telling her remaining siblings of her pregnancy during her celebration, it had been brought up. To her surprise, there were a lot of cheers and even more hugging. She had noticed her father even seemed to be taking it better.

I'm pretty sure telling Daddy three hours after getting off an international flight that he was going to be a grandfather was a pretty huge surprise. I really should work on my habit of blurting out big news. I'm fairly certain jet lag was the real reason his reaction was so contained. Then again, after the whole Cordwell thing, Mom has been pretty supportive of me. It only takes one, master vampire incident to help you reassess what is important in life. My sisters and Jill were pretty excited, and I think Dante is just still in shock. I'm kind of sorry Beth couldn't be here, but I doubt she could ditch her duties. Speaking of, I better step it up, or I will be late. I can't believe that old coot is making me do rounds on my birthday.

She finally made it out of the restaurant, after accepting all the well-wishing felicitations from the staff, and walked toward the southern end of Central Park. Light snow drifted in the air, making the sky sparkle. Kama decided to walk topside to her destination, instead of through the tunnels. It gave her a few more minutes of time to admire her surroundings. Fewer people braved the park at night in the chilly weather, so the atmosphere was soothing and rather calm. She made it to the carousel to find The Judge waiting there for her.

"About time you got here."

The words were punctuated with cigar smoke, and she coughed

"I'm not late," she grumbled. "You are poisoning my baby's air."

"You filter out all the bad stuff before it gets there," The Judge said, blowing another billowing cloud into her face.

Kama sighed and rolled her eyes. She waited for a few moments, looking around. After the silence got too heavy, she met his eyes. He stared at her, so she stared back, until the hairs on the back of her neck rose and the wolf paced in her mind. She had the feeling he would let her stand there all night, so she broke the stare off.

"Where am I patrolling tonight?"

"Down to the Lounge to get me some coffee," he said.

"But you don't drink coffee from the Lounge," she said in surprise.

"I do today," he said, waving her off. "And Kamaria…"

Aw, dammit. He is going to make me do something unpleasant.

"Yes?"

"No patrols on your birthday night. Go hang out with your friends."

Kama stared as The Judge walked away without another word. He had almost gotten out of visual distance before he turned back around.

"I was serious about the coffee. Come and find me once you have it. Some of us still have to work tonight. You will be able to, yes? Or has your baby taken all of the good brain cells?"

She shook her head and walked toward the nearby overpass. Along the walls was another tunnel entrance. After a quick look around, she pushed the third panel on the wall until the door slid open, and she ducked in. She made it to the Lounge ten minutes later and filled up a large cup of coffee.

"Kama!"

She looked across the room, and a grin covered her face. Beth, Olivia, Mary, Dan, Damien, and Lani all sat at a table. There were a few, small balloons on sticks and a white bakery box. She walked over to them and started to laugh at their deliberately horrendous, chorus version of "Happy Birthday."

"Thanks. That was really something," she said. "You don't have to sing every year."

"Yea, like we were going to try to pretend we could sing better than a diva?" Damien said with a roll of his eyes.

The others laughed, and Beth opened the box to reveal a dozen, purple and white cupcakes.

"Happy birthday, Kama," Beth said. "Choose one. We've been waiting ages to enjoy them."

Kama looked over the beautifully decorated cupcakes. Each one was slightly different, but all had some kind of purple, frosting flower. Finally, she chose the one decorated with a lavender and white swirled pattern and three, small, white roses with purple tips sat on the top.

"These are gorgeous," she said.

"Yea, Ajani worked all night to get them just right. He used purple for amethyst and your favorite color."

Kama's eyes filled with tears at the gift from her brother.

Stupid hormones. Stop it. We have certainly come a long way in the past few months.

"He's moved up to decorating cakes again?" she asked in surprise. "When did he start?"

"About three months now," Beth said with an affirmative nod of her head. "He decided he needed to do something with his life before your dad shipped him off to work in the diamond mines. Not to mention, he's good at it. And he always tastes sweet."

Kama made a gagging face, rolled her eyes, and then took a bite of the confection.

"Oh, wow. Pistachio. My favorite," she said, not caring about her rudeness of speaking with a full mouth. "This is amazing."

She looked around at her friends and smiled at the greedy looks on their faces.

"Despite my wanting to eat them all, please help yourselves to a birthday cupcake."

Kama sat down with them, and they fell into easy banter. A minor squabble broke out over the cupcake with a huge, fluffy, icing flower. She fixed it by swiping a freshly licked finger through the icing with no shame. Her friends each took a treat and left the spoiled one and another four for her. As she laughed at a particularly raunchy joke that Lani told, she spotted the long-cold cup of coffee.

"How did you talk The Judge into giving me the night off?" Kama asked.

She felt her stomach knot as Beth gave her a curious look.

"What are you talking about? I finished my shift, and we figured we would have to wait for you to take a break," Beth said. "I nearly had a heart attack when you showed up so early. I'm glad I gave all the decorations and cupcakes to Dan earlier tonight."

"Oh, damn," Kama said and stood.

She picked up the cup and realized she would have to pour hot coffee and then hope it didn't slosh out and scald her as she ran to The Judge, if she could even find him. As she tried to figure out where he might be, he walked into the Lounge with Jack and the other Betas. None of them looked particularly upset, but she wondered why they were all together. Kama stopped and stared at them for a moment and watched them continue their conversation. She put down the cold coffee, then picked up a cupcake from the box and walked toward them.

"Cupcake, Alpha?" she asked.

"Happy birthday, Kama," Jack said with a smile that stole her breath.

That's it? "Happy birthday, Kama?" How completely lame. I am eighteen, finally, and we still have to play this game of not knowing each other. I want a birthday kiss, dammit. This is the first time I have seen him today. Ever since I met this man, we have had to dodge being in the spotlight because others might not like our relationship. Well, I just killed a thousand-year-old master vampire. Not to mention, we're going to have a baby in a few months. This is our Mate. If someone wants to be upset, let them. I'm all done hiding.

"Thank you, Jack," she said with a smile and put the cupcake on the table.

Kama stepped in closer, wrapped her arms around him, and kissed him. She pressed in close and felt him wrap his arms around her and return the kiss. She felt like this was the first kiss they had ever had. As the kiss broke, she opened her eyes and heard whooping and cheering from the table where her friends sat. She had the grace to blush as Jack took her hand and smiled at her. She realized the Betas stood in front of them, staring at her.

Right. Now what? Oh, no. What if they don't approve?? Maybe I should have waited. Maybe…

Lorna took a step forward, and silence filled the Lounge. Kama met her gaze and held her breath.

"Alpha," Lorna said with quick smile and a short, formal bow.

Kama looked at Jack, who raised an eyebrow at her.

She meant me.

Despite her utter shock, Kama nodded her head to Lorna. "Alpha."

Aturus had stepped forward and bowed as well.

This is not really what I expected. I sure hope nodding at them is okay, because I've done it twice now. Oh, hey, that's what Gabe's voice sounds like. He's on board with this, too. Now The Judge. Why is he staring at me? I bet he still wants his coffee.

"Alpha."

Kama quietly exhaled a breath she had held. She waited for a plume of smoke that never came. She noted the cheering had gotten much louder, and as she looked around, she found that most of the people in the Lounge had joined in. She smiled widely and, when she chanced a sideways look at Jack, had no surprise when he pulled her in for another kiss.

"Let's go," he said quietly after the kiss ended.

She took the hand he offered her again and winked at him.

Kama walked with Jack and the Betas away from the Lounge and *her* Pack.

While I am surprised that we just did that, I am glad. I never could have imagined this would be happening today. What on earth is going on, though? Why are we, or at least why am I, being walked out like I'm going to my death or something?? Wouldn't they have just jumped me after I kissed Jack? Does he even know what is going on? Okay, okay. Yes, Wolf-girl, I think you are right. We should calm down and wait to see what happens. Lorna called me Alpha, and Aturus bowed to us, so they must be somewhat okay. Either that, or they are taking us to an isolated part of the tunnels to kill us both and bury the bodies. You calm us down. I can only think of being taken to my grisly demise for claiming this man. Yes, okay, we will breathe.

She looked over and found Jack smiling at her. He seemed calm, and she tried to take her cues from him. While the hallways stretched on before them, after two, quick turns, they walked into a room, and the door shut with finality. Kama blew out a nervous stream of air and tried to find an escape route. The room was fairly large, with a business-style table in the middle. Her heart sank just a bit when she saw no other way in or out. She looked up at Jack and met a schooled expression.

Well, that is no help. He just went from smiles to Mr. Stoic. What is happening here?

Kama watched The Judge as he walked over to the far end of the room, behind the table, and leaned over. He stood up and held out his prize, a black bottle with a gold label. He rounded the table, poured drinks in glasses that had appeared on the table, leaned back against it, and sipped his drink. Jack and Aturus joined him, and Gabe took a drink from his own pouch. Lorna stood scowling, shifting her glare between the men and the tumblers. The Judge handed her a Styrofoam cup.

Holy crap, I'm pretty sure she just tried to shoot lasers out of her eyes.

"It is about damn time you all got around to making it official," The Judge's voice grated out after a long sip of what smelled to Kama like scotch.

When she was reasonably certain her mouth no longer hung down gawping, she tried to pull the rest of herself together. A quick side look showed her the surprise on Jack's face, which he quickly covered.

"How long have you all known?" he asked with a dry tone.

"Let's see, you go off to Los Angeles to fix an alliance, but come back like a hound of hell with a bad attitude," The Judge said with a nod.

"I mean, really, Jack, we didn't expect you to bring a girlfriend home," Lorna said and then looked around. "I am going to be damn sick of apple juice if this is what I have to drink at every meeting."

"We barely even interacted in the first few weeks," Jack protested.

"Right, and yet Gabe had to declare the Alpha's corridor off limits to everyone but the special detail," The Judge drawled. "You all were loud."

"We never did that here," Kama said and blushed furiously as she realized what she said. She looked up at Jack for help and sighed as he was shaking from quiet laughter.

"Thankfully," The Judge said. "I would hate to hear how loud you get with sex, because your arguments are pretty vocal."

I really wish the ground would open up and eat me. I am the new Alpha, and we're talking about my sex life. How did that even happen?

"Why didn't you all say anything?" Kama asked.

"You weren't obvious to most," Aturus said. "But we would be some damn poor Betas if we didn't notice what was going on with our Alpha. I was just worried I wouldn't get you trained quickly enough to handle a Challenge before you claimed him. I'm sure, when my team hears the news, they will understand why I pushed you so hard. They were starting to think I liked you."

Kama nodded as things began to make more sense to her.

"Right. You built up her reputation by sending her on those missions," Jack said. "Everything is falling into place now."

"She is a good warrior, but no, I would have never sent such a new person out on missions this early, otherwise," Aturus said. "Though, she performed better than I had imagined. Not to mention, I do have to applaud your decision to claim your Mate now, seeing as no one can touch you for six months."

Kama nodded in confusion for a few minutes until Lorna absently rubbed her belly.

Right, I am pregnant. No one can Challenge me.

She took a deep breath and then smiled at Jack. He gave her shoulder a hug-squeeze.

"Well, if you are set for the evening, we are going home. We can start getting our new Alpha ready tomorrow," Jack said.

Good-byes and congratulations were offered, and the Betas left the room.

"What do you say we go celebrate?" Jack asked.

Kama smiled up at him.

"Did I really just become Alpha?" she asked.

"Yes."

"My Mate," she said and met his eyes. "I love the sound of that."

They walked out of the meeting room, and Kama noticed how busy the tunnels were. People weren't shy about staring at the two of them. Most smiled, but a few hostile looks were thrown her way. She smiled wider and grabbed Jack's hand. She had a million questions to ask him but knew she would have to wait until they had some privacy.

The snow had stopped falling topside, and the park was still. They walked the few blocks from the park to Jack's house. In the foyer, she shrugged off her coat and looked at it. Jack had gotten the button replaced for her. She smiled looking at it. She looked up to see him watching her. He leaned down and kissed her until they were breathless.

Damn, he knows how to kiss. I hope it's always like this. I can't believe what I did. I can't believe they all knew. If this is a dream, I'm not waking up. What? Oh, yes, he is looking at us.

"Happy birthday, Kamaria."

"Yeah," she said, still reeling. "I just claimed you, didn't I?"

"Yes," he chuckled. "Should I be saying happy birthday, *Alpha?*"

"How about some tea?" she blurted out, noticing the bemused look on his face.

"Okay. I'll wait in the living room. I'll make a fire," he said.

She walked straight to the kitchen. Eight minutes later, she had composed herself and brought tea to the living room. She handed him his mug and sat on the couch. Kama took a sip and looked at the fire he had started. When she was done avoiding him, she put the mug down and turned to face him. She had millions of questions to barrage him with.

"Kamaria Celeste DeKosse, will you marry me?"

She looked at him and then to the ring he held out. The ring had a 4 carat, oval, colorless, flawless diamond in the center. The stone was flanked with twenty-four, accent stones, spiraling down to a four-strand, thin-roped shank.

"Yes."

She barely managed to squeak out the word. Kama almost jumped with nervous energy as Jack took her hand and slid the ring on to her finger. She wrapped her arms around his neck and kissed him. She pulled back and looked at her ring, then stared at him wide-eyed.

"How did you—You got my sisters to make my ring?"

"They didn't know it was for you," Jack said with a grin. "First of all it was difficult to find their shop. Secondly, I had to convince them to work with me. They are something, though else. I felt like I was going through an inquisition during the design phase."

"Wait a minute," Kama cut him off. "They let you help design the ring? They never let people help."

"In the end, the only idea they kept was the stone size," he said with a shake of his head.

Kama looked down at the ring and back up at him.

"Wow."

Tears spilled out before she realized they were even coming. She snuggled into his embrace.

"Happy tears?" he asked.

"Yes. Incredibly happy."

Kama stared at the fire and smiled.

So, this is eighteen. Not a bad start. Oh, I agree. We can shift into a lower gear. We've had enough excitement for a while. I'm not sure what happens next, but I do know it will be amazing.

"Jack?"

"Yes, Kama?" he chuckled.

"Do werewolves mate for life?"

"This one does."

"Okay," she said. "I think my family is going to be surprised. Oh, my gosh, I have to tell them. I—"

Her panic was interrupted with a soft kiss. She met his eyes and laughed when he winked. She leaned her head on his shoulder

"Kama?"

"Yes, Jack?"

"I love you."

"I love you, too."

Epilogue

Her feet pounded against the debris littering the forest floor. She ran through the twisting paths with ease as she pushed forward. She could hear his mating howl, feeling its intensity course through her. Pressing forward, she ducked the tree branches in her way. She opened her mouth and laughed, a sensual sound carried on the wind back to him.

He caught her and pulled her up against his chest. She felt his hot breath against her neck as he leaned in to kiss her nape. He grabbed her shoulders, turning her to face him, and captured her lips with his. She leaned into his chest and melted against him in a perfect fit as if meant to be there. She broke the kiss and stared deep into his eyes.

"Mine."

Kama sat straight up, her heart pounding, and stared at the clock. She calmed when the blue numbers only showed eight in the morning. She still had plenty of time. She lay back down and stretched. She had half drifted back to sleep when pounding at her door startled her awake again.

"I know you can hear me," Ajani said.

"Yes, I can. You bastard," Kama muttered as she sat up.

"Oh, she's up," she heard Beth say in a chipper voice. "She just cursed at you."

"You two better have brought some coffee," she said.

Kama stood and pulled on a robe. She made it to the front door and yanked it open. A steaming mug of coffee was thrust under her nose. She took the cup and turned to walk to her dining room, expecting her guests to follow uninvited. They remained blessedly quiet, even though Ajani poked around in her kitchen. She finished her peace offering and looked at her brother and best friend.

"Why are we up at eight in the morning? I have until three you know," she said.

"Mom wanted to make sure you had enough time to get everything done," Ajani said. "She told me to make sure you had breakfast. She followed up her dictate with a menu of what I should prepare for you. So, here we are."

"I can eat breakfast at ten," Kama muttered.

"No," said Beth. "At ten you have an appointment with your sisters. At twelve, a meeting with your parents for lunch, and then at one-thirty, it will be time to get ready."

She sighed and rested her head on her arms. She figured she could doze while Ajani cooked for her. She peeked up at Beth, who seemed to vibrate with excitement. She knew more caffeine would be needed and nudged the mug over to her friend.

"Happy wedding day, Kama," her friend said brightly.

The morning had gone well. Her brother had outdone himself with her breakfast. Even though the hour of the morning had been ghastly, dining with him and Beth had been fun. Ajani brought up old memories, and they laughed as they reminisced.

"...and then Mom and Dad had to explain to six-year-old Kama that not everyone knew how to speak Italian," Ajani laughed. "She spent the rest of the flight teaching basic phrases to the lead marketing manager of World Banking Systems."

"Oh, wow. I had forgotten about that," Kama said, trying to catch her breath.

From there, the day moved into pampering. Twin and Jill met her at her favorite day spa. Beth tried to excuse herself from going in with them with the weak protestation of not being family. Kama was glad she wasn't the only one who laughed.

"Oh, stop. You enjoyed spa day at the park. As for being family, give it time," she said to her friend. "Ajani is smitten."

Before Beth could duck out, Twin flanked her on either side and escorted her in. Kama nodded to Jill and went in to enjoy the spa with her sisters.

Lunch with her parents had been good. Kama had expected tears from her mother, however to her surprise, they had a quiet conversation. She knew her father was still trying to make sense of all the rapid changes in her life. But instead of the tension she had expected, her parents also took a jaunt down memory lane with her. They sneakily took advantage of the alone time to present her with a pre-wedding gift.

"Something old and something blue," her father said, handing her a box.

Nestled inside, lay an antique hair comb made of platinum. It resembled a delicate leaf, with diamonds as the blade and sapphires creating the veins. Kama lifted it out, speechless.

"It has been in my mother's line for four generations," Malik said, his voice thick with emotion.

"Thank you," Kama whispered, and she leaned across the table and hugged him tightly.

"Something borrowed," her mother said, handing her another box.

Inside, laid the snowflake necklace she had coveted since childhood.

"Mind you, I did say *borrowed*," Brenna chided. "I see the greedy look in your eyes."

"Thanks, Mama," she said. "And you shouldn't call the bride greedy on her wedding day."

"And something new," her mother said, ignoring the last dictate.

She accepted the flat, rectangle box, curious as to what it held. Kama had assumed the new part of the rhyme had been covered with her wedding dress and shoes. She unwrapped the box and opened it. She pulled out a piece of satin. Her face flamed red as she stared at an ivory slip.

"I…I…Mom?"

"Kamaria. You are getting married," her mother said.

"Be thankful," her dad chimed in. "She wanted to get you the corset set."

"The ones with the edible panties," her mother chimed in and, after giving Malik a sly look, faced Kama with a grin. "He wouldn't let me. Apparently, there is a rule that says I cannot mortify you on this day. Not even a little. I'm not sure why."

"I will never be old enough to have this discussion with you. Oh, look. One more box," Kama said, grabbing for it.

I swear, if it contains a thong, I am gone.

She opened the final box and smiled at the handcrafted garter made with satin ribbons and diamonds in a scalloped weave pattern.

"It's gorgeous," she said. "Thank you both. For everything about today."

She embraced her parents and felt a small pang.

Yes, it, it is the happiest day of our life, but still, it means moving even further away from them. Let's focus on the happy, or I will be a sobbing mess before the ceremony even starts.

Kama stood in the canvas tent and paced. Her dress slid around her in silken waves as she moved. Her hair fell in ringlets down her back. She couldn't believe it was taking so long.

"Kama?" Jack called out.

"No. Stay out there. You know the superstition about seeing me before I walk down the aisle," she said brusquely. "I just want to talk to you."

"What's wrong?" he asked.

"What's wrong? How can you even say that?" she said, panic fully kicking in. "We're getting married, and I don't know a damn thing about you."

His hand passed through the curtained doorway and waited until she walked up and grabbed it.

"What would you like to know?"

"Everything. Something. I mean, what is your favorite color?"

"Black."

"Okay. Well, I know your birthday is in July, and you like jazz," she said. "What hobbies do you have?"

"I like saltwater fishing. Canarsie pier in Brooklyn is a great place. Or if I want to charter a boat, I go out to Montauk Point on Long Island."

"Really? Fishing? Wow, it sounds so boring. Until you get to the gutting them part. And then it sounds gross," she said.

"Being Loup is exciting enough," Jack said, and it sounded to Kama like he tried not to laugh. "My hobbies have to be boring to bring balance."

"How old was Melissa when you married her?"

Kama could have sworn she heard a chuckle, albeit a light one.

"Eighteen."

"Jack Twist, what is it with you marrying eighteen-year-olds?"

She knew she sounded exasperated and felt the wolf roll her eyes at their pre-wedding jitters.

"I was eighteen at the time," he said, definitely laughing.

She grinned.

"You were never eighteen," she said and took a breath.

"All better?" Jack asked.

She felt him squeeze her hand and nodded. Kama laughed at herself, because she knew he couldn't see the action.

"Yes. Much," she said.

Kama released his hand and found her bouquet. A few seconds later, her father walked into the tent.

"Ready?" she asked.

"To give up my baby? Never," her father said and swept her into a hug. "But I love you, and I know this is what you want."

Kama heard the music start, and they walked out of the tent. Her eyes widened at the gorgeous set-up before her. She had allowed her mother the freedom to plan the wedding. She was also certain her father might not have yet forgiven her for the six-week deadline. Large fans made of ostrich feathers parted in time with the music and formed an arch as she walked underneath. The crowd made appreciative noises while she passed by. Her smile grew wider and more genuine as she drew closer to Jack. The last of the feathers moved, and she saw him, handsome, handsome in his tux, with a tear caught in his eye. Her father handed her off to Jack with the minister's prompting and a kiss on the cheek.

They turned to face each other and began the ceremony. After the vows and rings were exchanged, their family and friends broke into applause, and howls were heard on the wind. Kamaria looked around and realized in finding her true self she had found her place.

~~FIN~~

ABOUT THE AUTHOR

Jennifer Fisch-Ferguson has been writing and publishing fantasy stories since 2003. Publishing credits include short fiction, writing contests and novels.

She attended the Eastern Michigan University and graduated with a B.A in African American History and promptly went to work with AmeriCorps on a literary initiative. She went to the University of Michigan and got her Master's degree in Public Administration in 2008 and while she finished writing her thesis, also got a Masters in English – Composition and Rhetoric in 2009. She recently is working on her PhD at Michigan State University in the field of Writing and Rhetoric. She has been teaching collegiate and community writing classes since 2003 and loves the variety and inspiration her students bring.

She currently is moving forward with new WIP's and dutiful writes on her blog space about her journey.

She lives in the Midwest with two amazing sons, one coffee supplying mate and acts as staff-in-residence to four needy cats.

See more at: http://warriorsofluna.com

https://www.facebook.com/ETM.JFF/

Team Cade

For those who have asked— yes, there is much more to Cade's story. We only ever got to see him from Kama's point of view – and some readers needed to have more. Don't worry- it's already in the works and Cade has some amazing adventures. I'm still working on a title because everything I have thought of so far hasn't been cool enough for him.

Enjoy the sneak peek.

Chapter One – April

"Cade Xavier, step forward for visitation."

Cade sighed and slowly walked towards the double doors. He put his arms up in habit and didn't resist as the guard patted him up and down. He didn't understand how a woman so short could emanate an aura of "kick-your-ass" so strongly. He towered over her tiny frame.

"Do you have any weapons?"

"Only my good looks," he said with a smile.

He waited for one in return, but it didn't come. He hadn't really expected one, even though he had been trying for years.

"Any recreational drugs, prescription drugs or cigarettes on your person?"

"No. I don't do stuff like that."

"ID, change and keys in the basket."

"Yes, ma'am. Although, I have to admit, you looking way too young for such a stuffy title. However, I I've got to respect the badge, and you."

He almost got a smile. Cade handed Officer Mack the paperwork packet. She looked through it carefully.

"I promise it's all in order," he said. "I know how you like it."

He met her gaze, and swore she was biting back a grin or a chuckle. He didn't push the line too much.

"Meaning you trained me very well in how you like to see the packet."

"You may enter."

"Thank you. See you next month," he said.

He pushed open the doors from the inspection area, waited in a small ante chamber and waited for them to close. A buzzer sounded and the second set of doors, leading into the prison visitor center opened. Cade looked around and smiled as spotted his father, waving from the table at the back corner. He walked over to him and hugged him tight.

"Did you get her to crack?"

"I think I am breaking her down," he said. "I am pretty certain I will get a smile before you get out of here."

"I doubt it. She has been here for three years now and I've never seen any more than a scowl from her."

"You're old and married, she has no reason to smile at you," Cade scoffed.

"It's good to see you too, son," his dad said. "Smack doesn't like anyone, married or otherwise."

"Probably because you and your other unfortunately incarcerated pals makes jokes about her name."

"I, for one, have never offered to smack her ass. I am not that low brow."

"Right. Stealing cars is fine. Making low brow comments is not…" Cade said with a smirk. "Have you figured out what the 'S' stands for yet?"

"Sourpuss, I am pretty certain. And while I may have stolen cars before: one- I have been reformed and two – who in their right mind would insult the woman in charge of your freedoms."

His dad chuckled and gave a short cough. Cade didn't comment on it, but filed the information away for later. There was no point in making their short time together tense.

"It's gotta be Stephanie, Sara, or Shannon. From what I have figured, she was born '75 or '76, since she's only been on the job four years. I heard her talking about what her five year bonus would be last month."

"Enough about her, I have at least five more years to figure it out. Tell me, son, what's good and new in your life?"

Just like the five years and three months of visits prior, Cade sat back and began to share what had happened in his life since their last visit. Though he spoke non-stop for almost twenty minutes, he related the stories on autopilot. Instead he looked his father over, in concern. They shared dark brown hair and eyes, that one girl had said looked like melted dark chocolate. He had really thought she was cute; until he found out she only wanted him to do her homework. He shook his head over that debacle and continued to check his dad's physique. Their faces were oval and they each had the chin butt. Except now his father showed signs of gray around his temple and new creases around his eyes. Unwelcome changes of stress.

"Are you on track to graduate next year?"

His father's softly spoken question brought him fully back into the conversation.

"Absolutely," Cade said. "Mom is trying to plan a party of something, but I really don't want one. Can you convince her that a nice dinner is all I need? Or a Spyder. Either one will be fine."

His father snorted and Cade returned the smile.

"In all the remembrances of your short life, have I been able to convince your mother of anything? If she is planning on throwing you a big party, I suggest you take the next year to get used to the idea."

"Maybe plant the idea of a nice quiet party here, during her next visit?" Cade implored.

"And waste my time with her?" his father snorted. "We have better things to do."

"You have like two hours…"

He let his voice trail away and ended the conversation before he could open the door wider for any innuendo laden conversation to happen. His dad leaned back and laughed openly at his expense. Cade took it; far too often there wasn't any reason for laughter. He kept the momentum going with another story, glad to provide a distraction from their surroundings.

"Okay, so I'm going to head home," Cade said as a loud buzzer sounded.

"Love you, son," his dad said, while standing.

"Love you too," Cade said, and accepted the too brief hug.

Hugs were begrudgingly accepted, but the shorter the better. He didn't want to give any guard any reason to react.

"Be good and take care of your mother."

"Absolutely."

Cade gave walked through the double doors, shot Officer Mack one of his best grins, and headed toward the parking lot.

www.ingramcontent.com/pod-product-compliance
Lightning Source LLC
Chambersburg PA
CBHW060132130626
46556CB00006B/2324